Singing River Publishing

CHOSEN BY A KILLER

LAURIE L NAVE

Cover Image: Photo by Molly Mears on Unsplash

SINGING RIVER PUBLISHING
Florence, Alabama
www.singingriverpublishing.com

First Edition

Prologue

January

Theater seating was a macabre choice for a room used to witness an execution. Celia swallowed her nausea as she walked past several worn chairs, selecting one in the front row. The creaking of seats unfolding behind her was like scratches on a chalkboard. The closed curtains behind the glass were a muted pattern of maroon and navy blue, leftover from the 1990s.

Celia's gaze dropped to the dark, sensible pumps she wore, willing the curtain to stay closed. Voices whispered behind her, but Celia listened to her breathing; she didn't want to know what the voices were saying. The murders, the scandals, the stories, none of that mattered to Celia. Her friend was about to die.

Light falling over her shoes meant the curtains had opened. *Look up*, Celia thought. Look at her. Her gaze lifted just in time to see Natasha's head turn toward her. The two women, one seated in front of the glass and one lying on the gurney behind the glass, barely nodded at each other.

An orderly stood over Natasha and inserted an intravenous line into her right arm.

Celia winced as her own right arm twitched.

She blinked and held her arm protectively as the same orderly walked to the opposite side of the gurney and inserted an additional line into Natasha's left arm.

"The inmate has waived her right to a final statement."

Natasha was still watching her. The actress smiled at Celia, and Celia mirrored her expression. When Natasha made a fist, Celia gripped the arm of her chair.

The fast-acting barbiturate came first. Its job was to render the inmate unconscious. Celia watched Natasha relax, and she looked away when the actress closed her eyes. She knew what came next – a paralytic, and then the poison. Someone behind a thin wall was pressing a series of pumps, and her friend would quietly suffer cardiac arrest.

In four counts, out four counts. Celia breathed robotically, watching the second-hand jerk slowly. With every movement, her heart rate accelerated, even as her friend's heart slowed.

Four minutes after she closed her eyes, the physician and warden pronounced Natasha Bronlov dead from a lethal injection. The orderly disconnected the lines as the curtains began to close.

Not yet!

Celia pressed the glass as the room tilted. She swallowed bile and she was certain the others observing could hear the ringing in her ears.

"Can you stand?" Keith was beside her.

She nodded and allowed him to help her out of the creaky chair. They walked up the concrete steps and out the door.

"Are you okay?"

But Celia didn't hear him. She was already stumbling toward the ladies' room. She slammed the stall door and began retching as she bent over the toilet.

After the wave passed, Celia leaned against the stall door. There was no way she was sitting on the dirty floor in her suit. She bent over further, putting her head between her knees as she fought another wave. Except for the ringing in her ears, it was quiet.

That could have been me.

Chapter 1

September

I swear to God if that blowhard made me miss my flight…

Celia jogged to her gate, cursing the CEO she'd just interviewed, and was relieved to see that people were still boarding. As she flashed the attendant her boarding pass and headed down the jetway, her cell phone rang. It was her boss, John, micromanaging again.

"Celia Brockwell."

"Hey, you on your way back yet? How was the interview? Did he cave?"

"I'm boarding the plane, John."

"Good, so you got the story?"

"I always get the story. Can this wait? It's been a long day."

"Just checking," he chuckled. "This is the biggest thing we've got this week."

"It's under control. You've got your lead story, and he's gonna need more lawyers."

"Good, as I said, you're the biggest one we've got, as usual. I like to make sure."

"I heard you the first time, John." Celia rolled her eyes. "I've got it, John. Look, the flight attendant is walking this way. Cell phones have to be off now." Without waiting for an answer, she ended the call and dropped the phone into her briefcase.

"Don't you hate these small planes?" The older lady beside her remarked. "No business class."

"They aren't built for comfort, that's for sure." Celia adjusted a small neck pillow.

"You're smart, sleeping through takeoff. It always makes me nervous." She rifled through her purse. "Gum? It keeps your ears from popping."

"Thank you." Celia took a piece.

As the attendant droned on about safety and oxygen masks, Celia tried a power nap. Dozing kept her anxiety at bay. Strange that she still felt it after a decade of flying.

"Takeoffs and landings are the worst," she'd told a therapist years before.

"It's because you aren't in control." That was the therapist's 200-dollars-an-hour conclusion.

Celia glanced over at the older woman, who was engrossed in a book. Then she pulled out her tablet and opened her interview notes. As she listened to the interview recording, she began a loose outline for the article she would write about the corrupt businessman.

Hayward Ingleson had been skittish at first. He was under investigation for more than a few violations, from ethics to corporate regulations, and he was defensive. They always were in the beginning.

"Your career has been successful, and your longevity impressive, Mr. Ingleson. Don't you think the business world, your colleagues, would benefit from hearing your story? I mean, you've been a leader and a mentor for so long. I think they need to hear your voice amid all this noise. Don't you?"

Celia smiled as she listened to Hayward begin talking. The tactic worked. As always, the best way to lower the guard of a narcissist was to tell him how important he is. And let him think you're on his side. They can't resist talking about themselves.

"So, what do you think about this assertion that transferring Lydia Gross was an ethics violation, based on your prior...involvement?"

Hayward was still pontificating when Celia slipped in the first tough question, and he just kept going. By the time Hayward realized Celia wasn't on his side, he'd said too much. All she had to do was spin his words back to him, and after an hour, there was enough for a lead story. He was furious, of course, and his backpedaling had nearly made her miss her flight. Arrogant bastard.

"Aren't you Celia Brockwell?" An attendant asked as she served drinks.

"I am," Celia smiled. "I'd like a chardonnay."

"Oh my goodness, I love your articles. I'm taking classes part-time to become a writer. I would love to do what you do. Traveling all over, writing important stories."

"I do love my job."

"I bet you do. Any tips for a new writer?"

"Work your ass off." Celia laughed.

Celia sipped the wine as the attendant walked away. *There's no way she's a writer. Maybe a future mommy blogger, but not a journalist. Too much sorority and not enough spine.*

Remembering her own brief sorority experience, Celia chuckled. It had been at her mother's insistence; she was a legacy. Maybe it would look good on a resume, especially if Celia was an officer. But Celia dropped out her sophomore year. Thursday night swap parties and gossip were not her things, and the restrictions were stifling. Not to mention the president was a pretentious bitch.

After she had quit, Muffy—or whatever her name was—spread the rumor that Celia was the sorority slut.

Celia had her chance to get back at Greek life the next year, however, when a pledge accused a senior fraternity member of sexual assault—a guy who also happened to be the president's boyfriend. The fraternity and sorority had sided with him, and they blackballed the poor pledge. So much for sisterhood. Then a few more girls came forward, and Celia wrote a scathing article in the campus paper demanding that the University take action. In the end, the senior was expelled and charged, and Celia was the new chief editor of the newspaper her senior year.

Mom was right. Greek life was a benefit after all. *And look where I am now.*

"So, you are Ms. Brockwell," the middle-aged man across from her said.

"The one and only." Celia kept scrolling.

"Still at *The Journal*?"

She looked up then. The blond man looked familiar, and his suit was expensive and well-fitted. "Still there. And you are?"

"William Keller. CEO of – "

"Multicorp, yes. I thought you looked familiar." She shook his hand.

"I didn't mean to interrupt your research. It looks serious."

"There's always work to do," she turned over the tablet. "I'm sure it's the same for you."

"Definitely. You're quite the writer. Very astute and straightforward."

"Thank you."

"It's rare to read a story that isn't editorialized or emotionally manipulated these days."

"True," Celia sipped her chardonnay.

"I'll let you get back to work." William closed his eyes.

By the time the plane began its descent, Celia had a tight outline of the article, along with a list of damning quotes from Mr. Ingleson. John would run it as the lead, and Celia would probably have another award to hang on her wall. God bless corruption.

The airport arrival area was crowded; however, Bart waved to get Celia's attention once she rounded the corner toward the exit. She smiled and waved back. He insisted on picking her up, even though they'd only had a couple of dates.

"How was your flight?" Bart took her bag.

"It was fine. You didn't have to meet me here. I could have taken a cab."

"You had a long day. I didn't want you to have to fight for one."

"Thanks, I am a little tired." Celia slid into the passenger seat as Bart put her bag in the trunk.

"Are you hungry, or do you just want to go home?"

"I just want to get comfortable. Home is fine."

While Bart navigated rush hour traffic, Celia listened to him prattle on about his job, a new intern, and his great golf game. He pointed out a couple of places that had good takeout, but Celia ignored the hint. She wasn't in the mood for company or romance. When they arrived at her place, he hopped out and grabbed her luggage.

"I'd ask you in, but I'm just beat." Celia smiled as Bart handed her the overnight bag. "Are we still on for dinner at 7:00 tomorrow?"

"Sure thing," Bart kissed her lightly. "Get some rest."

Lucille, Celia's neighbor, greeted her as she walked toward her house. "Hello, dear. Have a good trip?"

"I did. Glad to be home."

"I have your mail ready. I can go get it now for you." Lucille left before Celia could comment.

"Thank you." Celia took the stack.

"Here you go, dear. Have a good evening."

After dropping her bag in the foyer, Celia flipped through the mail. There were bills, a couple of catalogs, the usual. Then a manilla envelope caught Celia's attention. The address was written in a flowing script, and the postmark was from Delaware. Who did Celia know in Delaware?

Then she looked at the return address. There was no name, but there was a place: *Baylor Women's Correctional Facility.*

Chapter 2

Who would be writing to me from prison? Celia studied the writing, trying to play a guessing game with herself. The script looked vaguely familiar.

After ripping the envelope, Celia turned to the last page of the handwritten letter. She wanted to know who had sent it before reading; it was a practice she'd begun early in her career. When she saw the name, her curiosity skyrocketed. It was from Natasha Bronlov.

Celia didn't know the famous model and actress personally, but she knew her work. She'd seen a couple of movies. The Oscar-winner was supremely talented. However, it was Natasha's arrest and conviction that truly made her a household name. In 2007, the world watched as Natasha was arrested, tried, and convicted of the murder of five men, the last of whom was her father. The evidence was overwhelming, and it had only taken the jury three hours to come back with a guilty verdict.

The sentencing had been another shock. In an age where the death penalty was more and more controversial, the judge sentenced the actress to death by lethal injection. "Yes," Celia thought aloud, "I'm definitely reading this letter."

Dear Ms. Brockwell:

I am sure you are somewhat surprised to receive correspondence from me. I will, therefore, come to the point. As I am sure you are aware, my last appeal was denied, and so it seems that my execution will take place soon. I loathe the vultures of the press and have declined to give them a single breadcrumb of my story. However, I have followed you and your career closely for quite a few years, and I have immense respect for you.

The flattery was obvious, something Celia might have done herself. Still, it made the reporter smile to think of the actress sitting on death row, reading her articles.

I understand that you prefer to maintain a distance from the stories on which you report. This, in my opinion, has been one of the reasons you excel. However, I would like to grant one authentic telling of my story before I am executed by the state of Delaware, and I would like you to conduct that series of interviews.

Celia smiled; Natasha had read her mind. Celia didn't do melodrama and emotion, which is what a story about an immigrant beauty turned serial killer would need. This story would be the only story; Natasha hated the press. Why choose a facts-only writer, Celia wondered as she continued to read.

I am sure you are puzzled by my request, but I believe you to be the only one who can correctly tell my story. I ask that you consider my request, as I would very much like to meet you and speak with you.

So Natasha Bronlov wanted Celia to conduct not just one interview, but a series. After closing the door to the press following her arrest, the actress was swinging it wide open, but only for one journalist—Celia. She imagined the faces of her colleagues, especially John.

I do not want this story released until after my execution. This will not be a sordid retelling of the crimes' physical details. All of those were available during the trial. I ask for the utmost discretion and that no details be released until the series is finished. I have included an outline and tentative calendar, which of course can be adjusted to accommodate your prior engagements.

The letter closed with contact details for her lead attorney, along with procedures for drawing up a contract. If Celia took the story, she would have three months to conduct the interviews. Three months to get to know an enigma and tell her story. It wasn't a lot of time.

However, Celia could hardly resist. It would be the crime story of the century, and she would be the only reporter who would ever be given true access to the actress's life. This would be the one that propelled Celia's career to world-famous status. She couldn't turn away the opportunity to interview the nation's most beautiful psychopath.

As she crawled into bed, Celia reread the letter. She wasn't telling John about this. She wasn't telling anyone. And first thing tomorrow, she was calling Andrew, Natasha's attorney. She picked up her tablet and crafted an email before turning out her light.

****

At 10:00 the next morning, Celia was on hold, waiting to speak with Natasha's attorney. As the poorly chosen music played over the phone, she doodled on her notepad. She had a scheduled call to discuss the particulars of her first interview with Tasha, and in typical fashion, the lead attorney was keeping her waiting. She was used to the tactic; he wanted her to know who was in charge. However, after having read the initial correspondence and tentative contract, Celia knew exactly who was in charge: Natasha Bronlov. Oh, she was demure enough to let the attorney *believe* he was, but Celia recognized the ruse; it was one she had used several times in her own career. Powerful men generally liked to believe they held sway over an attractive woman, even if they did not, and it was often advantageous to let them believe it.

"Hello, Ms. Brockwell." The attorney's voice was deep and well-crafted. "I am sorry to have kept you waiting. I trust you have had time to go over the tentative contract and the requirements for visiting Mr. Bronlov."

"I have, Mr. McMillian," Celia answered. "I'd like to know what to expect when I enter the prison."

"Yes, well," the attorney paused and sounded surprised by her directness. "I suppose we can discuss that first. Of course, you will not be allowed a computer, and you will likely be searched. You may, however, bring a recording device. I would also be happy to assist you with notes."

Celia spun away from the phone, smiling, and looked out the window behind her desk. He was already negotiating. "It was my understanding that Ms. Bronlov did not want anyone else in the room while we conducted our interviews," she said.

"I had hoped we could encourage her to compromise on that point, Ms. Brockwell. As her attorney, I am not completely comfortable with her talking to the press without me present."

Smiling, Celia turned the page in her notepad. Of course. "And as the person whom Ms. Bronlov has asked to be her sole interviewer, I do not feel comfortable asking her to compromise her boundaries."

It was quiet for a moment, and Celia continued to doodle. The longer he was silent, the more certain Celia was he would acquiesce. She knew if he cleared his throat, she had won.

"Well," the attorney said, clearing his throat, "as Ms. Bronlov has been insistent on this point, I suppose we should accommodate her. Now, regarding the contract, are you satisfied with the preliminary terms, or do we need to negotiate any particulars?"

"I feel satisfied with the terms Mrs. Bronlov set forth," Celia answered.

"Well, then, since everything seems to be in order, I will have the final contract sent for your signature, and we can schedule the first interview."

"Thank you, Mr. McMillian," Celia said. "I look forward to speaking with your client."

Once the call was over, Celia walked across the street for lunch. She told her assistant she would be returning at 1:30 and reminded her of the 2:00 appointment with her editor. John was proficient at what he did, but he was notoriously late for appointments. Celia's assistant, Gladys, would make sure he was on time.

While she nibbled on a salad, Celia explored the notes she had taken researching the actress's crime. The interviews were sparse and brief, and even the tabloids were guessing at what went on in the actress's life. The stories contained an array of photos, all showing Natasha with the same cool, closed expression on her face. Funny that all the journalists and hacks chose such stark photos when there were hundreds of more attractive photos out there.

Natasha Bronlov was arraigned at 1:00 this afternoon, and bail was set at two million dollars. She is expected to post bail this afternoon before returning to her Greenwich home until the trial begins. Her legal team had no comment as to their defense strategy.

A few stories were detailing the trial and verdict. Again, her attorneys had no comment. And, of course, the most recent story was about the denial of her last appeal.

Natasha Bronlov's legal battles may finally be over, as her last appeal was unsuccessful. After a decade on death row, it looks as if Delaware will execute its first woman in decades.

Eventually, Celia gave up on her research and concentrated on her salad. The patrons around her were noisy; it was a popular lunch spot with its varied menu and casual atmosphere. The owner had been a fixture for four decades, and he traveled from table to table greeting guests. Celia had no idea of his real name; everyone called him Pop.

"Ah, Ms. Brockwell, only a salad today? You'll wound my cook!" Pop's thick accent carried through the restaurant.

"Last time I was here I ate so much, all I can have is salad this time. Your cook is bad for my figure."

Pop laughed and ambled to the next table.

The sight of the owner caused Celia to imagine Natasha's father. He'd been her final victim, the one who led to her arrest. It was strange to Celia that Natasha had chosen to kill him. Surely she'd known it would seal her fate. Why had she? Was he abusive, a stage father, or worse? The actress might not want a retelling of her crimes, but Celia was determined to get answers to her questions.

At 2:08 John entered her office, still eating the sandwich he had ordered for lunch. It wasn't typical for the boss to come to the employee's office for meetings. However, John's office was so cluttered, it was all but impossible to find room to work, much less have anyone in for a meeting. He would rather not have to put things in order. It also meant that if he was running late, no one was at his office door waiting.

"So, Celia, what's happening with the CEO piece? Did you crack him yet?"

"He tried to put me off, saying he needed to talk with his attorney to craft a statement. I let him know how that would play in a story. He agreed to make a brief comment. An hour later I had enough for an article."

"I swear you could have been a detective." John tossed his napkin into the wastebasket. "You don't need a bad cop. So when do you think you'll have something ready?"

"It should be ready to go by the end of the day. That means it can run in the next edition."

"Perfect!" John pushed himself out of the chair and began pacing a bit. "So when do you plan to fly out to Phoenix? Later in the week?"

"About that," Celia had rehearsed her speech. "I need to visit a friend in Delaware on Friday. I was planning to take the train Thursday night, and I can fly into Phoenix from there."

John stopped and frowned. "I was hoping you'd be able to do the Phoenix bit Thursday or Friday."

"I already have the appointment set up in Phoenix for 9:00 am. on Monday. I'll be back in the office writing Monday night."

"Do what you need to do then. Your friend sick or something?"

"Something like that."

John grabbed a handful of candy off Celia's desk and left. Celia took out her recorder and headset and began working on the CEO article. A revealing article by day's end would appease John. Not to mention, it was time this man's shady practices were exposed. It was just dumb luck that he hadn't already been prosecuted. He wasn't nearly as smart as he thought he was. How he had managed to rise in the ranks to run a company was beyond Celia's understanding. It certainly wasn't his intellect.

It was almost 6:00 when Celia sent her article, and she was supposed to meet Bart for dinner at 7:00. She'd been seeing the widowed attorney for a couple of weeks, and she still found him pretty charming. They'd passed the third date mark, and he wasn't getting antsy the way most men did, as if the number three entitled them to something. Celia had insisted on splitting the bill on their first date, and though Bart had expressed appreciation, he had told her it wasn't necessary. Butterflies weren't fluttering in her gut, but they rarely did. He was attractive and interesting, and she was looking forward to the date, which was more than she could say for the last few men she'd met.

"I'm taking off, Gladys. You should shut down too and enjoy the weather."

Gladys grabbed her purse. "I think I'll walk out with you. Maybe I can take the dog for a walk."

Since she had a few minutes before Bart picked her up, Celia decided to take a short walk. The weather wouldn't be this warm for much longer. She walked down JFK, watching as people milled in and out of buildings. Once she reached 15th Street, she saw the familiar buskers setting up their guitars or keyboards outside the park; soon it would be filled with music. Love Park was relatively quiet; it was too late for the summer tourists and too early for the fall tourists. A couple of families were there, their children playing in the water feature. Celia sat away from them in silence, scrolling through her phone. She put her earbuds in so that no one would try to strike up a conversation. Small talk wasn't Celia's favorite thing. Finally, just before 7:00, she made her way back to her building, where Bart would pick her up.

"Glad you're back," Bart gave Celia a quick kiss before opening the car door for her. "I hope it was a good trip."

"Oh, it was. You'll read about it in the next edition."

"Vermillion's okay?"

"Sure, I love their gazpacho." Celia turned off her cell phone. "So what about you? Anything you can share about the tax case?"

"It's a real mess. I'm not sure how much longer I'll be taking depositions. I've got three more this week."

"Sounds fun. No wonder you wanted a night out."

"Exactly. And I missed you." Bart squeezed her hand.

They chatted about small things during dinner. Bart was attentive and engaging, and Celia felt herself enjoying the date again. He reached across the table to touch her hand, and she could read his body language. Celia found herself wanting to ask him back to her townhouse. She felt energized having finished another article, and she was feeling some excitement about the upcoming initial meeting with Natasha. Expending some primal energy might be just what she needed. She smiled as she sipped wine and pictured Bart without his expensive suit.

"So, since I'll be ready to get away from work after these depositions, and you'll have another big article under your belt, I have an idea." Bart poured some more wine for both of them. "How do you feel about the mountains?"

"I enjoy them, especially for skiing. Why do you ask?"

"My fraternity buddy has a chalet in Ashville. I thought you might like to get away for the weekend. You've been so busy. We could go down on Friday and come back Sunday evening."

Celia felt a little twinge. They hadn't slept together yet, and now he was suggesting a weekend away? Of course, she was planning on rectifying that after dinner, but still. His invitation sounded a little warning bell in her brain. Thankfully she had an appointment at the prison.

"That sounds wonderful, but I have to take a short trip to see someone on Friday, and I may not be back until Saturday morning. Maybe another time?"

"Sure." Bart frowned slightly. "So where are you going?"

"I'm visiting a friend in Delaware. I'm not sure how long I'll be there, so I had planned to spend the night."

"Too bad, we'd have a great time." He smiled. "Of course, I'm having a great time tonight, too, having dinner with a beautiful woman."

Celia leaned forward a bit, closing the space to distract Bart. "So are you interested in dessert?"

It only took Bart a second to register the double entendre. "I'd love something sweet."

Celia excused herself to the restroom while Bart stayed back and took care of the check. They met outside and Bart opened the door for her when the valet brought his car. Before starting the engine, he leaned over and gave Celia a long kiss. She pushed him away playfully and sat back, crossing her legs so that her skirt rode up just enough. It had the desired effect, and Bart revved the engine before pulling away from the curb.

When Celia and Bart arrived at her house, her neighbor Lucille was outside looking for her cat.

"Hello, Celia. I'm out looking for Jerry. You know how he wanders away."

"He does seem to wander, Lucille. I hope you find him soon."

"And who is your friend?" Lucille asked, smiling.

"I'm Bart." He stepped forward and shook Lucille's hand. "It's nice to meet you."

"Why thank you. I'm Lucille." Jerry ran out from beneath some bushes. "Oh, there he is! You two have a nice night."

Celia bid Lucille goodnight and unlocked the door to her house. Once it was closed, Bart kissed her long and hard, and they made their way to the bedroom.

"Let's try not to disturb the cat," Celia laughed.

Chapter 3

Natasha's attorney, Andrew McMillian, was in his late forties, but it was apparent he was trying to retain his youth. He was very fit, with a trendy haircut and a fitted suit. Very metro, Celia thought. Of course, Natasha had several attorneys, but he was taking the lead with the interview contract. Celia read it carefully in his office. There were the tentative dates, her remuneration in addition to what the paper would be paying her as staff, several requirements and restrictions, and some prison-specific guidelines.

"It's just as we discussed." Andres gave her a pen. "There will be regular visits involving only you and Me. Bronlov. No leaking of the story or teasers beforehand. The story will run after the execution."

"Everything seems to be in order," she said. "Is there nothing left to be done about her appeals?"

Andrew shook his head. "It's in the hands of the governor and the powers that be now. I'm still looking for options. I know someone close to her has written letters, and I thought he might have some pull, but so far nothing."

"It's been a long time since a woman was executed."

"Yes, it has. You know, I wonder sometimes if the privacy that was so important to Natasha during her career might be hurting her now. People don't have the emotional investment in her that they have with more open celebrities. Considering her crimes, I guess the privacy made sense, but now I think it's a liability."

"I can understand that," Celia said. However, inwardly, she understood the actress's desire. Celia was the same way. Her business wasn't everyone's business. Luckily, people didn't fawn over journalists the way they fawned over actors.

"I have wondered if running this story before her execution might be beneficial. What do you think?"

"That isn't what is in the contract."

"I know," Andrew said. "But contracts can be amended. I was hoping that maybe both of us could encourage her to go in that direction. She seems to value your instincts."

"I haven't even met her yet," Celia replied. "But I have to say, I'm inclined to do what she wants at this point. I suspect she thought a lot about granting interviews before she extended the invitation. I'm not going to jeopardize that unless there is a chance she might agree."

Andrew sighed. "I can see why she thought you were the perfect choice for interviews. You sound just like her."

Celia smiled. "I think I'll choose to take that as a compliment."

"Well, she is a formidable woman."

"That she is. I am looking very forward to meeting her."

"Good, great," Andrew replied. "We have the first appointment set up for 9:00 am. It would be smart to arrive a few minutes early if possible. Do you need transportation?"

"No, I have that arranged."

"That's fine then. Would you like me to accompany you to the first interview?"

There it is, Celia thought. One last attempt to get into the room. "I appreciate it, but I'll be fine. I may not have visited a death row prisoner, but I have been in prisons before."

"Alright then." Andrew frowned. "If you have any questions, just give me a call."

After leaving the law office, Celia met Bart for lunch downtown. There was a new café close to his office, and she'd been wanting to try it. The chef was said to be able to do wonders with vegan cuisine. When she walked into the restaurant, Bart was already seated, and he waved at her.

"Glad you could make lunch." Bart pulled out the chair for her.

"Thanks for the invitation. I've been wanting to try this place. A couple of my colleagues have raved about it."

"You look great."

"Thanks, you too. How's work?"

"I'm billing so many hours on this I may retire early," Bart chuckled. "How about you? Anything exciting?"

"Just the same old same old. Expose corruption, report the truth, all that jazz."

"You're very talented. I read the latest piece, and it's a work of art."

Celia smiled. Bart certainly was good for the ego. "Thank you."

The waiter arrived, and they placed their orders. Bart ordered a zucchini pasta dish, and Celia ordered a salad with roasted tofu. She laughed when Bart wrinkled his nose a bit, and she explained to him that tofu takes on the flavor of whatever it is cooked in, so, despite its appearance, it doesn't taste like Styrofoam. He looked skeptical, but he said he might try a bite if he felt brave enough.

"So do you have any big plans for the weekend?" Celia asked.

"I'm going to a fundraiser. My former in-laws run a non-profit in Wilmington."

"Sounds interesting. So you're still close with them?"

"We stay in touch. Stella and I were only married for five years, but her parents really needed support after her accident, so I stuck around for a while."

"That was kind of you. I guess you probably needed support as well. Do they know what caused the accident?"

It only lasted for a second, but Celia noticed it. Bart's face darkened and then blanked. She'd seen interview subjects do the same thing. There was something under the surface. "There was a problem with the car. It was a curvy road at night. I think she just lost control," Bart smiled thinly. "So how is your friend? The one you are visiting?"

"Oh, I'm sure she'll be okay. She just hates being cooped up."

"So what's wrong with her?"

Celia shrugged. "It's a woman thing. I don't want to violate her privacy."

Bart's jaw tightened. "I see."

Their food arrived, and they began eating. Celia was surprised at how delicious it was. Bart's looked good as well. He was brave enough to try a bite of her tofu, but he wasn't a fan, he said. Celia laughed as she finished her meal. They chatted about work and the goings-on in the city. Bart asked her to dinner on the following Tuesday, and she accepted. He was a lot of fun, and the sex was fun. She was hoping they'd go out regularly without becoming too serious. Getting attached wasn't on Celia's to-do list. She'd have to keep Bart at a distance; he was definitely the attaching type.

"Let me get this one," Celia said when the waiter brought the ticket. "Please."

Bart didn't look completely comfortable, but he agreed. Celia didn't want him to get the wrong impression, being the one to pay every time. Everything in life was a transaction. She handed the ticket and her card to the waiter, and then she excused herself to go to the restroom.

"Hey, Celia, I thought that was you," Julia, a colleague, said as she washed her hands.

"You were right about this place," Celia replied. "The food is great."

"I enjoyed looking at your date," Julia teased. "Where'd you find him?"

"He's an attorney in town. Yeah, he's easy on the eyes."

"Hot is more like it. He needs to invite Dan to his gym a few times. Get rid of that dad-bod."

Celia laughed. "See you back at work."

Bart had her card and was standing by the door. He'd taken care of the tip, and they walked outside together. He leaned in for a kiss, but Celia gave him a friendly hug instead. "It was great to see you. Enjoy your weekend fundraiser."

"Thanks. Have a safe trip," Bart answered quickly, but Celia noticed it. That same dark look. What was wrong? Perhaps his relationship with his former in-laws wasn't as cozy as he claimed.

When Celia arrived back from lunch, Gladys had a stack of messages for her. Most people used digital means, but after a controversial story broke, Celia liked to have a hard copy as well. Threats sometimes happened, and the paper copy of the number and name of the person who had called made Celia feel more in control of the situation.

Several of the messages were from the law office that represented the subject of her latest article. She wasn't worried about those. She'd covered all the bases, her ass, as well as the publication's. She recognized one name as a family member and a couple of others as victims of his unethical behavior. Those would go unanswered; Celia didn't do emotional displays and pleadings. The rest she'd have to check into before making a decision.

"You're back, I see." John poked his head into her office. He saw the stack of messages and smiled. "You caused another stir, didn't you?"

"Who, me?" Celia chuckled. "You know I aim to please."

"That you do. This will send our sales up for sure. Everyone likes to see a rich man get screwed."

"True. Except for the ones who want his money."

John laughed. "Working on anything new I should know about?"

"Just tying up some ends and getting ready for the interview in Phoenix."

John studied her for a minute, then slapped the door frame. "Okay then. I'll let you get back to it."

Celia shook her head after he walked away. Good grief, he was nosy! Every journalist had at least a tinge of paranoia now and then, but John's could be incredibly annoying at times. He was fishing, Celia was sure of it. But she wasn't going to take any bait until she had something solid from her next project—a cold-blooded, beautiful killer.

When Celia arrived home, her telephone was blinking. Sighing, she pressed the button. The messages could only be from one person. *I really need to get rid of this landline.*

"Celia, it's me again. I know it's been a long time. I want to talk to you. Please, it's important—"

She erased the message without hearing the rest.

Chapter 4

The night before her appointment at the prison, Celia reread the requirements and restrictions the prison had concerning death row inmate visits. It would probably be a no-contact visit, which meant she and Natasha would be separated by a partition. There was a list of prohibited clothing, but since Celia didn't wear sundresses or revealing clothing to an interview, she wasn't too worried about that. The attorney had assured Natasha that she could have a pad, pen, and recording device. She would likely be at least informally searched. Most of it wasn't new information; Celia had visited prisons before, though this was her first death row visit.

"License and pass. Be sure to sign the log after you finish the paperwork." A grandmotherly woman sat at the desk behind what was likely bulletproof glass. She typed loudly at a keyboard and handed Celia a clipboard without looking away from the screen.

"Please step this way." A corrections officer wearing gloves directed her. He gave her a quick pat-down and took her purse and phone. After examining her recording device, he nodded.

"I'm Robert. Follow me please." He used a code and badge to open the first set of doors. Both their shoes echoed along the hallway, and Celia made a note to wear different shoes next time.

"Does Natasha get many visitors?"

"Her attorney visits, of course. Other than that I can't discuss. Wait, please."

Of course, he can't tell me that. Celia watched him swipe the badge and enter another code, and the second set of doors opened. Another officer joined them until they reached a set of doors.

"Keith will take you from here. See you in an hour."

Keith was a tall, lean man who was probably about 40. He shook Celia's hand.

"Nice to meet you, Ms. Brockwell. We'll be visiting Mr. Bronlov in Room 4. I need to remind you that you are to remain across the table from the inmate at all times. Both of you are to remain seated. The visit will be for one hour, and I will be outside the door. I will knock once when you have ten more minutes and once when you have five minutes left. There is a button on your side of the table should you need anything."

"Thanks. I thought there would be a partition."

"Ms. Bronlov is allowed contact visits with her attorney. We will allow contact visits in this case too unless they become a problem."

"I assure you I do not plan to create any problems."

Keith smiled again and unlocked the door to Room 4. "Celia Brockwell is here to see you. Celia, Natasha Bronlov. I'll be outside the door. You have one hour."

"Thank you for coming, Celia. I apologize for not standing to shake your hand, but the prison has so many rules." She laughed. "Have a seat."

Natasha sat at the table, her legs crossed casually and her hair swept back into a band. The bland prison uniform blended with the neutral walls. Natasha, however, was anything but neutral. Even without her makeup, she was still stunning.

"Thank you for the invitation. Do you mind if I record? It will give me the most reliable record."

"Of course, I assumed you would. I like your suit. I think decent clothing is one of the things I miss the most. Well, that and cigarettes."

She's going to be executed, and she acts like I'm from Harper's, interviewing her in her living room. Celia wondered how much was practiced and how much of it came from resignation to her fate.

"I'm sure. I smoked for 10 years. Quitting was a bitch." Celia opened her notepad and pressed record on her device. "So in your letter, you said you wanted an authentic telling of your story. I'd like to start wherever you are most comfortable; however, we do not have to go in chronological order. I can fix the timeline later. I'll type up notes after each meeting, and then I'll write a draft. You will have some input, but I'll make the ultimate decisions for the final draft."

Natasha raised an eyebrow and then smiled. "Yes, that sounds fine. You are very straightforward, aren't you? Not too much for small talk."

"I am. I think it tends to prevent any misunderstanding."

"I agree. I despise reporters who try to trick their way into your secrets. I assume I can request that some things be off the record, should discussions meander?"

"Of course."

"Before we begin, there are some things I want from you."

Taken a little by surprise, Celia sat back and studied the actress. "I'll see what I can do. What do you want?"

"First, I want this to be a conversation. There is no one truly intelligent to have a conversation with here. Yes, I will answer your questions, but I want to know you as well."

"I don't usually get personal with interviewees."

"I'm going to be executed. Who would I gossip to?"

"It's just a professional boundary.'

Natasha sighed. "It won't be much of an interview with neither of us talking."

"Perhaps I'm not the best choice to write your story," Celia challenged.

"You are aware that you are the only reporter whom I have allowed access?'

"I am aware that you reached out to me and invited me to the prison to interview you, and that your letter didn't mention any requirement that I bare my soul."

"So dramatic," Natasha shook her head. "That seems unlike you. Perhaps I misjudged you, and this was a mistake."

"Perhaps it was. I don't commiserate and share feelings. I write stories based in fact." Celia gathered her recorder and stood to leave.

Natasha started, and Celia couldn't tell if she was angry or impressed. "Wait. Sit down," Natasha finally said. "I won't ask for any secrets. You may have your boundaries. But if I am going to tell you mine, I can at least ask about your career, or maybe you can tell me about your latest roll in the hay, as they say."

"I'm not the most exciting hay roller, but sure. We can talk generalities."

"Good. Now for the more important request. Bring me cigarettes. Good ones."

"Are death row inmates allowed to smoke?"

"Don't worry about that. Just bring them."

"No problem." Celia clicked her pen and wrote the date at the top of the page. "So, tell me about your life, your career, wherever you would like to start."

Natasha sighed and sat back in her chair. "I am sure you know from your research that my family came here when I was small. My father moved from Russia to England, and then my mother, father, and I moved here. I believe I was around 6 years old."

"Do you remember much of your life before moving to the US?"

"Not too much," Natasha replied, picking at a string on her shirt. "It was my father who most wanted to come here. He grew up in Russia, and I think Britain was not quite far enough away for him."

"And your father had a business?"

"He did, but first he worked for a university. That job provided the visas. He worked long hours, and my mother stayed home. I went to a neighborhood school."

"I see. So you went to public school."

"I did. I went to primary school and elementary school. Then I began attending a private school after I started modeling." Celia folded her arms. "Your turn."

"My turn?"

"Tell me about your parents."

Pressing pause on the recorder, Celia began. "Dad was a dentist. Mom was a teacher. Both were from apple pie families."

"And was your family apple pie?"

"Well, Mom did love to cook." Celia chuckled. "Dad liked to drink. It was what you'd expect of middle America."

"Interesting. So are they still married?"

"Not since I was twelve."

Natasha pushed her chair forward. "This doesn't feel like a conversation."

"Dad left for one of his hygienists. Very predictable." Celia sighed. "Mom stayed single. Our lifestyle changed dramatically. I chose a college across the country. Built a career. Never really looked back."

"Only part of the story," Natasha scolded. "But fair enough. Where were we?"

"Ah." Celia adjusted the recorder. "So the modeling. I have read some vague stories about how it began. Was it something you sought out? I know an agency approached you but was it a goal that you or your family had?"

"Honestly, no. My father told me often I was very beautiful, but it wasn't until someone asked him if I had tried modeling that the idea came to him. Once I realized that a modeling career could mean travel, money, and getting away from the boredom of school from time to time, it interested me. So we signed a contract with my first agency."

"This all happened quickly?"

Natasha nodded. "It did. My father had photos taken of me, and we went to several events. I don't know how he managed the invitations. Someone who knew someone saw me at these events. My father was thrilled when they offered me a contract."

"Yes, I read about that. They signed you and one other girl, correct? The two of you became close friends."

Natasha folded her arms. "Margaret, yes." Celia noticed a cooler tone. "We frequently worked together. Photographers liked the way we looked together, with my fair hair and skin and her dark hair and olive complexion."

"I've seen some of the photos. You two did make a striking combination. So working so much together, you must have been close."

"Oh yes, very," Natasha replied. "We spent a lot of time together."

"Was there a rivalry between you?"

"I'm not sure what you mean," Natasha said.

Oh, yes you are. "I mean, you were both young, both new talent. I know you worked together a lot, but surely there were times when you competed. Did that affect your friendship?"

"Not at all," Natasha quickly answered. "As I said, we spent much time together, and we did most of our work together. Each of us did other things too, of course, but that is part of the business."

Celia paused and reviewed her notes. "Yes, you did work together very regularly until your first runway show. The two of you competed for that spot."

Natasha shook her head. "We did not so much compete as understand that there would not be room for both of us. It happens at work." Natasha spread her hands on the table. " In the end, the producers selected me because Margaret was in the hospital."

"That's right. Relapse of an eating disorder, I believe."

"Such a shame. We discussed her concern over weight gain. I had noticed that her eating habits had become laxer. To stay competitive, you must be vigilant about your size. I suppose knowing she was teetering on the edge sent her into more anorexia."

Celia wrote quickly in her notebook. "In the end, that show was a turning point in your career."

"It was. I knew it would be." Natasha sighed. "But do you truly want to know about my modeling career? It became boring."

"I'm just laying a bit of a foundation. The more I understand about your early life and career, the more I can understand what came after."

"You mean the murders."

"Yes," Celia replied. "You must know one of the biggest questions people ask in these crimes is what made the person into a murderer. They all want to recognize the signs."

Natasha laughed. "Yes, they think if they can unlock the psychological mystery, they can catch people early or prevent crimes."

"It's a popular subject that fascinates many. More than one television series has cashed in on the fascination."

"Those television shows," Natasha laughed. "They do all seem to fit a certain caricature, don't they?"

"Of course. The exaggerations make it dramatic. People make a study of the psychology of murder. Of course, the goal of my piece isn't to psychoanalyze serial killers. I only want to understand you."

"I wonder if you could understand," Natasha mused. "None of the other reporters who begged to interview me would have. They were so focused on the tragedy, the drama. They wanted to use their gift with words to elicit some display of emotion, I am sure. You know how some journalists love making their subjects cry."

Celia laughed at that. It was true that many of her colleagues felt a story wasn't a story unless it had made someone cry or someone angry. It was one of the reasons journalism had stopped being what it used to be: reporting of facts. Celia never understood it. "True. And that isn't the kind of story you wanted."

"Not at all," Natasha said firmly. "I do not want my entire life dissected with emotion. Languishing and hand-wringing change nothing about the past or the future." Natasha sat back and folded her arms. "Okay, it's your turn again. What about you? How did your career begin?"

"My story isn't nearly as interesting."

"Somehow I don't agree. Everyone's career has decisive moments, turning points. I would be interested in hearing about yours. After all—" Natasha spread her hands—"Who am I going to tell?"

The final knock came, and Keith walked into the room. Smiling, Celia tapped her notebook with the end of her pen. "Maybe next time. I appreciate you talking with me. I'll see you next week?"

"I very much look forward to it," Natasha said. A second officer walked in and escorted Natasha out of the room, and then Keith walked with Celia to the security doors.

Once back in the waiting area, the desk clerk gave back her phone and purse. Celia placed the recorder and notebook in her bag, waved to the clerk, and exited the building. Driving to her hotel, she assessed the initial interview. It had almost been boring. Somehow Celia had expected more. She thought the actress might toy with her or probe her for more personal information. True, Natasha had asked about her early career, but she didn't push. She'd probably ask again, though. *You've watched Silence of the Lambs too many times, Celia.*

Celia settled into her hotel room and ordered room service. Her phone buzzed, but she ignored it. She'd received quite a few messages since the CEO expose came out, and she was tired of responding "no comment" or reminding one of the businessman's attorneys that he was the one who granted the interview and spilled his secrets. Was it Celia's fault the man had no self-control? There were also the usual bleeding hearts wanting her to advocate on their behalf. That wasn't what Celia did. She told the story. She knew her manner seemed cold to some of her colleagues. But emotion cheapened a story, Celia believed. Getting emotionally involved was not part of the job.

Her room service order came, and as Celia ate her salad, she listened to the recording. There were always things she noticed about conversations after the fact that helped her compose the next interview. In this case, Natasha had revealed a little more than Celia thought. From the tone and mood of her voice to the way she stated things, there were clues in what she said. Natasha's tone was controlled throughout much of the interview, but there were a few times she sounded tense or as if she was working out what to say. Celia paused the recording when she came to the part about Margaret and her relapse. Something about it seemed off as if Natasha wasn't saying everything.

"We discussed her concern over weight gain. I had noticed that her eating habits had become laxer. To stay competitive, you must be vigilant about your size. I suppose knowing she was teetering on the edge sent her into more anorexia."

For someone whose close friend was hospitalized, Natasha had been very matter-of-fact. True, it had been years, but the actress didn't seem very sympathetic. Celia couldn't help but wonder if there was more to the story. Was it truly just pure good luck that Natasha's friend had relapsed, making the way for the opportunity? She wanted to chide herself for being jaded, but then again, Natasha had killed five people. Manipulating a few circumstances wouldn't be a stretch. Celia knew how easy it was to use someone's behavior or circumstances to her advantage. *After all, it's how I got my break too.* She made a note of it, reminding herself to explore it more later.

Chapter 5

"So how's your friend?"

Celia looked up and smiled at John. She'd expected him to come by at some point to check on her. When he was focused on one of her projects, he was a pest. "Much better, thank you for asking. I'm working on the next article now."

"Good. When do you think it'll be print-ready?"

"Probably tomorrow by lunch."

"I was hoping for today, but tomorrow will do. Too bad you had that side trip."

"Well," Celia said sweetly, "the more I focus, the faster it'll be ready."

Taking the hint, John grunted and walked away. He was annoying sometimes, Celia thought, and a bit of a slave driver. However, the job paid well and afforded her many benefits. She could usually charm John out of her way. She was relieved he didn't press for information about the "friend." The man was like a bloodhound, almost as bad as Celia was. She had a plan if he did, though. All she would need to do was begin a sentence about "gynecological problems," and he'd run for his office. The thought made her laugh.

The phone rang as Celia was finishing the first paragraph of her article. It was Bart. He'd called the night before, but it was so late she'd ignored it.

"Hi, Bart."

"Hey babe, glad you're back in the office. How was the trip?"

"It was fine. I got home late last night. Working on the article now and trying to get it done by close of business."

"You mean your business closes?" Bart laughed at his own joke. "How about lunch around noon?"

"I can't, Bart. I have to finish this. But dinner later this week?"

"Sure babe. I'll call you later. Don't work too hard."

"I'll try not to. Oh, and Bart, I'm not the biggest fan of being called babe. It's just not me." Celia doodled in the margins for a few seconds.

"No problem, Celia. Just a pet name. No more babe then."

"Thanks. I'll talk to you later on."

Why did the pet name bother her so much? Celia wasn't one of those who thought all pet names were demeaning, but *Babe?* It was presumptive, somehow. Sure, they'd slept together before she left for Delaware, but "Babe" implied an intimacy she didn't feel comfortable having with Bart. Women were thought to be the ones who got clingy. In Celia's experience, it was the opposite. It was why she had never married or had a true long-term relationship. They were invasive.

On Tuesday at exactly noon, Celia submitted the finished article. She'd had most of it done by Monday afternoon; however, John had stopped by two more times hounding her, so she held it until her original deadline. He was happy enough once she submitted it, and once that was off her list, she could look toward her next interview with Natasha. She hadn't been able to get their initial conversation out of her mind, and the woman fascinated Celia.

After two more phone calls, Celia agreed to meet Bart for dinner Tuesday evening. They decided on a Tex-Mex place near his apartment, and Celia was looking forward to some queso; it was her weakness. He was waiting at the bar when she arrived, and she had to admit he looked hot. His jeans were just tight enough, and the sweater fit in all the right places. Now that she knew what those shoulders looked like unclothed, she appreciated them even more.

"Hey B—Celia." Bart gave her a quick kiss. "Want something to drink?"

"A margarita would be perfect, thanks."

"Done." He signaled the bartender, ordered, then turned back to her. "You look great."

"You too. I definitely approve of those jeans."

Bart slipped an arm around her waist. "Maybe later you'll take them off."

Celia stiffened a little, uncomfortable with public affection, but she managed a smile. Margaritas made her horny. "You never know," she teased, pretending to push him away in a flirty manner.

They sat at a table and began perusing the menu. Celia always ordered the same thing, but she felt compelled to survey the menu as some sort of ritual. They ordered drinks and cheese dip, and then Bart pulled her menu down slightly to look at her.

"So do you have plans this weekend? I'd love to take you somewhere."

"I wish. I'm going to be traveling several weekends in a row."

"Man, John keeps you busy, doesn't he? Doesn't he know his star reporter needs vacations too?"

"It's not all work. My… friend still needs my help." Celia pulled the menu up slightly and pretended to keep browsing.

"That must be some friend if you're willing to sacrifice weekends," Bart grumbled.

"Meeting with a friend is not a sacrifice," Celia said.

The waitress took their orders and menus, and Celia asked Bart about work to change the subject. She supposed she could tell Bart about her interviews with Natasha and swear him to secrecy, but they had only been out a few times. She had agreed to keep them confidential. Besides, she didn't owe an explanation to a man she had only gone out with four or five times.

Bart told her a few funny stories about crazy clients—no names, of course. He did have a way of telling a good story. Celia found herself relaxing and laughing freely. The three margaritas probably helped. He touched her hand from time to time, and she enjoyed watching his arm flex under the sweater. By the time dinner was done, Celia was happy to take a walk with him and then invite him back to her place. He might be a bit too enthusiastic, she thought, but enthusiasm had its positive sides.

The next morning, she got up while Bart was still asleep and showered. He was still snoozing when she finished and while she dressed. Celia had an early meeting with another writer, and she was going to need to leave soon. Finally, after her hair was done, she sat on the edge of the bed and shook Bart gently. "Wake up, sleepy."

"What time is it?"

"It's only 7:00, but I have an early meeting. I need to go soon."

He sat up and stretched before smiling. "You look good. I'll go ahead and get up. I need to shower."

Celia looked at her watch and frowned a bit.

"I won't make you late," he laughed. "Or, you could always just give me a key, and I'll lock up when I leave."

"I'll tell you what, if you can get ready quickly, I'll take you to breakfast." Celia stood and walked away from him. "It's the least I can do," she flirted a bit.

"Sounds like a deal to me." Bart threw back the covers and gave her a quick kiss before heading to the bathroom.

Celia exhaled as he shut the door. A key? He was moving far too quickly. No one had a key to her place except her, and she liked it that way. If he kept up the insistence on going away and hints about keys, she'd have to put the brakes on. Those were the kinds of conversations Celia was never good at; someone always got angry.

After a quick breakfast at a diner, Celia headed to work as quickly as possible. She was going to be almost ten minutes late for the meeting, but it was better than giving Bart a key or even leaving him there alone. She didn't want people alone in her space. Luckily, Julia was patient, and they got started and made up the time. By the time everyone else got to the bullpen, they were almost done. Celia headed to her office and checked messages. Other than the fact that her assistant was home with a bad cold, the rest of the messages were nothing of real importance.

"So, Celia, can I come in?" John knocked on her half-open door. It was 10:30, and Celia had become so engrossed in writing she didn't look up immediately.

"Sure, John. I'm just making some notes."

He sat down slowly and looked at her. "Notes about Natasha Bronlov?"

Caught off guard, Celia sat up and stuttered a bit. "Wh—what?"

"Your assistant is sick, so when her phone rang and I happened to be walking by, I thought I'd answer, help out, take a message for you. You were meeting with Julia."

"I see," Celia said.

"Someone from the prison asked if your next visit could be moved to 1:00. They are having some sort of official visit that morning. Want to tell me what's going on? Or do you have a close friendship with a serial killer that you failed to tell me about?" He folded his arms.

Crap! Celia hadn't wanted to tell John yet. She knew he'd hound her and press her to give people a sneak peek. "Look, John—"

"I get it. I know all of you are going to do some sleuthing of your own from time to time. I also know I'm not the biggest game out there. Though I'm pretty freaking close." John leaned forward. "What I don't get is why my favorite ice queen reporter would be interested in serial murder, especially when everybody knows that woman won't talk to anyone about anything."

"John… she asked me to come."

"Bull," John said simply.

Celia sighed and pulled out the letter she'd received from Natasha. He read it, and as he did, his expression changed.

"Well, I'll be! This is amazing! This is big news! This is going to make me and the publication the biggest out there." He slapped the edge of Celia's desk gleefully. "When can you get me something tantalizing to run as a teaser?"

"It doesn't work like that. You read what she wants."

"Yeah, and to hell with that. She can't get to the pub anyway. Hell, those death row people can't even watch the news, can they? We can't sit on this for three months. What if one of those jailers leaks it?"

"They aren't going to leak it. Natasha will pay them if she has to. She won't keep talking to me if I don't do it her way. I've got this, John. Just be patient and we'll be the big game. The only one with this story."

"Is something else going on here?"

"What do you mean?"

"I mean am I even the game you were gonna pitch this to? I know you, Celia. You're ambitious. You travel all over. I also know the two biggies have been courting you."

"What, how did—?" Had John been reading her email?

"No, don't change the subject. Are you keeping this quiet so you can use it to make the next step up?"

"No, John." Celia was getting exasperated. "Good grief you're paranoid. I didn't want to talk to you about it until I'd done enough interviews to get something good. I've only met with her once!"

"You're under contract. And I have some clout in this business."

Now Celia stood. "Get out. Now. You don't get to threaten me. This story is for us. Here. At this publication. And you're acting like a child."

John tossed the letter at her desk and stood. Celia didn't sit, so he shook his head and left her office, slamming the door behind him.

Chapter 6

On Friday, Keith led Celia to an empty room and waited with her until Natasha arrived. When she did, she blew the officer who was escorting her a kiss before sitting. He didn't look amused. Keith raised an eyebrow at Celia before walking out with the other officer.

"Good morning," Celia offered.

"God, I hope you brought cigarettes." Natasha ignored the greeting.

"I did. I bought the brand that used to be my favorite."

"You don't smoke anymore. I had forgotten."

"I don't. There's a history of lung problems in my family. I quit after my mom got cancer."

Natasha leaned forward when she saw Celia take out a small book of matches. "I'm sorry to hear that."

Celia smiled and shrugged. "She smoked two packs a day after my father left. I guess it's unwise to tempt fate."

"So you're not a smoker. You work very hard. You dress… conservatively." Natasha smiled. "What do you do for fun?"

"I have some pastimes. Just not much time."

Natasha laughed. "Time is all I have. So, do you knit? Cage fight? Fool around?"

Celia laughed as she set up her recorder. "So this is the part where we talk about me, huh?"

"I'm bored. Humor me, please."

"Well, let's see. I run. Not in marathons, but I do the occasional 5K. I like photography, though I'm not all that good. And I love to bake."

"Baking?" Natasha brightened a bit. "You look too fit to bake."

"I don't usually eat what I bake unless testing the batter counts."

"Hmm, maybe you could bake me a cake and hide a file inside or something. Didn't that work in old movies?"

Celia laughed, imagining Natasha in a black and white striped uniform, picking the lock of her cell with a file. "It might set the metal detector off, sadly."

"Too bad. I could have used it to poke the new guard a bit."

"I noticed he didn't seem too friendly."

Natasha rolled her eyes. "He is very by the book. Has something to prove I think. He let me know very quickly that my 'being a big star' wasn't going to get me any special treatment. As if the prison death row has special treatment. He probably has 'little man' syndrome."

"But he's over 6 feet tall," Celia chuckled.

"Dear, that isn't the kind of little I mean."

There were a few seconds of silence, and then both women burst into laughter. Celia tried to contain herself. Natasha was very disarming, but the journalist didn't usually break her professional manner this way.

"We only have an hour, so let's go ahead and get started." Celia pushed the record on the player and looked at Natasha. "I have to admit, I've been thinking about what you said about Margaret."

"What about her?"

"Well, there was something about the way you put it. You said you had noticed her eating habits. Did the two of you talk about that?"

Natasha smiled. "Of course. Models talk about eating and not eating pretty regularly."

"So you told her she was eating too much?"

"Oh, I wouldn't do that. In fact, just the opposite."

"What do you mean?"

Natasha drew imaginary circles on the tabletop with her finger. "I told her I was jealous that she could eat the way she did and not worry about a muffin top."

"I see." Celia looked down at her notebook to write. So there was more to the story. "So was she worried?"

"I have no way of knowing. I assume not, since she kept eating, at least for a while. We were going to do a swimsuit shoot together, and I remember telling the assistant how unfair it was that Margaret could eat like a horse and still fit into almost as small as size as I could."

Celia wrote slowly, thinking about what Natasha had said. She knew passive-aggressive when she heard it. All women know that "I'm jealous you can eat so much" was code for "be careful dear, you're getting pudgy." And there was no doubt Natasha knew it.

"Is there something on your mind?" Natasha asked.

"Did you know that Margaret had struggled with an eating disorder?"

"Oh God, yes, everyone knew. She was very vocal about overcoming it."

"Yes." Celia looked up. "It's a shame she had that relapse."

"It certainly is," Natasha replied.

They looked at each other in silence. Celia thought Natasha might say more, but it was clear the actress was waiting for her out. She was not going to share. Celia figured she should drop the subject. "So your modeling career took off. What was it that made you want to make the jump to movies?"

"That was initially more my father than me. He used to call me his chameleon. So I started auditioning for very small parts and television commercials. I had some luck with those, but he pushed for more."

"I read one piece that stated he was a bit of a stage dad."

Natasha laughed. "He did have that reputation. My father was used to getting what he wanted."

"So he wanted you to get a bigger role in something, and then you got it."

"It wasn't quite as simple as the modeling. There were many things my father could do, but convincing the world I could act wasn't one of them. It's hard to make that jump from a few lines and a perfume ad to a real role. I felt I had talent, but in Hollywood, that isn't always enough."

"I'm sure. Who you know plays a part in all that."

"Yes, who you know." Natasha looked at her pointedly. "And who you allow to know you."

"Surely you don't mean the proverbial casting couch."

"I prefer to call it an intimate audition. One that gave me some leverage. Lots of married directors cheat. Some of them don't want their wives to know. Or the executives."

"Ah, I see."

"I only did that once. My first big role was a success, and I got great reviews. After that, it was all about marketing and hearing the right things at the right time."

"And you didn't feel… violated?"

"Oh, I wasn't coerced. I knew exactly what he wanted. I just made sure I had one of those little recorders like yours."

Celia shook her head. "You are very calculating, aren't you?"

"Well, we have to be, don't we?" Natasha placed her hand on the notebook. "Are you saying that all you did to get here was work hard?"

"I'm not judging at all. Just making an observation. But for the record, I haven't slept with any supervisor. They don't exactly have the charm of the Hollywood types."

"Yes, I've seen pictures of your John Talbot. Quite the little troll, isn't he?"

"I think of him more like a hobbit, actually."

Both women laughed again, and then the guard knocked at the door and entered.

"Alas," Natasha said. "Just when it was getting interesting."

They parted ways, and Celia followed Keith down the hallway.

"She's a pistol, isn't she?" He remarked.

"That she is. I feel a little sorry for the new guard."

Keith laughed. "Oh, he could use a little humbling, trust me. And she'll get the job done."

"So has she been this way since she got here?"

"She was kind of quiet at first. She observed everything closely. Some of the guards were either star-struck or determined to take her down a peg because she was famous. You know how that goes."

"Oh really?" Celia's reporter senses went up. "Did anyone mistreat her?"

"Oh, nothing like that," Keith answered quickly. "Just sarcasm and trying to make sure she knew who was boss." He chuckled a bit. "Of course, one guy asked her for an autograph."

"How did that go over?"

"She gave him some creative ideas about what he could do to himself."

Celia laughed. "Why doesn't that surprise me? So she adjusted, then what?"

"Honestly, she's pretty calm most of the time. She meets with her attorney. She occasionally asks for papers or magazines. She asks for your paper a lot."

That explained how Natasha had followed her career. "I'm flattered… I think."

"Yeah, she likes the way you write. She showed me a couple. You're pretty talented."

"Thanks. So she seems to be pretty calm about the execution. Is that an act?"

"It probably is, but it's one she keeps up 24/7. If she's afraid, she's not showing anybody. In fact, the only emotion I've seen her show lately is the obvious dislike she has for that new guard."

"Yeah, that was obvious. Poor guy."

"Eh, he'll be fine." He pushed a button and the last door slid open. "Have a nice afternoon Ms. Brockwell."

"It's Celia and thanks. You too."

After a full afternoon, Celia headed home and called a local Asian place for delivery. Bart had called, but she decided to turn off her phone for the night. She needed a little space after his overnight earlier in the week. Solitude was calling her name, along with a bottle of wine she'd picked up at an upscale little shop. After a long shower and dinner, she took the bottle of wine with her to her desk and got out the recorder. As her voice and Natasha's droned on through the small speaker, Celia's mind drifted away from the interview to her days in graduate school.

"I saw that you were up for the Abbot Award, Celia. Congrats. I am too!" Paul said.

"Thanks, Paul. Have you decided what you're going to submit?"

"I think so. I have a piece about the issues at the recycling center that Dr. Ross complimented."

Celia tilted her head purposefully. "Really? You're submitting an opinion piece? That's gutsy."

"You think? I mean, the guy the award is named after was an editor, right? He was best known for his byline."

"Oh yeah, he was. I'm just impressed you aren't worried it will come off as a cliché. Good for you," said Celia. "I wouldn't have the courage."

"Hmm, maybe I should rethink..."

"No, no, go with your gut. I'll probably just play it safe with a straight fact piece."

Paul looked less enthusiastic. "Thanks, Celia. I guess I'll see you later."

Celia shook her head and rewound the microcassette, annoyed with herself for getting distracted. What had made her think about that? It was so long ago. She'd end up submitting a pointed and opinionated piece about campus safety and double standards against women, and she'd won the award. Paul's piece about the upcoming city elections didn't even make the top three. Oh well, was it her fault he second-guessed himself? He'd been a year ahead of her and several years older. He should have trusted himself. It also wasn't Celia's fault the award got her a great internship that turned into her first job.

After finishing her notes, Celia turned on her phone. It was almost 10:00, and she had three text messages from Bart. He was at a bar around the corner listening to some live music and invited her to join him. The wine was beginning to wear off, and Celia decided a little music might be fun. Besides, she felt energized, and maybe she and Bart could work up a sweat. At his place this time, though. She didn't want him spending the night again. Celia put on something sexy, grabbed her purse, and headed to the bar.

Chapter 7

On Monday, Celia did something she rarely did. She called in sick. The weekend had been frustrating, and she'd overindulged for the first time in almost a decade. She knew she could work from home once her headache subsided, and she was getting tired of John lurking around trying to get some nugget from her about the prison interviews. If he was going to persist for the entire three months, she was going to have to sit him down and set him straight. To hell with his temper and control issues. She couldn't deal with that after the weekend she'd had.

For starters, it had been a mistake to join Bart at the bar. He was already a bit drunk once she got there, and he was handsy. Celia hated PDA, and she had to get firm with him to make him stop. Of course, by this time, she was drunk and needy, so she went ahead to his place to blow off some steam. He'd gotten angry when she wouldn't stay, and they'd fought. She'd called him pathetic and clingy, and he'd called her an ice queen. Once she left, Celia stopped by a store and bought some more wine.

On Saturday her phone had blown up with calls from Bart, and she'd ignored them all. The man behaved like a teenage girl. Once she'd had enough of the incessant interruptions, Celia took the train to the opposite side of town and meandered in and out of shops until dark. There was a billiard room at one corner, so she decided to see who she might hustle. Not that she needed the money, but her father had taught her how to play, and it was fun to watch some guy's ego swell up and then deflate when she took his money. Luckily, she was one of the only women there, and decidedly the best looking, so she had plenty of players to choose from.

One man, Thomas, was almost as good as she was. He had a bit of a swagger and a quick wit. He bought Celia a couple of drinks, and then he let her buy him a couple. After three games, he led her to a booth so they could both sit for a while.

"So when you're not hustling drunk guys, what do you do?" He asked.

"I rob banks," Celia quipped, sipping a glass of bourbon.

"Oh really? Me too! Have you hit the Bank down on Robinson, 'cause I've been casing that one for a week."

Laughing, Celia shook her head. "No really, what do you do?" She asked.

"Boring things with numbers. Mostly glorified accounting. And you?"

"I write for The Journal."

"I thought you looked familiar." Thomas looked at her closely. "Yeah! You did that big piece on the crooked CEO, didn't you? That was awesome."

"Why, thank you. I hope you weren't his accountant!"

"Definitely not," Thomas laughed. "Let's play another game."

"I'm tired of hustling," Celia teased. "What should we play for?"

"How about your place or mine?"

Celia raised an eyebrow, but she smiled. "Sounds good. Rack 'em up."

Thomas was good, but she was still better. After two games, they ended up at her place. She barely got the door closed before he was kissing her roughly. She pushed him back and held his shoulders. "If I say no, you stop. Got it?"

"Yes, ma'am," he replied. "And if you don't say no, I'm not stopping."

She let him push her backward to the bedroom, and then everything became a frenzy. Bart was tender and romantic and passionate, which had its benefits. Thomas was nothing like that. Celia hadn't intended to let him stay, but she was so exhausted she fell asleep.

A banging at the door a few hours later shocked Celia from sleep. Thomas was out, sprawled on his back and snoring. "I'll be right back. Stay here." Celia shook him just a bit until he mumbled and rolled over. She put on a robe, closed the door to the bedroom, and walked to the entryway. "Damn," she whispered when she saw Bart through the peephole. She didn't undo the chain but opened the door just enough to talk to Bart.

"You haven't answered your phone since the night before last. I was wondering if you were okay."

"I'm fine, Bart. Just a little busy. What are you doing here?"

"I just wanted to apologize for the other night. I was over the line. I shouldn't have had so much to drink, and I shouldn't have pushed." He tried to look around her through the small gap. "Can we talk?"

"It's not a good time Bart. And it's early."

They both heard movement and a bit of stumbling. Thomas's curse was muffled, but there was no doubting Bart heard a man's voice.

"What the hell, Celia?" Bart's voice rose. "You went out and—?"

"Look, Bart, I'm not having this conversation right now."

"You screwed someone else? Who is it? Your boss?"

"Good god, Bart, of course not! It's none of your business!"

"Like hell! We're together. It's absolutely my business!" Bart pushed against the door.

"You break the door, I'm calling the police. And we are not together. You made that choice when you became an ass Friday night. Besides, we only went out a few times."

"I swear to God, Celia, you better open this door." Bart's voice was low.

"Go away. Do not come back. I will not have this conversation." Celia put her full weight against the door and slammed it closed, locking it while she leaned against it. Bart pounded the door once and cursed, but he left. *Good riddance*, Celia thought.

"Angry boyfriend?" Thomas came out with his jeans on and his shirt in his hand.

"Just some idiot who can't take no for an answer."

"Well, can you blame him?" Thomas smiled, pulling on his shirt. "I gotta go. Want to give me your number or no?"

"It was great, but no," Celia answered.

"No problem," he shrugged. "You know where I hang out if you want to try to hustle me again."

Thomas left, and Celia went back to bed. She flipped through channels until she wasn't pissed anymore. Thomas was the kind of guy she needed. Fun, no questions, no expectations. Good for a romp, an ego boost, and then gone. It was Bart's own fault he was upset. No one invited him to drop by like that. It was for the best. Now he'd leave her alone.

Celia spent the rest of her Sunday morning watching trash television and working on her laptop. Her stomach was too unsettled from a night of drinking to make any lunch, so she just chugged coffee all day. Late in the afternoon, she went for a run, and then she stopped by the store. For some reason, she felt like baking. She supposed it was her conversation with Natasha. Celia decided she'd make a cake and take it to the prison, but with no file.

Celia wasn't sure why she enjoyed baking so much. Maybe it was because her mother didn't let anyone in the kitchen. She'd told Celia it was her domain, and she didn't want Celia going in there making a mess.

"You don't know what you're doing, Celia. Cooking is an art." Mrs. Brockwell said.

"But I want to learn to cook! It's my kitchen too."

"Actually, it isn't. I pay the bills. There's more to cooking than following a recipe, you know. You have to be creative."

"I can be creative!"

"Celia, honey, you're good at many things, but you aren't creative. Just let me fix dinner, and you go do your homework."

Celia had surprised her mom by learning to out-cook her. She'd also created a good little side business baking cakes for friends and family's birthdays, anniversaries, and such. Not that she was a big fan of gatherings, but it was fun to see someone's face when she brought out a perfect cake, especially her mother's.

The phone rang, and Celia hoped it wasn't Bart. It wasn't; it was her neighbor, Lucille, asking if Celia had seen her cat. The woman was beside herself. Celia told her no, she hadn't seen the old tabby, and she hung up before the woman started crying. Celia was not a fan of most animals, especially cats. However, this tabby was too old to cause much trouble, and she didn't wail the way some cats did, so she didn't bother Celia much. Not like that stupid tomcat that used to roam in the alley. That thing wailed half the night and left his paw-prints over everyone's cars. Thank goodness a bit of antifreeze had solved that problem. Feral cats were one of the issues the city had tried to do a better job of addressing the past couple of years, and Celia was glad. Still, she'd go ahead and put up a flyer at the corner like her neighbor asked. It never hurt to have the neighbors on your side. The lady was always willing to watch Celia's place or get the mail when she traveled. Her daughter rarely visited, and the elderly woman appreciated the fact that Celia always said hello.

Once she had the cake on a cooling rack, Celia decided to catch up on some office work. Natasha Bronlov wasn't her only story, and she wanted to finish a couple of outlines. She was saving a draft when she heard a knock at the door. She pulled aside the curtain and saw Bart's car parked on the street. Rolling her eyes, she kept working. He knocked a couple of times, and then she heard a car start, and she watched him through the window as he drove away. Good, she thought. Maybe he'll take the hint.

By 9:00, Celia's stomach was growling, and the screen on her laptop had started to blur. She needed something to eat, but cooking was out of the question. Instead, she grabbed a sleeve of crackers, some peanut butter, and a beer and sat on the sofa to watch television. She fell asleep there and barely moved until Monday morning when the headache that kept her home awakened her.

Chapter 8

Natasha was more than a little surprised when Celia walked into Room 4 with a cake in hand at their next visit. "They x-rayed it, so no file. Sorry," Celia said dryly.

Throwing back her head to laugh and slapping the table, Natasha asked, "Did you at least bring some forks?"

"No forks, sorry. But I did manage a few spoons and some napkins," Celia replied, pulling them from her pocket. She laid out a napkin for each of them, sloppily cut two slices with one of the spoons, and invited Natasha to taste the cake. It was a strawberry cake with buttercream frosting.

"Oh my God, I may have a sugar orgasm," Natasha moaned after taking a bite. "Why are you a reporter when you could be doing this full-time?"

Celia smiled and picked at her own piece of cake. "It wouldn't be fun if I *had* to do it."

"True," Natasha said, pointing at Celia with a spoon full of frosting. "Still, I think I may request this for my last meal. The frosting alone is worth dying for."

Celia laughed, but then she considered Natasha's flippant remark. "Not to ruin our treat, but how *do* you feel about losing your last appeal?"

"You mean facing the fact that I am going to die? I try to be pragmatic about it."

"I think I would find that difficult."

"I did too, at first. I wanted to win. Winning meant thwarting the death penalty. I poured an ungodly amount of my money into winning."

"Success has its benefits, even in prison."

"Exactly. However, after my second appeal failed, a chaplain came to visit me. I had managed to avoid such things during the trial and afterward, but I guess he slipped in," Natasha rolled her eyes. "He asked me about the state of my soul and the afterlife."

"Interesting." Celia wrote swiftly, *found out the name of the chaplain,* and then returned her attention to Natasha. "What *are* your thoughts on that?"

"I understand how religion might give some people security. But I don't need it, nor do I believe it. I believe he was sincere, and I wasn't rude to him. But I did tell him I had no concerns about my eternal soul and let him know there would be no need for him to visit again."

"I see," Celia replied.

"Do you believe in a god or afterlife?" Natasha moved her napkin to the side and leaned in with interest.

"Not really. I mean, I know objectively it cannot be proved either way. I suppose I'm agnostic. I just don't see the relevance except, as you said, it gives comfort to some people."

"I didn't think you seemed like the religious type," Natasha nodded with approval. "I think I'd like another piece of that cake."

"Really?"

"If there is no god, then gluttony is not a sin," she teased.

Celia cut another slice for Natasha, but she didn't finish her own. "So you feel settled about the inevitable?"

"After the chaplain visited, I thought about things. I realized that if there is no afterlife, I have nothing to fear from death. And truly, what most people want for those on death row is for them to be afraid. To suffer. By refusing to fear this, I am still winning, in a sense."

"I never thought of it that way, but it does make sense."

They sat in silence while Natasha savored her second slice of cake. Celia watched her and thought about what she had said. It made sense in a way, but it was also a bit odd. Natasha had shifted her thinking so that she could still win somehow. Celia supposed that made sense too. The actress was used to succeeding, getting what she wanted. Of course, she would spin what most people might consider a loss into a win.

"You haven't eaten your cake," Natasha pointed out. "It isn't poisoned, is it?"

Celia laughed. "Not at all. I am just not a big eater of sweets. I mainly learned to cook to prove my mom wrong."

"Well, that sounds like an interesting story."

"It's not very. My mom didn't want anyone in her kitchen. She was rather obnoxious about it. So I learned to cook out of spite, and then so that I could render her speechless."

Natasha laughed. "Well, well, it looks like I'm not the only one who likes to win."

Celia shrugged. "Most of life is a competition, after all."

"Yes, it is, one that I intend to win until the end."

"Some might consider getting away with four murders winning. In a strange way, of course."

"Well, except I didn't get away with them, did I?" Natasha sat back and licked her fingertips.

"You only got caught after killing your father. If that hadn't happened, you would have gotten away with them."

Natasha's expression darkened, and she shifted in her chair. "I guess in that way, my father won. Damn him."

"Why *did* you kill him?"

"We're not ready for that part of the story," Natasha replied shortly.

"I'm sorry, I didn't intend to touch on it yet. I was just curious since we were discussing him."

"I do plan to talk about him, but not today. I don't want to have indigestion after this lovely cake."

Celia scanned her notes. "In that case, let's go way back. I asked you in our first interview if you remembered much about your life before you moved to the states."

"Yes, I remember the question. I do remember some things. I remember my mother. I remember being told stories, and I remember that one time when I was sick, I slept in the bed with her. I don't know where my father slept. I have a vague memory of people I assume were my grandparents."

"Would you say you were happy as a child?"

Sighing, Natasha crumpled her napkin and then brushed the crumbs onto the floor. "What is a happy childhood? My parents took care of me. My father provided for us. My mother was very attentive. Until she left, I lived what I assume was a life like anyone else. I was an independent child. That is what my father always said."

"So no abuse or trauma?"

"That is always the hypothesis, isn't it? No one ever beat me. My parents' marriage was less than ideal. There were fights, which mostly consisted of my father yelling and my mother cowering. I remember slipping through the back door and escaping to the yard or somewhere down the street from time to time."

Celia smiled. "Would you say you were an obedient child?"

Laughing, Natasha tapped the table. "What do you think?"

Celia thought for a minute. "I think you were very good at seeming compliant."

"Who, me? I was the model child!"

Celia laughed. There was no doubt Natasha knew how to wrap others around her finger, even at a young age. Who wouldn't use that to their advantage?

"I generally did what I wanted; however, I learned how to work the house rules to my advantage I suppose. Most young people do, at least once they become teenagers. It did get harder after my mother left, but I eventually learned my father's methods too."

Natasha wouldn't have been openly defiant, Celia thought. It didn't fit with her cool nature. Not that Natasha didn't likely get angry at times. There had already been a couple of moments where Celia had sensed an undercurrent of it. The day the new guard walked Natasha in, for example. The actress had been smarmy and flirty, but it was apparent she was not happy that the guard tried to control her in a domineering way.

"So now it's your turn again." Natasha pointed. "Tell me more about your not-so-apple-pie family. Are they nearby?"

"Oh, god no," Celia replied. "I was raised just outside the Bible belt."

"Churchgoing family then?"

"Mom and I did go to church a bit when I was very young. She was involved with some ladies' group there. All that changed when my father left."

"How so?"

"For some reason, once he left, we were different. Our status was tainted, I guess. All those ladies group women dropped her, and we stopped going. I didn't mind; it meant I could sleep in on Sundays."

"So, you and your mother were close."

Celia studied Natasha; the actress already knew they weren't close. "No. Mom got bitter, and my father became insufferable with his trophy wife and a new set of kids."

"I take it he wasn't a good part-time dad." Natasha chuckled.

"Hell, no. I stopped visiting him when I was fourteen. I think he was relieved."

"And no touching reconciliations years later."

"Hardly," I snorted. "I assume my father hasn't traded up in the last several years. My mother died in 2010."

Natasha's sad expression seemed almost sincere. "I'm sorry about that."

"I was in Haiti. I didn't make it back for the funeral."

"So…" Natasha smirked. "No desire for marriage or family?"

"Is it cliché to say I am married to my career?"

"Maybe a little. But a career gives you tangible rewards, and it doesn't demand sandwiches."

Celia laughed so hard her eyes began to water. "Oh my god, so true. Sex is nice, but—"

"But it's a fairly steep price to pay for sex."

"Also true. And no variety."

"Poor Bart. Does he know his hopes for fairy tales are futile?"

"He'd better."

The five-minute warning knock came, and Celia began to wrap the cake in the cellophane she'd used to bring it. "We have two weeks until our next interview. I'd like to start talking more about the jump from actress to murderer. I'm no psychologist, but I have trouble believing that you went from a controlled professional straight to a serial killer. I want to explore that."

"I assumed you would. You'd be surprised though. Sometimes a controlled professional is just a cover for darker impulses. There are more ways to win than killing. Success is the ultimate win. Don't you agree? You've certainly won in your field."

"I suppose I have. I'd like to think I'm still winning."

"I'm sure you are. Your career is as important to you, as mine was to me. Staying where we are and not moving forward isn't who we are." Natasha pouted a bit. "I suppose I can't keep the rest of the cake, can I?"

"No, they told me I'd have to bring it back out with me. I wondered if they just said that so they could have a slice too."

"I wouldn't blame them. After a slice of that, Keith will *really* want to get into your pants."

"Oh god, no more men please!" Celia rolled her eyes. She knew Keith had an eye on her, but prison guards were a no-fly zone.

"Hmmm… sounds like there's a story there. Maybe I'll want to explore that in our next meeting."

Keith knocked, and they both laughed. "You ladies must have had fun?" He looked confused.

"Oh, Celia is a lot of fun," Natasha said, winking as the other guard led her out of the room.

Keith and Celia walked down the hallway in silence. He entered the code, and the doors opened. They were almost to the entry when he turned to her. "Hey, Celia—"

"Want some cake?" She interrupted. "I have some spoons in my pocket. I was planning on leaving it with the clerk at the desk."

"Oh," Keith said. "Sure, it looks great."

When they got to the front desk, Celia cut a piece of the cake for Keith and the clerk, Myra. Myra's reaction to the first bite was similar to Natasha's, and Celia told her to take the rest home. Keith enjoyed it too, though he looked a little disappointed that she had interrupted him in the hallway. *Sorry, Keith, no-fly zone.* She told Keith to be nice to Myra so he could take some home too.

Her cellphone rang as she walked to her car. It was John.

"Hey, Celia, are you heading back from the prison?"

"I just walked out. I should be back after lunch."

"Okay then. I'd like a status report when you get here. I also have something else I'd like you to look into. I think it's your kind of thing."

"Sure," Celia replied. "I'll text you when I get back."

Celia tossed the phone onto the passenger seat and started her car. Ever since she'd set John straight, he'd avoided her a bit. This new story was probably a way to get back into her good graces.

Or it was a carrot to convince her to spill all the details about her interviews with Natasha. Either way, Celia knew she'd need to be on her guard. John never did anything without an agenda.

"So I was thinking about how long you've been here," John began as Celia walked around her desk as sat. "I've been thinking about how we can expand the writing you do."

"That sounds interesting." Celia smiled.

"You're adept at outlining the implications of things like corruption, negligence, and topics that sometimes go over the public's head."

And often yours, John.

"I'd like you to consider a weekly byline, sort of a general inform-the-public series, almost educational. You could do what you do best, lay out the facts."

Celia's smile froze in place as she thought about John's words. It was typical. It seemed like a compliment, but there was also a dig. This time the dig was in reference to her drama-based interviews with Natasha.

"I think it would really bump up our numbers, yours included, and you could share your expertise."

"I'll think about it," Celia said. "I'll have to see if it will fit in with the other stories I have in progress and the exclusive interviews with Natasha." *See, I can dig too.*

"I understand," John smirked. "You do that." He left the office, closing the door loudly on his way out.

Celia opened the folder titled "Prison" and began typing up her notes from the day's interview. She'd listen to the recording later. When she got to the word *parents*, she paused She knew her father was single again; his trophy wife had taken the kids and left. That probably explained why he kept reaching out, continuing to reconnect. And somehow, knowing he was alone made Celia even less inclined to return any of his calls.

Sorry, Dad. You used up your chances.

Chapter 9

It was the fourth time Bart had called. Celia sighed and turned over her cell phone. He'd left repeated apologetic messages, hoping to talk with her to "straighten things out." At first, Celia had considered indulging him. However, after the third rambling voicemail, she became completely turned off. Hopefully, if she ignored him, he'd just give up eventually.

As she worked, Celia periodically eyed the file labeled "Prison." Every time she interviewed Natasha, she listened to the recording, consulted her notes, and created a transcription of sorts. Then, she printed the transcription and placed it in the file folder. It was the only story she was working on that wasn't digital storage only. For some reason, Celia felt compelled to print each transcript, in case some unheard-of technology travesty erased the digital records. It was a bit obsessive and paranoid, but Celia couldn't seem to help herself. Today, however, she resisted the temptation to open it.

John was pleased with the bits and pieces of her visits with Natasha that Celia had chosen to share. He still didn't like the fact that they were sitting on the story; he was paranoid about getting scooped or having one of the prison employees leak Celia's visits. Any early preview of the story, however, and Natasha would halt the interviews. Delayed gratification was not John's strength, but he grumpily agreed.

As soon as Celia got home, her phone rang. She swore, but wasn't Bart this time; it was her friend, Marlene.

"Hey Celia, you've been a stranger!" Marlene was almost always upbeat.

"I know," Celia said. "I've been churning out story after story. You know I work for a slave driver."

"John can be an ass, but I think your biggest slave driver is you," Marlene countered. She had worked for him for years; it was how Celia met her.

"You could be right," Celia laughed. "How's the restaurant business?"

Marlene and her husband owned an authentic Italian restaurant; she'd left The Journal to open it. Dave, her husband, was a great businessman, and Marlene had her grandmother's almost magical gift for cooking. Even Celia couldn't replicate Marlene's Italian cheesecake, and she'd repeatedly tried.

"It's crazy too. I was worried in the beginning when things started slowly. But now Dave is trying to figure out how to make more space for us without moving locations."

"That's great! I saw the piece in the paper about it. I need to get over there to sample the new dishes."

"You do! Of course, you'll get the friend discount if you wash some dishes."

"On second thought, maybe I'll just have it delivered."

Marlene laughed, and her dogs started barking in the background. "Shut up Rossini! Puccini!"

"I still can't believe you named your great Danes after Italian composers. Or that you have two Great Danes in that townhouse."

"That's actually why I called," Marlene said. "We bought a house. We're moving."

"Congratulations," Celia said. "I thought you'd live in that townhouse forever."

Well," Marlene giggled, "we need more room…"

Celia didn't answer for a few seconds. Then she understood what Marlene meant. "Oh my goodness. When?"

"About six months from now. We'd all but given up. I wasn't even taking shots anymore."

Marlene was 39, and she and Dave had been trying to have a baby for almost as long as Marlene had known her. Celia didn't relate to the urge, but she always tried to offer the appropriate support. "You'll understand when your clock starts ticking louder," Marlene always said. Celia was 38, and her clock had never ticked. However, she was glad Marlene and Dave were getting what they wanted.

"I'm glad for you and Dave, Marlene. About the house and the baby."

"Thanks," Marlene gushed. "I want you to put the 27th on your calendar. We'll be in the house, and we're having a housewarming and gender reveal."

"Oh…wow."

"I know, I know. We used to make fun of those. But now that I'm finally pregnant, I want to do everything."

"I'll be there," Celia promised. "Let me know what I can bring."

"Actually, I think we need a girls' night before the party. I want to hear all about your love life!" Marlene teased.

"I'd be glad to have a girls' night, but it'll be a boring night if that's the only topic."

"Oh come on, I'm married. I have to live vicariously. Surely you have some drop-dead gorgeous man in your life."

"Drop dead gorgeous doesn't necessarily mean sane and normal," Celia said dryly.

Marlene's voice changed. "Oh, it sounds like there's a story there. What's his name?"

"His name *was* Bart. He got clingy and then kind of crazy. I can't seem to shake him."

"That sounds a little disturbing, Celia. Is he stalking you or something?"

Celia laughed. "You've been watching Lifetime again, haven't you? It's fine."

"Your problem is you are just too irresistible. They just can't stay away from you."

"Oh god, you already have a pregnancy brain, don't you?" Celia smiled. "So when do you want to have this girls' night?"

They set a night to meet, and then Marlene chatted for a few more minutes before saying she needed to throw up, so Celia ended the call. Marlene was sharp and loyal, and her husband had his finger on the pulse of a lot of the business in town. Their friendship had been enjoyable and beneficial. They deserved happiness.

Celia was considering what to bake for the housewarming when someone knocked at her door.

"Oh great, you're home," Bart said as Celia opened the door. He was holding a bouquet. "I think we should talk."

Anger was Celia's first impulse, but she forced herself not to react. "Bart, there's nothing to talk about."

"But I need to apologize. I was an ass. You were right. We weren't exclusive yet."

"Bart," Celia held up a hand. "It's fine, you're forgiven. I think we should both just move on." She began to close the door, but Bart stepped forward.

"Please, Celia," he said. "Just one conversation to clear the air. Then, if you still don't want to see me, I'll leave you alone."

Celia opened the door wider and stepped back so that Bart could walk into her place. She followed him to the living room, and when he sat on the sofa, she sat in an armchair.

"You look great," Bart said.

"Thanks, you too. So what's on your mind?"

"I've been thinking about our argument. I was wrong. I was moving too fast. We were having a good time and I was pushy."

"It really is okay, Bart. It was a stupid move on my part too. I was having a rough weekend." Celia hoped if she took some blame he'd be appeased and finally drop it.

"Me too," Bart said, moving closer. "It was all a stupid misunderstanding. Can we just forget it, pretend it never happened?"

"I'd like that too," Celia carefully responded. "You're a great guy, Bart. I'd hate for us to leave it on bad terms."

"Thank you, Celia," Bart said, taking her hand. "I think you're pretty awesome too." Celia withdrew her arm, but Bart continued. "Would you be interested in dinner Saturday night?"

"Bart, I don't think—"

"No expectation. Just friends. Dinner only. I have two tickets to the hospital gala. I know how much you like Nora Jones."

Celia seriously doubted Bart only wanted to be friends. However, she'd love to see the singer perform in such an intimate setting. And it a gala would be much more public than a dinner for two. "Sure Bart. That sounds great."

"Great!" Bart stood and handed Celia the flowers. "I'm glad we got things fixed."

"Me too," Celia said. "These are beautiful, thank you."

Bart walked toward the door, and Celia followed. "The gala starts at 8:00, so I'll pick you up at 7:30."

"Sounds good," Celia said, keeping a bit of space between her and Bart. "I'm looking forward to it."

After Bart left, Celia went to the kitchen and looked through her cabinets until she found a vase and filled it for the flowers. Then, instead, Celia opened the cabinet under the sink, pulled out the garbage can, and dropped them inside.

Chapter 10

On Friday night, Celia and Marlene met at Zahav, an Israeli restaurant they both enjoyed. It was a bit crowded, but because the owner knew them both, they managed to get seated quickly. After ordering drinks and hummus, Marlene pinned Celia with a serious look.

"So tell me more about this Bart."

"Well, I think he's fine. I was still pissed off when we talked before."

"What does that mean? What happened?"

"We went out a few times. He's pretty charming. Then I met him at a bar one night and we had a fight, parted ways. We were both drunk."

"Okay, following," Marlene nodded.

"Well, I went out the next night to a pool place. You know I love to play pool."

"I know you love hustling," Marlene laughed.

"True. Well, I played a few games with a guy. He was funny and hot. We ended up back at my townhouse. Let's just say we were both exhausted and fell asleep."

Marlene sighed dramatically and pretended to pout. "Ah. Memories of wild sex."

Laughing, Celia continued. "Well, we were both still asleep, and someone knocked at my door."

"Oh, I know where this is going. It was Bart, coming to grovel."

"I don't know why he was there, but he heard Tom in the background, and he blew up. I get why it bugged him. But we never said we were exclusive, and we'd had that fight and ended things."

"Yeah," Marlene shook her head. "That isn't how they think. You were both drunk. He thought it was just a fight. And I assume you'd been sleeping with Bart, right?"

"I had been."

"Sorry, hon. You two were a couple. At least in his mind. But still, he didn't have to act like a jerk."

"Well, he tried to apologize and I ignored his calls. Then he showed up again."

"Wow. What did he say?"

"He apologized. He apologized for the fight and for making assumptions. He fell on his sword."

"Okay…" Marlene sounded surprised. "Is that all?"

"Well, he said he wanted to be friends. He invited me to that gala tomorrow night."

"You didn't say yes, did you?"

"I wasn't going to, but Norah Jones is singing."

"Oh Celia," Marlene scolded. "You know he wants to be more than friends."

"Probably, but it's a public venue. I will not let him come back to my place. And it's Norah Jones."

"For someone so brilliant, you don't always understand nuances, do you?"

Celia was a little miffed. "Look, I'm a big girl. I can handle an evening with a man who said he only wanted to be friends."

"I know you can. But don't go out with him after this. Something about him seems off."

"Yes, Mom," Celia teased. "Boy, those maternal hormones are kicking in, aren't they? Do I have a curfew?"

"Bitch," Marlene teased. "I am getting hungry, though. Don't they know they can't keep a pregnant woman waiting for food?"

After dinner, the two of them walked in and out of random shops, catching up and gossiping. Marlene was an expert gossip. She told Celia more backstories about the staff at The Journal than she'd ever wanted to know, including stories about John's antics before Celia began working there. Celia talked about some of her travels, and Marlene expressed jealousy. Celia laughed at Marlene for needing to pee at every place they visited. But she felt herself relax for the first time in a while. She'd been so busy traveling, interviewing killers, and navigating Bart's ego, she hadn't realized how much she needed a mindless night with a female friend.

"So, are you thinking of names yet?" Celia asked.

"Well, we're talking about it. Dave wants a family name if it's a boy. I would like to use my Nona's name if it's a girl."

"What was your Nona's name again?"

"Olivia."

"Oh, I like that. I can't stand these strange new names people choose. Especially celebrities. What are they thinking? Can you imagine the news in twenty years? Senator Astral took the floor today to champion a new gun control bill. This is Plum Johnson-Evanovich reporting."

Marlene giggled. "Hmmm, I kind of like Astral."

"Don't you dare! I will adopt that child myself."

By 10:00, Celia could tell Marlene was about to fall asleep standing on the sidewalk. They said their goodbyes, and Celia drove home. Predictably, Lucille was in her front yard calling for Jerry when she got home.

"Oh, hello dear," Lucille asked. "Have a nice evening?"

"I did. Dinner with an old friend."

"Oh, I see. Your young man was here earlier. I thought you might have been out with him." Jerry walked out from behind Celia's bushes and rubbed himself on her legs before allowing Lucille to pick him up.

"Not tonight. Just the girls. Goodnight, Lucille."

Celia was a little irritated as she unlocked her door and walked inside her townhouse. They were going to the gala tomorrow night. Why would Bart just drop by like that? Marlene was right. He probably hoped he could convince her to be more than friends. She would have to make that clear at the gala, and that would be the end of it. Nora Jones or no Norah Jones.

The light was blinking again. Celia almost deleted the message without listening, but she couldn't quite do it.

"Celia, I'm going to be in the Philadelphia area for business next week. I figure you live somewhere near The Journal office. Please call me back. There are some things you need to know."

A little curious, Celia listened again. What could her estranged father possibly have to tell her? And why didn't he just spill it in a message? It felt like manipulation, and she bristled. She was well acquainted with his manipulation; Celia had learned the skill from him. She pressed the delete button and went to bed.

On Saturday, Bart arrived at 7:30 exactly. Celia gave herself a once-over in the mirror before answering the door. She looked amazing, she had to admit. The blue dress fit her in all the right places, and her hair had just the right amount of loose curls teasing her neck. She opened the door and smiled. Her date was equally stunning.

"You look wonderful tonight," Bart said, kissing her cheek. She stiffened a bit but smiled.

"Thanks, you look pretty good as well. Shall we go?" Celia held her wrap with both hands so he wouldn't try to take her arm. No touching or affection, she thought. Very clear boundaries.

Once they arrived, a valet took Bart's Mercedes, and as they walked in, Celia could feel a few stares. She straightened and walked with a bit more hip movement. Too bad Bart was such a clinger; they made a breathtaking couple. They found their assigned table and sat down, greeting another couple already seated there.

The dinner was delicious, and Celia managed to keep Bart at arm's length. A few important people had their say, and then Norah Jones was introduced. Celia applauded along with everyone else, and she relaxed as the artist began to play and sing. After several selections, she took a break, and the house band began to play. Several couples began dancing, and Bart turned to Celia.

"Would you like to dance?"

"Yes I would," she smiled.

Bart was an excellent dancer, and Celia enjoyed following his lead. She kept a bit of distance between them, despite Bart's attempt to pull her closer, but he didn't react. After a couple of dances, she said she was ready for something to drink, so they made their way to the bar.

"Celia? Is that you?"

Celia turned to see Keith, dressed in a security uniform, walking toward her.

"Hello, Keith, how are you?" Celia shook his hand.

"You look great!" Bart stepped beside Celia as Keith gave the compliment. "I'm Keith Rhodes." He shook Bart's hand.

"Bart Vandiver," Bart said with a thin smile. "Nice to meet you."

"You too. I hope you two are having a nice evening."

"We are," Bart said. "We were just headed to the bar."

"I won't keep you then," Keith said. "Nice to meet you."

Bart began walking to the bar, but Celia stayed back. "Good to see you. Moonlighting I see."

"Yeah, prison guards don't make the big bucks," he joked.

"I'll see you next week," Celia said, and then she joined Bart, who didn't look especially pleased. Oh, well, she thought, that's his problem. It's not like Keith was a rival. No one was a rival because they were just friends, right? She smiled and ordered a drink, ignoring his expression.

They danced for a little while longer, and then Nora Jones began performing again. Celia enjoyed her immensely, but when she bowed for the final time, Celia was ready to go home. She hoped Bart wouldn't suggest a nightcap.

"This was wonderful, Bart, thank you. But I'm exhausted for some reason."

"Probably all that dancing," Bart smiled. "I'll take you home."

It started to rain as they drove back to her townhouse, which Celia counted as lucky. Once they pulled into the driveway, Bart reached for his door handle.

"Oh, you don't have to get out in this weather. I can see myself in. I'm so tired I'll probably fall right into bed and sleep. Thank you for a wonderful evening." She exited the car before Bart could protest.

Once she was inside, Celia shed her dress, took down her hair, and scrubbed the makeup from her face. She was tired, that hadn't been a lie. Two nights out in a row were enough for her after a busy week. Shaking her head, she thought, *So this is what forty feels like.* Once in bed, she flipped through a few channels and then settled on a documentary. However, she was asleep before the narrator even finished the introduction.

Chapter 11

Even though Celia was looking forward to the next interview with Natasha, she had to admit the week without travel to and from the prison was a nice change. She had other pieces to finish, research to do, and several meetings, including a quarterly staff meeting—"all hands," as John liked to call it. It would have been a nightmare to add travel and an interview into the mix.

At 10:00 on Wednesday, the entire staff gathered into the too-small conference room. All chairs pointed toward the podium, where John would lead things. Celia tapped her pen on her notebook and watched the stragglers trickle into the room. John wouldn't begin to talk until everyone was there and he had their undivided attention. He hated being interrupted. Finally, the last couple of people took their seats in the back.

"Okay, everybody, let's get started. I'm gonna ask you to turn off your phones or put them in your pocket on silent. We need to focus, and none of these stories needs to get out of this room." It was the standard speech he gave at the start of every meeting.

"First," John continued, "the numbers. Our readership is up, which is good news. Thanks for the hard work. Two-thirds of our stories were picked up internationally this quarter, and a few of our reporters are working with the big three. Let's hear it for Omar Sirami and Celia Brockwell.

"Now, we have a lot of work to do. I don't want anyone—anyone—one-upping us on a story. We get it first. Always. That means nobody sleeps on the job, and nobody talks about the big stories outside these walls.

"Now, let's talk about stories and collaboration." John pointed to a reporter. "Hannah, how's the piece about the gala going? You got your pass and the research on the spending of funds from previous galas?" Hannah nodded, and John moved on. "Great. George, the vet story? The guy who euthanized pets without permission? Where are we on that?"

"I've got testimony from three clients and an assistant who doesn't want to be named. The vet is stalling with the records."

John looked down for a moment, gripping the podium. "Who's in charge of the office there?"

"An older lady." George consulted his notes. "Her name is Jeannie Grey."

"Okay, I'll get someone from animal services to lean on her. Don't even bother with the vet. He's just trying to cover his ass."

The meeting continued, with John asking for specifics about various stories, recognizing those getting the job done, and berating those dragging their feet.

"Finally, Celia," John said, grinning. "You're last because you've got some big stuff going. How's the case with the CEO going? Subpoenas, dates, what you got?"

"Right now they're deposing people, lots of people. I expect more lawsuits. Of course, their lawyers are trying to stay tight-lipped, but I'm pushing. I won't stop."

"I know you won't. You're relentless. What about the state legislation piece? You and Julia on track?" Celia looked across the room at Julia and nodded, and Julia gave her a thumbs up. "Good." John looked around and then leaned forward a bit. "And what else have you got for us?"

"That pretty much covers it," Celia replied.

John walked around in front of the podium and folded his arms. "You sure? Nothing else you want to share with us?"

Celia looked at John and raised an eyebrow. "I'm absolutely sure, John. There is nothing else to share in this meeting."

After holding Celia's stare for several seconds, John smiled and leaned back against the podium. "Okay, then, folks. Get your asses back to work."

Celia walked back to her office, and she was about to close her door when John placed his hand on the panel. "Can we chat for a minute or two?"

"Sure," Celia nodded. She sat at her desk and offered John the chair in front of her, but he remained standing.

"So you don't even want to let the rest of the staff in on the big story?"

"I'd prefer it was just between you and me for now. Just to make sure nothing leaks."

John shook his head. "So, you trust the underpaid prison guards to keep their lips sealed but not your own colleagues?"

"I can't control what happens at the prison. I have no choice but to let them do what they will. However, I can control who knows what outside the prison. It's not a matter of trust."

"How about this—you give me a preliminary write-up, and I'll sit on it."

Celia leaned forward. "John, why does this bother you so much? You've never asked for anything like that. This isn't the first hush-hush story we've done."

"Everything about this bothers me. Why did she pick you? Why all the secrecy? Why is she even telling a story now, when she's set to be executed? This is a woman who lived in the limelight her whole life, and I just have to wonder what her angle is."

"She performed in the limelight," Celia corrected. "She did everything a celebrity can do and then some to live as far from the limelight as she could. As for why she sought me out, I have no idea. I'm not a bleeding heart emotional, bent on overturning her sentence. Hell, I was practically the only stoic reporter after 9/11. I'm not worried about her angle. The story will be good for us."

"Good for you, you mean."

"And that's another thing, John. When one of the people here succeeds, you succeed. The publication succeeds. When has that ever been a bad thing?"

John looked at Celia for so long, she wondered if he was having some sort of stroke. Finally, he placed his hands on her desk. "I just think you need to remember who is in charge here."

"You can go now, John. This is ridiculous." Celia wiggled her mouse to wake up the monitor and began typing. After a few seconds, John left her office, closing the door quietly behind him.

Less than a minute later, someone knocked. Celia looked up from her laptop, and Julia was standing in the doorway. "Got a minute?"

"Sure, have a seat." Celia smiled. "Want some water?"

"I'd love one," Julia answered. "What's up John's butt today? He didn't look happy just now."

"Oh, he's having one of his phases," Celia sighed, passing Julia a bottle.

"Ah, one of his 'I'm the boss' moments?"

"Exactly. He does it every time he doesn't get his way."

Julia laughed and sipped her water. "True. I think he's still mad he didn't grow to be six feet tall."

"You're terrible. I love it." Celia laughed. "So what's up?"

"I wondered if you'd hear anything about a bigger media company trying to buy us out."

"No, I haven't heard anything like that. What did you hear?"

"Well, you know how inept John is with technology sometimes. I had to help him the other day, and I happened to see part of an email from over his head."

"What did it say?"

"I didn't see much, and he was not happy at all when he realized I caught a glimpse. But it would explain why he's been such an ass the past few weeks."

"Well, you know," Celia got up and closed the door. "We're getting more and more attention. Omar and I aren't the only ones getting called upon by the bigger pubs anymore. Not to be a jerk, but I think we're outgrowing John's ability to manage things."

Julia sipped more water and placed the bottle on the desk. "You could be right. You know, I've been here ten years, and sometimes I'm still not sure how John landed the position he's in. Not that he doesn't get things done. But his controlling tendencies and his manner…"

"I know. He's a bit like the manager of a mom-and-pop store who was thrust into running Walmart headquarters at times. And that's when he gets like this."

"Any idea who would be running things if we did get absorbed?" Julia sounded concerned.

"If they replace John, they'll want someone with name recognition and big story guns."

Julia sat back and smiled. "It could be you."

"I dunno. It's kind of a boys' club."

"Julia, you have more balls than any man in this office. I don't know everything you're working on, but I got the idea in our meeting that John seems a little rattled."

Celia considered John's words. If something was stirring, it might explain his paranoia. "Oh well, there's no use speculating. If something that big is going on, it won't be a secret for long."

"True." Julia grabbed her water bottle and stood. "Thanks for the water. I'll let you get back to work."

Once Julia was gone, Celia thought about what she'd said. Was John worried about his job? Was that why he was so skittish and testy? Celia had to admit, the thought of moving up appealed to her. She was doing well now, but a promotion within a bigger media corporation would give her more freedom and more clout. And she'd be one of the few women in that position. A buy-out would also explain why John was so worried about this story that had fallen into Celia's lap. Being the only journalist with real access into Natasha Bronlov's life was a distinction that would certainly come with some perks and recognition.

As she returned to her tasks, Celia imagined what it would be like to have a more authoritative position. She liked the idea. Maybe it was just gossip, but if not, she was going to throw her hat into the ring, forget about John. This was her livelihood and her passion. A moody man operating above his pay grade wasn't going to get in the way.

Chapter 12

"I saw you in the newspaper this week," Natasha said as Celia sat and began setting up the recorder.

"You read the newspaper?"

"Not typically," Natasha replied. "Occasionally a guard will leave me theirs. This time Keith gave it to me with the request that I return it when I was done."

Celia opened her notebook. "Ah, you must have seen photos from the gala. I did see Keith there. He was working security."

"Yes, he mentioned you were there. I do hate that newspaper photos are black and white, though. What color was your dress?"

"It was navy blue. I'd worn it before."

"You looked great, and that date of yours was certainly hot. Someone new?"

"No, not new. It was just a date for the gala."

Natasha smiled. "Is he the one you had the date with before? The recorder isn't on yet. Surely you can give me a first name."

Celia sighed. "His name is Bart. Yes, we've been out a few times."

Natasha put her elbow on the table and leaned forward. "He looks very professional. Potential long-term material?"

Celia laughed. "The jury is still out. I thought yes, then no, and now I'm undecided. He's a bit… enthusiastic for my tastes."

"Lucky him," Natasha teased. "I've never had much luck with long-term. Of course, I also never had much desire."

Celia turned on the recorder as Natasha continued. "My parents' relationship was less than inspiring."

"Yes, you mentioned there was conflict."

"I'm sure someone like my father would be hard for any woman to live with. My meek mother was certainly no match for him."

"Yes, I've noticed that when you dated before your arrest, you tended to be paired with men who had a strong presence."

Natasha laughed. "That was very tactful. What you mean is that I had a thing for handsome, arrogant pricks."

"True," Celia chuckled. "But none of them lasted."

"Maybe they were no match for me," Natasha joked.

"You know, I can see that. You were formidable and successful. That could threaten even the most confident man."

"That was a problem for some of them," Natasha agreed. "Although a few were just too desperate for a lifelong commitment. Which is all but a delusion in Hollywood."

"Yes, why is it that we women are seen as clingy when so many men are so eager to lock it down?"

"I have no idea," Natasha replied.

"It has to be difficult navigating a relationship in front of the whole world."

"The press is incredibly annoying. They feel entitled to everyone's most private details." Natasha raised an eyebrow. "No offense, of course."

"Of course," Celia said. "I tend to agree."

"And yet you certainly seem to be adept at convincing corrupt CEOs to spill their secrets."

Celia shrugged. "In my mind, there is a difference between exposing a criminal or cad and hiding in the bushes outside a celebrity's home."

"The paparazzi don't think so," Natasha's voice sounded tense, and Celia saw her fingers press into the table.

"I have to say, you were much more successful than most at keeping them at bay."

"It was certainly difficult. They are like roaches. Stomp one, and three more skitter out from the dark."

"Sounds like you have some personal experience, despite your best effort."

Natasha sat back and studied Celia in silence. "I'm definitely going to need a cigarette to tell this story."

Laughing, Celia pulled one from the package and lit it with a match. She handed it to Natasha, who smoked it quietly. Celia sat back and waited. Natasha would begin talking when she was ready. As she waited, Celia thought about how Natasha's slow control would drive John up the wall. It would drive several of her colleagues up the wall. Patience had usually worked well for Celia, however.

"One of the things any public person has to learn to deal with is the less than professional so-called reporters," Natasha said. "Don't misunderstand me. Nothing is stopping a journalist from the Times from being a pain in the ass in their way. I'm sure your recent CEO subject would agree."

"Good point," Celia said. "I'm sure you're right."

"I am. But those small parasites who wait for a glimpse of your undies or a temper or for you to appear just a little too drunk," Natasha flicked ash at an imaginary example. "They are the first to truly make life difficult, especially if you are young and female."

"That makes sense," Celia agreed. "They probably figure you're an easier target."

"Exactly. And they can use their fake charm and flattery to take an inexperienced person off-guard. It's a clever ploy, providing they don't overestimate themselves."

"Overestimate?"

"You'd be amazed at how many people will assume you are naïve simply because you are blonde and pretty."

"Being a mousy brunette, I wouldn't know," Celia grinned.

"You are very attractive, so I have no doubt you have been underestimated as well." Natasha shifted and smoked for a moment. "But there's something about that blonde stereotype that amplifies it. People assume you're a less intelligent Marlene Monroe character or the farmer's daughter."

"Or, in your case, the immigrant daughter naïve in the ways of the world, with an overprotective father."

"You understand." Natasha crushed the cigarette. "His name was Paul, and he worked for one of those grocery checkout rags."

"Paul Singleton?" Celia asked.

"Yes. You know him?"

"We both attended the same school. He was a few years older than I was and already working."

"Well, he obviously lacked your talent. He was there, and you are here." She waited for Celia to respond. When the reporter remained quiet, Natasha continued. "I had just finished filming my first movie. I had been successful as a model, but the jury was still out on my acting."

"And Paul followed your career?"

"Apparently. He was flattering, but a bit of a pest. It became clear that he wanted to know how I had gotten such a big role so quickly."

"I see."

"Once I realized he was fishing for a scandal, I told him to leave me alone. Then my father told him to leave me alone. He ignored us both."

Celia took notes and pictured a younger Paul hounding the young actress. He hadn't seemed like that type, but he'd had some bad luck early in his career. And he certainly wasn't a fan of Celia's. "So what happened?"

"Well, he began to hound the casting director and one of the producers. He even went after one of their wives, assuming I had slept with her husband since he was a notorious philanderer."

"And you didn't sleep with the producer?"

"Not that one," Natasha replied. "But he was becoming more than a nuisance. He was a problem."

"I imagine so. Sounds relentless."

"I knew he had an alcohol problem. He'd been arrested for drunk and disorderly and had a couple of DUI's. He was on the brink of some real legal trouble, even prison time." Natasha smiled. "So I invited him for a drink."

"You did?"

"He probably thought I was going to proposition him to leave me alone. I let him think that as I filled him with good scotch. When I suggested we drive separately to my place, I knew he was intoxicated."

"Ah, and did he get to your place?"

"He never made it. I called in a report of a blue Taurus driving erratically, and I gave the license plate. I knew another DUI would complicate his life the way he was complicating mine."

Celia sat quietly as Natasha watched her, waiting. After a few seconds, it dawned on Celia, and she widened her eyes. "Was that the night of the accident?"

"It was," Natasha replied. "He must have been very excited to get to my place. He drove too fast around a curve, and the road was wet."

Paul Singleton had died in a single auto accident in 2005, running off the road and into a tree. His blood-alcohol level had been well above the legal limit.

"It was not exactly what I had planned, but he never bothered me again. The police did question me. People had seen us together."

"And what did you say?"

"That I had agreed to meet him to do an interview, that he had been drinking heavily and ignored my pleading that he call a cab."

The story was a little chilling, and Celia was shocked. But she was also fascinated. The actress's plan was pretty clever, considering the circumstances. Still, it resulted in Paul's death. Was Natasha responsible, though? It was clear he was an alcoholic who made some pretty bad choices.

The five-minute warning knock startled Celia a bit, and she directed her attention back to the actress. "Do you think that incident deterred other reporters? I mean, they couldn't have known."

"I don't know. The owner of the tabloid tried to ask me about that night, but I shut him down, citing trauma." Natasha shrugged. "Mostly, it taught me to treat everyone holding a press card or camera with suspicion. I also found a very forceful attorney."

Celia finished her note-taking and shut off the recorder. She offered Natasha one more cigarette. When Keith knocked, Celia was ready to leave. "I'll see you next week."

"I look forward to it," Natasha replied. "I want to hear more about Bart."

"We'll see," Celia laughed. "If he doesn't give me some space, there may be nothing more to tell."

Celia was still thinking about Paul when she got home. She hadn't known him to drink that much in school, but then again, they weren't close friends. He never got that one big break. Of course, had he won the internship over Celia, he might have had a successful career. Did that failure impact his drinking? She shook off the thought. All she did was win a contest. If Paul had been more confident in his writing, he wouldn't have been so easy to rattle.

As she was washing her face, Celia heard the landline begin to ring. "Damn." She picked up her toothbrush, determined to ignore her father's call again. But it wasn't her father's voice on the phone.

"Your phone number is unlisted, but unlisted numbers aren't that hard to find. Why didn't you give it to me earlier? I'd like to get together this week. I was hoping the gala could be a new start. Call me."

Oh my God, I knew that was a mistake.

Celia climbed into bed and turned off the light. First her father, now Bart. She was absolutely going to have to get rid of that line.

Chapter 13

"You got more flowers," Gladys greeted Celia when she returned from lunch on the Thursday after her interview with Natasha.

Celia groaned and walked into her office, closing the door behind her. She looked at the large arrangement on her desk. This time it was Gerber daisies. It was another gift from Bart, who had sent her something nearly every day since the gala. After reading the note, Celia picked up the large pink vase and walked back out of her office.

"What am I supposed to do with this?" Celia asked her assistant. "My office isn't a greenhouse!"

"I'll keep them out here if you want," Gladys replied. "I love daisies."

"Thank you," Celia said, placing them on the corner of the desk. "I'm going to have to put a stop to this."

"He is very persistent, isn't he?

"That's an understatement. I feel like I'm in junior high school. What grown man does this?"

"Not my ex-husband, that's for sure," Gladys laughed. "But you're right. It is excessive."

"I never should have gone to that gala. Just dinner, my ass," Celia grumbled. "He just put himself in the definite no category."

"What?" Gladys asked.

"Never mind. I better go ahead and deal with this."

Once she was back in her office, Celia took out her phone. There were several messages from Bart, a couple she had answered but most she had ignored. He called on Wednesday night and left a message. Celia was hoping he would give up, but that wasn't going to happen. Celia dialed his number and braced herself.

"Hey Babe—Celia," Bart answered on the first ring. "You've had a busy week! How are you?"

"I'm good," Celia answered. "Thank you for the flowers. You didn't have to."

"You deserve to be spoiled," Bart said. "You looked so beautiful Saturday night. The only thing I could think of to compete with that was endless flowers."

"It's thoughtful, Bart, but it's too much. I really can't accept any more. I thought we agreed that Saturday night was just dinner."

"We had such a good time," Bart continued as if he hadn't heard. "We clicked all night. And the way you danced with me, I could tell the spark was still there."

"No Bart, it's not," Celia said firmly. "Look, I'm glad we cleared the air. I'm glad we had an enjoyable evening. But this isn't going anywhere. It's done."

There was silence on the other end. "Celia, you're my friend…"

"I thought we could be," she said. "But friends don't send flowers every other day and send endless text messages. We can't be friends. I'm sorry. You need to stop calling me."

"Is it the rent-a-cop?" Bart's voice was quiet, but Celia could hear the anger.

"What are you talking about?"

"The tall security guy you had that intimate little conversation with on our date."

"Intimate conversation? Do you mean Keith? We just said hello. You were right there."

"How did you even meet him? Traffic court?" Bart scoffed.

"No, I… It's none of your business. You need to back off."

"Did you screw him like you did that other guy?"

Celia stood up and willed herself to remain calm. "Listen. This is done. You will not contact me again. You will not come near me. I am making this plain. Stay away."

"You don't get to control me, slut."

"Goodbye, Bart," Celia swiped to end the call. It felt surprisingly unsatisfying. Sometimes Celia missed the catharsis of slamming down a receiver. "What a psycho," Celia muttered. She gathered the flowers in her office and walked past Gladys. At the end of the hall, Celia dumped them into a large garbage can.

"Everything okay?" Gladys asked when she returned.

"Sudden allergies," Celia said. She sat down and blocked Bart's number. Hopefully, this would be the end of it.

She spent the afternoon transcribing her interviews with Natasha, trying to put Bart out of her mind. As she listened to the actress's story about Paul again, she felt sympathy. Bart was just a determined suitor, not a dime store reporter, and Celia would love it if he ran off the road. In fact, if she saw him right now, she might run over him herself. While it was on her mind, she contacted the phone company and arranged to have her landline disconnected. She should have done it ages ago.

Gladys managed to intercept everyone who wanted to see Celia throughout the afternoon; it was one of the things Celia loved about her. Even John wasn't permitted an audience. By the time 6:00 arrived, she was ready to finish things up and soak in a hot bath at home. After she unplugged her phone.

Chapter 14

Celia read her notes as she handed the corrections officer her purse, sunglasses, and briefcase. After spreading her arms so that she could be checked for weapons, she nodded to the clerk behind the glass and followed Keith through the heavy doors and down the hallway. Checking the batteries on her recorder, Celia listened absently to Keith's small talk, commenting during the proper pauses. The inmates either ignored her, slept, or made half-hearted attempts at getting her attention. She had been there so often by now that no one gave her much notice anymore.

Natasha was brushing her hair when Celia walked into the interview room. She nodded to Celia but didn't stop, taking her hair layer by layer because the brush was too soft to go through her thick tresses. Natasha had complained about it numerous times, but a real brush was "too dangerous," she always said with a roll of her eyes. Celia set up the recorder and opened her thick folder, and then she just read her notes, giving Natasha time to finish brushing. They had an hour. Sometimes Natasha talked the whole time; sometimes she did other things until she felt like talking, and Celia had learned not to be impatient.

"So," Natasha said, taking the seat across from Celia. "How's Bart?"

Celia chuckled. She wasn't sure when her social life had become part of their conversations, but Natasha was very interested in the men Celia saw and why she saw them. "I hear he's fine."

"Oh my, another one by the wayside. You're almost as ruthless as I am."

"Well, I never had the chance to date Chip Rogers," Celia said good-naturedly as she turned on the recorder.

"Men like him are why it is necessary to be ruthless, trust me," Natasha said dryly.

Celia had learned to pretend to laugh at these comments while listening closely. Often, there was something substantial behind the humor. "Oh really? So he's nothing like his romantic comedy persona then, I assume."

"Are they ever?" Natasha shifted in her seat. "I know you don't smoke, but…"

"You do," Celia finished. She pulled a pack of Natasha's favorite brand out of her jacket pocket. Natasha smiled and took the pack. She pulled out a cigarette and held it out so that Celia could light it with a match from the small packet she had in her other pocket. "You know, I still can't believe they let you smoke during our little visits."

"They'll do anything if you flash them," Natasha quipped, and Celia dropped her jaw in surprise. "I'm kidding, hon." She leaned forward. "You have to pay them for that." Then Natasha sat back and laughed.

Celia didn't probe because it was usually impossible to tell when Natasha was lying. Besides, her earlier quip about men was much more interesting. "So which man-made you ruthless first? Obviously not poor Chip."

Natasha sighed with annoyance. "Not that old song again." She took a long drag, blew smoke to the right, away from Celia's face, and flicked the cigarette against her chair. "Everyone always thinks it's dear old dad."

"Well, he was your final victim, so you can understand my curiosity."

"Are you saying all little girls whose daddies play in their panties end up murdering them? It'd be a lonely world." Narrowing her eyes at Celia, Natasha licked her lips.

Studying her notes, Celia continued. "So no hanky panky with dad. But again, he was your final victim. Sexual abuse isn't the only way to be abusive."

"Daddy loved me, in his way. He didn't touch me, he didn't beat me. He loved me, loved my face, loved my talent, and especially loved the money and fame. The more I mattered to everyone else, the more I mattered to him." Natasha shrugged. "Proud papa."

"So then, why—"

"I didn't specify what he was proud of," Natasha said, crushing her half-smoked cigarette. "He disappointed me. So what happened with Bart?"

"He disappointed me," Celia said dryly.

Natasha stilled for a moment, the pack of cigarettes in her hand. Then she threw back her head and laughed. "And that's why I chose you," she said, lighting another cigarette. "At least you didn't kill him."

Celia laughed and changed the subject. "So enough about your father for today. You talked about some of your earlier crimes, the small ones. I'm just going to ask, will you tell me about your first murder?"

A buzzing sound interrupted them, and Celia jumped slightly at the vibration in her jacket pocket. She'd placed her cell phone there, and the officer hadn't frisked her today. They seldom searched her closely anymore. In any other situation, she would have celebrated the oversight. Today it annoyed her. She was even more annoyed when she saw that the call was from John. He knew where she was, and he had already called twice before she arrived at the prison. His intrusiveness was a problem.

"Your admirer?"

"My boss. I never should have told him about our interviews."

"He's jealous?"

"You know, I think he actually is. He's nosy and overbearing in a way he never has been, and he's dying to slip some sort of teaser into the paper."

"You know what the contract says."

Celia turned off the phone. "I do, and so does he. He's angry. He's redirected stories to some other journalists as punishment. It's a ridiculous temper tantrum."

"Surely the petty bastard can't hurt your career?"

"You know, I've stopped being surprised at what petty bastards can do." Celia turned a page in her notebook and resettled. "Enough talk about bastards and admirers. I don't want to ruin both our days. So let's get back to the story. We're ready to talk about murder."

"I think it's time, yes. Of course, you know I've been sizing you up just as you have been sizing me up during our conversations. I feel confident I was right about you. Now we can begin talking about the murders."

Celia tried not to lean forward too eagerly. She knew she was being tested in each interview, and she knew that if she had failed, the interviews would be terminated. That was the primary reason she still had not told John about the story. Celia wasn't going to get anything good until she had passed the tests. "Whenever you're ready."

"There's a diner I like to go to for coffee very early in the morning," Natasha began, crushing her half-smoked cigarette onto the table. "It is very quiet there, and almost always empty. I am not entirely sure how the owners stay in business. But they are a shy old couple, and they do not follow Hollywood or gossip or any other type of privacy invasion, so they never knew who I was. It was my private haven, and I went to great lengths to keep it that way."

"I can understand that," Celia said, nodding. "I'm sure there was almost no place you could go and not be recognized and hounded."

"Exactly." Natasha pointed her unlit cigarette at Celia. "This was very important to me." She waited for Celia to light it and then took a long drag before continuing. "That is why I could not let anyone change things."

"And your first victim, he changed things," Celia finished Natasha's thought.

"It was more than that. Tom Hayles, had he been a stranger, would have been easy enough to tolerate. I always dressed inconspicuously, and I never had my hair done or makeup on, so to most people, I would not have looked like the woman they knew from magazines. But Tom was a person from the past."

Celia leaned forward slightly and rested her chin on her upturned palm. "You already knew him?"

"Oh yes," Natasha waved the smoke around as she gestured. "He attended the private high school that my father insisted I attend. He was two years older, but still, I knew him. And he knew me."

Celia noticed Natasha's tone and slightly narrowed eyes betrayed her detached manner. "And what did he think he knew?"

Smiling, Natasha flicked ash onto the floor. "He thought I would worship him as the other girls did. And he thought I was naïve. He asked me to a school dance, and I said yes. Of course, he was expelled before the dance took place."

"Expelled? Why?"

"Before the dance, my father allowed me to meet him for a movie. He had a car, but Father believed I was too young to ride with him. Tom had some cigarettes and a bottle of vodka and suggested we go driving instead. I had hoped until then that he might have an interest in me, but when he suggested the drive and the alcohol, I knew. I knew what he was."

"So he got you intoxicated, and then he…took advantage?"

"He underestimated me. I had been sneaking a bit of Father's vodka for years. I was never intoxicated. And he would probably say I humiliated him, the spoiled bastard. In return, he threatened to tell everyone that we had sex." Natasha sighed. "It was fortunate for me that drugs were discovered in his locker on Monday." She smiled at Celia.

"Yes, very lucky," Celia smiled back. "Where did you get—"

"Of course, no one ever really knew where the drugs came from. You know how impulsive teenagers can be. He was expelled, and he slinked off like a kicked dog."

"Until you saw him in the diner."

"He did not notice me, so I began to watch him. He wore a suit that looked more expensive than it was. I noticed that he spoke to a wife on one phone and a mistress on another. He was the same as he had been. Of course, after several mornings he attempted to say hello. A man like this cannot help himself. Still too stupid to remember me, but I knew that my sanctuary wasn't a sanctuary as long as he was there. And one morning he would not be stupid."

Celia watched as Natasha smoked in silence for a few minutes. She had met with her enough times now to understand the undercurrent of anger in her eyes. Natasha was still cool, of course, but the slight hardening around the corners and the way her fingers gripped the cigarette made it clear that she was still angry remembering Tom. Natasha would take her time telling the story, however, always the consummate actress. Celia had learned to wait through the silence rather than probing.

"I followed him several times. He was always on his phone, telling his mistress what he would like to do to her, telling his wife he could not be home for dinner. The parking garage where he kept his car was older, with no cameras and very little activity. It was easy to approach him and ask him for a light. He never saw the gun."

"Yes, the gun," Celia noted. "They were never able to trace it."

"No. I can thank my father for that. He knew many things from living in Russia during the Cold War."

"And you only used it once."

"Of course. To use the same gun again would connect people. Only an idiot would use the gun more than once," Natasha shrugged. "I left the garage and went home. The clothing was washed and taken to one of those charity drop-bins. I did what many have done with the gun, I tossed it into the river."

Celia wrote in her notebook as she absorbed Natasha's retelling of the murder. There was a strange logic to her actions, and her story - so matter of fact, Celia almost understood how the murder made sense. She was learning that Natasha had a logic to every choice she made. Sure, the logic might be cold and criminal, but it was logical. Considering Celia's issues with the persistent and slightly creepy Bart, she could empathize with the actress's desire to have a part of her life that was safe from threatening interlopers.

"Have I shocked you?" Natasha interrupted Celia's thoughts.

"Actually, no. I was just thinking about how there is an understandable logic as to why you killed him. Which is a little disturbing," Celia chuckled.

"I thought you might see that. I'm sure you've encountered people who threatened your sense of personal space."

Celia didn't mention Bart; she knew Natasha was probing. "Yes, I think most of us have."

Keith knocked, and as he entered, Celia packed her things. Natasha greeted Keith and smiled as her guard entered. Both women exited Room 4 without a word.

"You look deep in thought," Keith said.

"She still has some of that dramatic ability," Celia said.

"That she does. She can almost make you feel sorry for her."

Celia didn't respond, but she agreed. In fact, the more they talked, the more able Celia was to see things from Natasha's perspective. She guessed it was because she too had a pragmatic way of looking at things, along with a strong sense of self-preservation. Not only had Celia learned her way of looking at things wasn't stereotypically feminine, but it also wasn't always traditionally black and white. After all, Celia had done a bit of maneuvering and manipulating to further her career, she thought to herself, remembering Paul Singleton. Sometimes you had to do what you had to do.

When Celia picked up her personal from the clerk, Sabria remarked, "I guess I forgot to get your cell phone. Or you didn't bring one. Let's keep that oversight to ourselves."

Celia chuckled as she powered up her cell phone, but her gut felt heavy as she typed in her password. There were almost 20 text notifications from an unknown number. Since blocking Bart's number the weeks before, she had received several calls from someone whose number was marked "Private Caller." She knew it was him, and these texts were probably him as well. How was she supposed to block him when he could just spoof another number or get one from an app? Celia screen-shotted each notification. She would read them when she returned to her office.

After locking her door and settling in her chair, Celia opened the string of messages. Just as she suspected, they were from Bart.

"Please talk to me."

"You blocked my number. I had to use another one to reach you."

"Why are you ignoring me? What are you afraid of?"

"You can't just unilaterally cut me out like this!"

"Who are you screwing now? Where are you?"

"Your car is not at work. Who are you with??"

"I'm not going anywhere! Talk to me!"

By the time Celia got to the last message, she was angry. What was wrong with him? She wished she had never agreed to go on the first date with Bart. Part of her thought she should be a bit afraid, but she was so mad, it overrode any sense of fear. He was not going to disrupt her life. She took a screenshot of every message before deleting them. She deleted the number as well. Yes, he'd probably get a new one, but she wasn't going to change her number; she'd had it for years. What a pain in the ass it would be to have to change it and notify everyone. Bart didn't deserve that kind of effort and inconvenience.

Pushing Bart to the back of her mind, Celia began to listen to her interview with Natasha and add to her notes. She had no doubt what Natasha would do if confronted with a man like Bart. Celia chuckled. The death penalty was way too high a price to pay for a pathetic man with a bruised ego. She'd had to think of something else to deter him.

At 4:00, A knock interrupted Celia's progress. "Yes, who is it?"

"Gladys poked her head into the office, and her expression was full of worry. "There's someone here to see you, but I'm not sure he is who he says he is."

Celia closed her laptop. "Who does he say he is? Atilla the Hun? I've never seen you so pale."

"He says," she paused and looked behind her. "He says he's your father."

"No way." Celia sighed and walked to the door.

It *was* her father. He was thinner, and he had less hair, but it was definitely him. He looked almost as concerned as Gladys. "I'm sorry to just show up. I knew you wouldn't be happy about it. But your landline was disconnected."

"You might as well come in," Celia sighed, opening her office door a bit wider.

"Should I bring in coffee?" Gladys asked.

"No," Celia said sharply. "Sorry, we won't be here long."

Celia's father, Stewart, looked around the office as he sat in the chair she offered. He couldn't meet her eye, and Celia had to admit that satisfied her a little. She didn't sit in her chair. Instead, she sat in front of him on the edge of her desk, wanting to be taller than he was. "So why are you here?"

"I needed to talk to you."

"Really, after all these years, you needed to talk? What happened to your new family?"

Stewart winced. "She left me. She left me two years ago."

"Hurts, doesn't it?"

"I deserve that." Stewart sighed. "I deserve much worse after what I put you and your mother through."

"You don't get to talk about mom. If that's what you came for, I think we're done."

"Wait," Stewart pleaded. "I need to talk to you about Melina's sister."

"Why in the world would I want to talk about your hygienist's sister? Is she why your new wife left?"

"No, well, possibly. But not for the reason you think."

"Then what? I have work to do. It's a paper. We have deadlines."

"Her sister's name was Judith. Judith Vandiver." He looked at Celia, expecting the name to mean something to her. "She's Bart Vandiver's late wife."

Celia opened her mouth, but she didn't speak. It wasn't what she'd expected her father to say. The walk back to her chair gave her the chance to hide her shock, and she sat slowly. "So you were married to Bart's wife's older sister? Did you know him? Does he know you?"

Stewart shook his head. "I met him once, at a family gathering. They didn't stay very long. I got the idea he didn't want to be there at all."

"What do you mean?"

"Well, they eloped, for one thing. Melina's family wasn't happy about that. And after they were married, Judith hardly ever visited. I know her parents traveled to where they lived, but they seldom came to town to see the rest of the family."

"Maybe he didn't feel welcome."

Stewart frowned and shook his head. "I don't think so. I know it's a touchy subject, but Melina's family was very kind. Even though..." he cleared his throat. "Even though Melina and I got together in the most selfish, wrong way, they accepted me." He looked down at his hands.

Celia wasn't moved by his discomfort at all. "Good for them. So why are you here?"

"Well, her parents never thought her accident was an accident. And Bart has shown up at some events lately."

"I know. He said they were still close. He was trying to be supportive."

"That's the thing." Stewart sat forward. "He wasn't. He didn't even want them to see her body. He wanted her cremated. It was the hospital that called them to tell them she'd died, not Bart."

"Well, I'm sure he was pretty upset," Celia said the words, but she wasn't sure she believed them.

"And the weirdest part? She was planning on leaving Bart."

"How do you know that?"

"Melina told me. She asked me if Judith could stay with us, and she wanted it to be a secret."

Celia looked at her father. He seemed sincerely worried. And yes, it was sort of nice that he cared about something having to do with right and wrong for a change, she thought bitterly. But what did any of this have to do with her?

"I'm sorry about Judith and all of it. I really am. But I don't have anything to do with this."

"Yes, you do. You're seeing Bart."

"Not anymore. We broke up. We only dated a few times." Celia folded her arms. "And anyway, how do you even know that?"

"I was at the event Bart attended. He was there, and he was bragging to someone about dating a big-name reporter. A reporter named Celia Brockwell," he sighed a little at the changed name.

"Yeah, we were seeing each other then. But we aren't now."

"Are you sure? I saw your picture in the news, at the gala. He didn't look like he was ready to give you up."

Celia didn't answer, but her father's observation caught her off guard. How could he tell from a picture?

"Let me guess, he's still pursuing you."

Celia laughed. "I have it under control."

"I'm not sure you do. The more Judith pulled away from him, the harder he pushed. And it wasn't love. He was angry."

She hated to admit it, but her father's words concerned her. Bart as an annoying pest was one thing. Bart as a man who had a pattern of not letting go was another. And Bart as—what—a murderer? That was laughable. He might have been angry about his wife, but Bart was too much of a coward to do something like that.

"Look," Celia said, rising and sitting on the desk again, "Bart is a pain in the ass, and he's been stubborn. But he's all bark and no bite. I've seen his kind before. His ego is bruised, but as soon as some hot paralegal catches his eye, he'll be on to his next conquest."

"Celia—"

"No. I'm sorry. I get that you're worried, and I can tell you feel bad about everything. But you don't get to try to protect me. You lost that right."

Stewart closed his eyes. "I know. I know you have every right to feel that way. I was selfish and stupid. I wish I'd never…" He looked at Celia. "I'm just telling you to be careful. And whether you hate me or not, please let me know if you need help. I gave your secretary my number." He stood and looked around again. "I guess I should go."

Celia didn't move as he walked out of the office. She heard him say goodbye to Gladys as he closed her door. "I don't hate you," Celia said before she turned back to her work.

Chapter 15

Celia was late for her appointment with Natasha. When she noticed Bart's car across from her townhouse, she altered her route, crossing and turning until Bart was no longer following. She certainly didn't want him knowing where she was headed. She was still receiving texts from strange numbers, so she had accepted the fact that changing her number was her next step. Keith could tell something was bothering her as they walked down the hallway, but he didn't ask.

"I was wondering about you," Natasha said when Celia walked into Room 4. "I thought maybe I scared you off last time."

"I'm sorry, I had some traffic issues. I'll be ready to go in just a moment."

Natasha watched Celia set up her recorder and turn to a blank page in her notebook. She didn't comment on Celia's clumsiness or her obvious tension.

"Okay, I'm ready. How are you?"

"Strangely enough, for a death row inmate, I think I'm better than you are today," Natasha said, smiling.

"Oh, I just hate being late," Celia replied.

"Really? I can't remember a time when there has been a traffic jam of people waiting to visit the prison." Natasha leaned forward. "So what really happened? Late night with a new suitor?"

"Hell no," Celia said a little too tersely. "Sorry, but men are the last thing I want to think about."

"Let me guess," Natasha said. "Your Bart is not giving up so easily."

Celia looked up sharply. "Why would you think that?"

"Even in black and white, I could see the… determination in him. People's body language betrays a lot. It was obvious he was more into you than you were into him."

"Is this a common skill among actors?"

"Not so much the acting, but my own skill development. You might have deduced that I am not inherently social. I've never been given to sappy emotion or sugary sympathy. Learning how to read people and assess situations was necessary for life and acting."

"I can understand that. I was a weird kid growing up, and I learned how to be like my peers over time. I still can't stand chatty small talk and effusive displays."

"Exactly. Which is why a clinger like your Bart would be especially annoying. I'm assuming he's bothering you."

Celia hesitated. The purpose of these interviews was to get Natasha's story, not share details of her own life. Still, Natasha was pragmatic, and she had experience with the persistence of the press. That wasn't too much different from Bart's antics. "He's annoying as hell."

"I assume you've blocked him, avoided taking calls, and made it clear that it's over."

"Yes. He's still finding ways to be a pest, though. Texts from other numbers, new email addresses. I saw his car this morning and took a longer route to the prison. I didn't intend to be late."

Natasha's eyes narrowed. "He's an ass, and you're going to have to get tougher. Change your number. And I can't believe I'm saying this, but file a report."

"A report of what? A bad breakup?"

"You told him to cease. He isn't ceasing. He is circumventing your attempts to stop contact. And he's following you. You have plenty to put into a report."

Celia shook her head. "This is ridiculous. He's just a guy with a hurt ego."

"Look, Celia," Natasha said. "I am not an empathetic person by nature, and I don't worry about things. But I was in the public eye long enough to know that stalking is not something to ignore. I know actresses whose lives were made hell, and these people need to be eliminated. Your space is your space, just like mine was mine at that diner."

Celia wanted to change the subject. "I already planned to change my number. I'll give the report definite thought. But I've already wasted part of the hour we have. If you're ready, I'd like to talk about the next murder."

"Fine. I've given my opinion. Just don't be late next time." Natasha smiled. "We can talk about Roland."

"Wer you concerned about killing a police officer?"

"He was retired. He took early retirement, in fact, and based on the way he had treated me, I suspected he'd been caught more than once being unethical. Men with his temper and God complex usually break the rules."

"What did he do to make you so angry?"

"Not long after I began driving, I was stupid and young and liked to speed. One night I was driving home from a party, and since the road was deserted, I thought I'd open up my little sports car and see what she could do, as they say. Roland was lying in wait behind some trees and pulled me over."

"A pain in the ass, but understandable I guess."

"Getting pulled over was irritating, but it was his manner that truly infuriated me." Natasha reached for another cigarette. "He made me get out of the car, asked about my citizenship, asked where I was going so late at night. I admit I was a bit of a smart aleck. He didn't want to give me back my license right away, and when I grabbed his hand to reach for it, he told me I was assaulting an officer."

"Good grief!"

"Yes, my father had to come to the station, and my car was impounded. Our attorney took care of it, but my father checked into Roland. Let's just say he wasn't squeaky clean. He had complaints against him for being overly rough and other infractions."

"Was he reprimanded?"

"A slap on the wrist at most. But it was enough to make him vengeful. I can't count the number of times I saw him follow me, the number of questions he asked every time there was an issue on a set or at a bar or restraint where I happened to be dining. I was glad when he retired."

"How did you get into his house?"

"That was quite easy. He was too arrogant to have a fancy alarm system. All he needed was a gun, you see. I visited his house more than once while he was out partying or with a lady friend. That was how I found the gun."

"Wait, so the gun was his? Why wasn't it traced back to him?"

"I could tell by the way it was hidden and its appearance that he'd lifted it from some crime scene. It wasn't stored the way his other weapons were, and it was dirty. A man like him would keep his legal weapons clean. I left it where it was and waited for the right time."

"So what happened?"

Natasha smiled. "I have to say, the first murder I committed was out of necessity. This one? This one I enjoyed."

Celia could tell by the way Natasha sat back and looked to be reliving it that she was telling the truth. "Do I need popcorn for this scene?"

"You might," Natasha laughed. "Too bad there's no spotlight..." She closed her eyes, and Celia smiled at the theatrics.

Roland sat up in bed, not sure what woke him. Had it been noise or just a sense that something was wrong? He tried chiding himself, but his heart continued to pound, and his dog whimpered in her sleep. It was quiet enough in his bedroom to hear the whirring of his laptop on the desk across from his bed. But the quiet didn't reassure him; it made him more skittish. Swearing to himself, Roland left the bed and went to his closet to retrieve the 9mm.

His mouth went dry when he discovered the empty box; it was missing. The gun was missing—not his issued weapon. That one was locked in its case beside his bed. This was the unregistered gun he had confiscated from a crime scene years before. He thought he might need it someday. And now it was gone. He was going to have to find the gun. Swearing, he headed to the bathroom. He rubbed his eyes as he stood at the toilet.

"Tsk, tsk officer. Doesn't this gun belong in an evidence locker somewhere?"

He turned, Natasha stood there. He watched her hands around the gun for some hint of shaking; shaking would indicate uncertainty. Her hands were as steady as his had been trained to be.

"I thought it might come in handy one day," he replied, not moving.

"And so it has. Did you bend the rules and beat the drug dealer or rapist you confiscated this from?"

Roland nodded quietly. "I shouldn't have done that."

"Why not?" she asked, tilting her head slightly. "He did do something wrong. That means it was okay for you to do something wrong, correct?"

"Natasha..."

"Shut up. Nobody wants to hear you moralize. Turn around."

He didn't move except to move his gaze from her hands to her face.

"Turn around, former detective, and put your hands in front of you." She cocked the gun. "Or don't."

Roland shakily turned and did as she asked, bile burning his tongue.

"Good boy. Don't worry. I know you were blinded by your ego, so I'll be quicker. And you don't claim to believe in God, so I can't hold you accountable

for breaking the very morals you claim to believe. Besides, you aren't very smart. You probably didn't have a choice."

Roland flinched at that last part. He heard her footsteps, and then the end of the barrel pressed coldly against the base of his neck, where his brain stem felt as if it was pulsing. "Please..." He heard himself whisper.

"I'm not sorry," she whispered back.

A loud, smoky explosion filled the room. Then it was silent.

Celia wrote in silence, absorbing Natasha's account of the murder. She could weave quite a story, and she didn't seem at all ruffled about killing a retired officer. And yet Celia found herself empathizing a bit with the actress. Roland had used his position to try to bully her and exact some kind of favor, probably the seedy kind. He was the type of officer who gave good ones a bad name. Celia wasn't sure murder was the best way to deal with a man like Roland, but she understood why Natasha held a grudge. Keith knocked on the door, breaking the silence, and Celia began putting away her things.

"I meant what I said about your problem," Natasha said as she stood to leave with the other officer.

"I appreciate the concern. I'll see you next week," Celia replied as she followed Keith out the door.

"So is everything okay?" Keith asked as they walked down the hall.

"Nothing I can't handle."

"The guy from the gala?" Keith chuckled when Celia looked at him. "It was obvious he wasn't thrilled I said hello to you."

"He's just a little persistent."

"It must be more than a little if you're getting advice from Natasha."

Celia laughed. "Oh, she just volunteered her input. She's not the most objective when it comes to dealing with stress."

"That's an understatement." Keith looked a bit concerned. "Still, if you need anything, let me know. I know there's a lot of disturbing gray between a persistent guy and what qualifies somebody for a restraining order."

"I'm sure it won't come to that. He just needs to meet someone else, and he'll forget all about me."

"Tell you what, just in case, I'd be glad to take a look around your place, see if I can offer some security device. You at least need to set up a folder to document all his contact. A paper file and a digital one."

Celia sighed. "Sure, that would be great. But like I said, he'll eventually forget about me."

"You may not be that easy to forget." Keith smiled.

"Thanks for the compliment, but I'll be fine. See you next week." Celia waved at the woman behind the desk, walked to her car, and drove home still thinking about what Natasha had said. She hadn't told Natasha or Keith about her conversation with her father. That would have led to a whole other series of probing questions that Celia didn't want to answer. And it would have given the actress more reason for concern about Bart.

Celia opened her mailbox and groaned. It was apparent from the packed box that she hadn't checked her mail for almost a week; she sometimes forgot when she was busy. After unlocking her door and dropping her briefcase and purse in the entryway, she began sorting through the thick stack.

Bills…bills…coupons…

Then Celia stopped. There was an envelope with no stamp and Celia's name printed on the front. She opened it, read it, and then dropped into a kitchen chair.

Celia:

You can't betray me. I will know. I love you. We belong together. I'm not giving up. Be careful how you reject me.

Celia's first impulse was to rip the note into tiny pieces. However, instead, she put it back in the envelope and placed it in the top drawer – her junk drawer. It was from Bart, and it bothered her more than the calls and emails. In those, he just begged to see her or tried to convince her they should be together. Sure, he was manipulative, but weren't most people that way when they wanted something? Celia had pulled more than a few strings in her own career, and Natasha certainly knew how to manipulate. Even John seemed to know which buttons to push.

But the threat in Bart's handwritten note was clear. And he didn't sign it. In all his somewhat pathetic attempts at romantic pleadings, he never hid who he was. Celia knew he was trying to scare her, but mostly she felt pissed. Bart wasn't going away quietly, and nothing she said or did seemed to deter him. It was late, Celia was tired, and she hadn't eaten since the prior evening. Bart wasn't going to ruin a quiet night home with takeout. She took the note out of the drawer and tore it in half before tossing it into the trash can. Taking the menu from Marlene's restaurant off of the refrigerator, Celia dialed the number to order her dinner.

Chapter 16

"So how are you?" Keith asked Celia as they started down the hallway toward Room 4.

"I'm doing pretty well. Ready for the weekend."

"Yeah, me too, I'm off this weekend, so I can finally enjoy some free time."

"Do you work many weekends?"

"Every other one," Keith replied. "I get time-and-a-half then."

"Nice." Celia smiled.

"That Bart guy giving you any trouble?"

"Keith, you don't have to worry about me. It's all good."

Keith shrugged and opened the door. "Enjoy your interview."

Celia smiled and nodded as Keith closed the door. Natasha was already sitting in her place.

"You look terrible," Natasha said. "You look the way I do when the noise in here prevents me from sleeping."

Celia tossed the notebook on the table in front of her. "Gee, thanks."

"No offense intended. I'm worried about you." She raised a hand when Celia raised an eyebrow. "Okay, I'm curious. Are you not sleeping?"

"Not really," Celia sighed.

"Why not? Your job? Your admirer?"

"I appreciate this, but I'd rather not talk about it." Celia realized she didn't have her recorder. "Well, crap."

Natasha sat back and watched Celia quietly. Celia considered knocking on the door and having the guard walk her back to get it, but that would take at least ten minutes from the interview time.

"Screw it," Celia laughed. "You may have to talk slowly today. We're going old school."

Natasha shrugged. "Or I could do the note-taking?"

"You write fast?"

"I know shorthand." Natasha chuckled at Celia's expression. "I learned it for the secretary turned agent role. I try to immerse myself into a character's skills."

Celia swore happily. "That's perfect. Great!" She slid the notebook and pen across the table.

"No problem. So where would you like to start?"

"I've been thinking about the murder you confessed to after your conviction. It was surprising at the time…"

"And?" Natasha laughed. "You aren't going to hurt my feelings."

"Well, now that we've had all these conversations, it's even more surprising. You were very, well, pragmatic about the other murders. Confessing to this one wouldn't have served you. You had already been sentenced, and confessing wasn't going to change that. It doesn't make sense."

"You've gotten to know me well, Celia. And you're right. There was no personal benefit to confessing." She put down the pen and sat back. "Would you believe I was just a little bit sentimental?"

"Honestly? Not really."

Laughing, Natasha picked up the pen again. "Well, maybe not in the way most people are. But an old acquaintance, the man's daughter, wrote me a letter."

"A letter. Did you keep it?"

"I didn't have to," Natasha shrugged. "I have a good memory. Occupational hazard."

"You memorized it?"

"You never know when someone is going to go through your things."

Dear Natasha,

I know you haven't heard from me in a long time. I'm sorry I lost touch when you were arrested. I didn't know what to say. It's not an excuse, but it's the truth.

I'm also sorry our friendship sort of fell apart after, well, you know. I guess I didn't know what to say then either. I felt too guilty. I figured you knew I knew, and I wasn't sure you'd want to be around me.

Tasha, my dad was a bad person. He hurt my mom, he hurt me, but I swear I never thought he would hurt somebody else. He had too much to lose. But I know he tried to hurt you. It's why I never invited you over again. I wanted to tell you how sorry I was, but I was scared and ashamed.

When he was found dead, I was relieved. I guess that's terrible, but he couldn't hurt us anymore. I wondered if maybe it was you, but then they questioned everybody, and they never did anything. My mom fell apart. I thought she'd be relieved too, but she loved him.

We moved, and life changed, and I just never really called you. I kept modeling, but once I turned 21 I quit. Too many bad memories. My mom never really got over it. We haven't talked in years. I can't stand the way she romanticizes him.

Anyway, I know they read your mail, so I won't ask you if you did it. I just wanted you to know I'm sorry. I kind of wonder if part of the reason you did those things was because of him. I hope not.

I just wanted you to know I was sorry for what happened. I hope you win your next appeal.

Sincerely,

Amelia Stratford

It was quiet for a while. "Wow, that's some letter."

"Yes," Natasha turned a page of the notebook. "I was surprised when I received it."

"So tell me about Amelia. The name isn't familiar. She was a model?"

"Yes, and she could wear anything. We knew each other fairly well. She wasn't catty and gossipy like most of the teenagers."

"So you were good friends. You visited her home?"

"More than once. When your father is like mine, it can be suffocating. I rarely socialized like a typical young girl. Not that it bothered me. But I needed time away from him. He thought Amelia was harmless, and he respected and admired her dad for some reason."

"Do you know why that was?"

"I'm not sure. Her father wasn't especially likable. Maybe they had that in common," Natasha chuckled. "Mr. Stratford was wealthy and had a certain amount of power in the industry behind the scenes."

"And he was abusive?"

"I never saw it. I knew Amelia's mother was quiet. But she never hesitated to correct a photographer or assistant who stepped out of line. I heard Mr. Stratford yell at her a few times when I visited. He ruled his house. But then so did my father."

"What happened?"

"I spent the night with Amelia. It wasn't the first time. Her parents went out and stayed out late. That wasn't unusual. They both liked to drink."

"Were they alcoholics?"

"Who knows. I heard Amelia's mother come in after midnight. She threw up in the bathroom and took a shower. But it was almost dawn when her father came home. He was loud. Amelia was still sound asleep, but I had a headache, so I went to look for some aspirin."

"You two drank as well," Celia smiled.

"We did. They never locked their liquor cabinet. And their wine was much better than my father's cheap vodka. But Amelia slept like the dead when she drank. It was impossible to wake her."

"So you went to find the aspirin."

"Yes, they had a cabinet in the kitchen with all their pills. I was looking for an aspirin when Mr. Stratford walked in. He wasn't wearing a shirt, and he had on these pajama pants."

"He tried something."

"At first he just said hello and asked where Amelia was. I was leaning against a corner of the L-shape counter, reaching for the pills. He got closer and told me how beautiful I was. Started stroking himself. It was disgusting to watch. I tried to get around him, but he trapped me, grabbed my shoulder, and shoved my hand down his pants."

"God!"

"For some reason, I didn't shout. He told me to keep my mouth shut or he would hurt me. Ruin me. He pressed me against the counter and moved my hand up and down. I stared into his face."

"You weren't afraid?"

"At first I was; he caught me off guard. Then I was angry. I knew he'd probably been doing it to Amelia too. She did not deserve abuse."

"So how did you get away?"

"I didn't. He came into my hand, groaned, and let go. Before he backed away, he warned me to stay quiet. He said he knew things about my father and that no one would hire me. Also, he said he hoped I came to visit again soon."

"What a… He was a monster."

"True. I went back to the bedroom. I lay there seething for a while and then dozed off. When I woke up, Amelia was crying."

"Why?"

"I'm not sure. I didn't say anything and neither did she. We had a late breakfast, and then I went home. I never got invited over again."

"Do you think she knew? Could she have woken up and seen something?"

"Her letter implies she knew somehow. I didn't care to go back, so it never bothered me when she avoided me."

Celia stood and walked to the small barred window. "And then you killed him."

"Even though I never visited, he was still at shoots and events. He'd corner me to remind me of his threats or try to touch me somehow. I knew he would be a thorn in my side. So I started to plan and wait to get him alone."

"And no one suspected?"

"I guess not. They questioned all of us, but I told them I was home with my father. They believed it."

"He was bigger than you," Celia said. "How did you overpower him?"

"I knew if I waited long enough, I could let him catch me alone. And when he did, I would trick him."

"But what about other people?"

Natasha shrugged. "I was young but not stupid. And I was patient. Sure enough, he came after hours to a site. I was there to escape my father. By then I was driving, though I was underage. He came to pick up something Amelia had left, or so he said."

"But still…no one else was there?"

"It was just us. He tried to flirt, and I let him. He tried to kiss me, and I let him. He pulled me close—"

"And you let him?"

"Yes. It was easy to stab him in the neck while he was distracted."

"Damn," Celia whispered.

"I ran off after taking off my shoes and smearing my footprints with socks. I snuck into my house and bathed, washed the clothes. I went to bed."

"What if your father had heard you?"

Natasha finished writing and put down the pen. "I hoped he wouldn't. He drank every night. Even if he wasn't asleep, I didn't think he would betray me. He knew I would be successful. And his ego wouldn't let him shame himself."

"So no one ever knew." Celia sat down again. "How old were you?"

"I was sixteen."

"You kept a murder quiet for almost 20 years. Then you confessed because of a letter."

Natasha smiled and shrugged again. "Amelia was a sincere person. She didn't even ask in the letter. I knew she wouldn't press for a trial, and I didn't think the state would go through all of that when I was already here. Now she knows the truth."

"It was very kind of you."

"Anyone can learn to be kind, Celia. You should know that."

Keith and Celia walked down the hallway in silence. Celia was still pondering the unexpected kindness Natasha had shown someone she hadn't seen for 20 years. Experts had proclaimed Natasha a sociopath, someone without empathy. So what made her confess to something she could have kept hidden forever? Was it truly just kindness without agenda? Then again, was anyone ever truly kind without an agenda. Celia had to admit, there were times when her interviews with Natasha left her unsettled, questioning herself.

"Must have been a deep interview," Keith remarked as he swiped his badge and input the code.

"It was a bit. I heard some things I didn't expect."

"Yeah, she can take you by surprise like that. Want me to walk you to your car?"

Celia was about to protest, but she thought about all the extra turns and stops she'd made on her trip to the prison. "Sure, thanks."

Keith walked with her across the lot. "So has this Bart guy done anything threatening?"

"Not really. Just a pest. He's the reason I was late today."

"What do you mean?"

"I noticed he was following me, and I didn't want him to know what I was doing, so I led him around until he gave up following."

Keith stopped and grabbed her arm to stop her as well. "He followed you?"

"I lost him. He's just trying to intimidate me."

"Celia, that's not normal. I'd consider that threatening."

"Come on, he's harmless."

Keith sighed. "You need to watch things. If he's following you, that means he's at least a little obsessed. Trust me, normal guys don't follow a woman around town just because she dumped them."

"I didn't dump him." Celia was defensive. "We only went out a few times."

"I could tell at the gala he was really into you. He didn't like us talking at all."

Celia rolled her eyes. "Yeah, that's part of what turned me off. We were just talking."

"I know that. I'm just saying don't dismiss the idea that he could be trouble."

"I won't. I'm not. But I'm not going to hide. He doesn't get to bully me."

Keith smiled and shook his head. "I can see why Natasha likes you."

"She likes you too."

"I'm not sure how to feel about that. But hey, two good-looking women like me."

Celia laughed. "Here's my car. Thanks for walking me."

"No problem. Take care. I'll be glad to walk you every time if you'll make me more of that cake."

"I'll see what I can do." Celia got into her car and locked the doors. She noticed as she drove away that Keith was watching her from the curb, making sure she made it out of the lot without any problem. He was a good guy. She could use a friend who could take Bart in a fight, she thought, chuckling.

Celia checked her rear-view mirror regularly on her way home, but there was no Bart following her this time. She'd lost him before she left the city, so he couldn't possibly know where she went. Still, she was glad when she returned to her office without a tail. Keith was right about one thing; it wouldn't hurt to be careful.

The deadbolt was unlocked. Celia always locked both the knob and the deadbolt. Part of her wanted to call someone before entering her house, but who would she call? Instead, she placed her keys in between her fingers and opened the door slowly.

It was quiet, and nothing looked disturbed. No disarray, no creepy gifts, and no notes. She set down her purse, turned on the entryway lamp, and walked through the kitchen and living area still holding the keys. The hallways were quiet as well. But she could see a glow coming from her bedroom. Her fist closed tightly around the keys as she inched forward. *If you're there, you're dead. I'm sick of this.*

No one was in her bedroom, but the bedside lamp was on, and there was something on her pillow. A flower. No leaves, no stem, just the bud. After looking in the closet and under the bed, Celia swore and grabbed the blossom. She tossed it in the toilet and flushed. Then she checked to make sure her windows were locked. Turning off the lamp, she left the bedroom and headed back to her purse.

Her father's card was in her wallet. She hadn't planned to call him, but now she wondered if he might know more about Bart. Was it worth connecting with the man she spent years hating to find out? She closed her eyes and pictured the tiny bud swirling around the bowl before disappearing. Yes, it was. If she was going to get Bart off her back, she'd have to play dirty. And that meant she needed to know more about his past. Celia dialed her father's number on her cell.

"Hello, um, Dad? It's Celia. I have some questions. Can we meet?"

Chapter 17

Stewart was already sitting at a small table when Celia arrived at the coffee shop. He was sipping something, and he waved when he saw Celia. She headed to the table without waving back.

"I'm glad you came. I wasn't sure you would. Would you like something?"

"No, it's too late for caffeine for me."

"So," he started to reach across the table, but hesitated. "What's going on?"

"I want to know more about Bart."

Her father frowned and leaned forward. "Has he done something? Has he threatened you?"

"Relax. He's just being a pest. Trying to intimidate me a bit."

"I told you he was dangerous. You don't need to underestimate him."

"I don't," Celia replied. "But I suspect he underestimates me. I can handle him, but I need to know more about his past. More about his possible secrets."

"Well, it was no secret he was an arrogant ass," Stewart said. "Judith's parents liked him well enough, but Melina never trusted him. She said he gave her a creepy vibe. I didn't know Judith that well, but Melina swore he was changing her. And not by choice."

"How do you mean?"

"Well, apparently Judith was the spunky one, the rebel. She had strong opinions and kind of went her own way. But she was fiercely devoted to her family."

"And that changed?"

"Over time it did. She went from speaking her mind to being more timid. Eventually, it was almost like she had to look to Bart for permission to say anything. And we saw less and less of her. She told us it was Bart's career, but she didn't come to visit by herself either. Melina wondered if he wouldn't let her."

"Was he abusive physically? Did you ever see bruises?"

"I never did. Melina never said if she did. But, as I said, We seldom saw her by the end."

"What about when she did visit? Was she quiet? Nervous? Did she wear long sleeves even when it was warm?"

Stewart nodded. "Now that you say that, yes she did. We had a cookout once, and everyone wore shorts except Judith. She wore pants and a button-down. I remember Judith commenting about it."

"I wonder if there were any trips to the ER," Celia said more to herself than her father.

"We'd have no way of knowing."

"I doubt it. He wouldn't leave marks you could see or hurt her bad enough to need medical attention. He'd stay under the radar."

"You're probably right." Stewart reached for Celia's hand. "He didn't touch you, did he?"

Celia put her hands in her lap. "No, never. If he'd done that, he'd be in jail. I'd know how to ruin him if it was that overt."

"I really think you need to get a restraining order. Do something."

"I wasn't going to, but now that he's been in my house—"

"Wait, what the hell? He was in your house? Tonight?"

"Not when I got home. But he had been there. I could tell. I'll have to get new locks I guess."

"I've got a suite," Stewart said. "Why don't you stay with me tonight? Stay there until you get the locks changed."

Celia shook her head. "No, I'm not running away. He doesn't get that. Besides, I have a meeting first thing in the morning."

"I could go with you, wait while you pack a bag. You don't need to be there if he can get inside."

"I'll use the chain, and I'll put a chair against the door if I need to. I'm not sleeping anywhere but my own bed tonight."

Stewart sighed. "I know where you got that stubbornness."

Celia smiled without thinking. "From you."

"You're right. Dammit." He smiled. "You're sure I can't change your mind?"

"Thanks, but no. You've helped though. I know where to dig now. If he's worried about being exposed as an abuser, he'll back off."

They said their goodbyes, and her father left the coffee shop. Celia decided to get a tall latte after all. *It's not like I'll sleep tonight anyway.*

****

At 9:00 on Thursday morning, every staff member, reporter, and assistant were crammed into the bullpen waiting for the meeting to begin. The email firmly requesting everyone's presence was cryptic, and the office had been filled with speculation all week. John was either in the dark about the meeting announcement, or he was using his office to hide from probing questions. He'd canceled all his meetings. On Wednesday evening when Celia locked her own office long after business hours, she'd noticed the light still coming from under John's door.

"I'm glad everyone could make it." A man dressed in an expensive suit stood to address them all. He was vaguely familiar to Celia, though she couldn't remember his name. "Let's go ahead and get started."

"Where's John?" Julia whispered as she sat next to Celia. Celia looked around and shrugged.

"For those of you I haven't met yet, I'm William Keller, CEO of Multicorp Media. As of Friday evening at 5:00, we acquired this publication as one of our affiliates, and I'd like to welcome everyone to the Multicorp Media family."

A few people applauded, and the rest of the room joined them. William smiled, lifted his hands, and continued. "Over the next few weeks, we'll be speaking with many of you in this room to discuss the direction we are planning to take and get your feedback. We want this transition to be smooth, so, for the most part, things will be business as usual. You will continue to work on your current projects." The room seemed relieved at the news.

"However..." William looked toward the back of the room. "We do have one promotion to announce. John Talbot has left us to pursue other opportunities, and we are appreciative of his contributions here."

"I told you!" Julia whispered, elbowing Celia. Celia shushed her and rubbed the rib where she'd just been jabbed.

"Your new editor-in-chief is a seasoned journalist with international experience and a stellar reputation. Everyone, please congratulate your new Editor-in-Chief, Celia Brockwell!"

Celia stood slowly, while Julia cheered loudly beside her. The applause this time was fairly enthusiastic, although Celia noted a couple of sour expressions on the faces of colleagues who had hoped the promotion would someday be theirs.

"Why didn't you tell me?" Julia asked as Celia sat and William continued his speech.

"Why didn't anyone tell me?" Celia responded.

After the meeting ended, people began to disperse, many of them stopping by to congratulate Celia on her new title. Once the crowd had thinned, William made his way to the back of the room.

"I gather from your expression during the meeting that you had no idea you'd been promoted," William chuckled.

"I didn't, sir, but I am very glad to be the new Editor-in-Chief."

"Yes, I didn't assume John would follow through and talk to you. I confess the shock on your face was priceless. Either way, we know you are the right person for the job."

"I appreciate that," Celia replied.

"I'd like to sit down with you if you have a few minutes. I want to get a feel for what you are working on to see if we need to reassign anything. You'll be taking on more as the Editor, so I don't want you too overloaded."

Celia checked her watch. "I'd like to talk about that as well. Unfortunately, I have a prior appointment at 10:30 off-site. Could we meet after lunch?"

"That sounds fine. 2:00?"

"Perfect," Celia said. "I'll make sure my assistant knows."

William walked away, and Celia walked toward her office. She was the new Editor-in-Chief, just like that! And Multicorp would afford her all sorts of exposure and opportunities. She couldn't help but speculate what the raise might entail as well. But now wasn't the time to daydream. She needed to be at the prison by 10:30.

When Celia walked into the familiar small room, she was surprised to see that Natasha had put on makeup and had her hair swept into a chignon. Other than brushing her hair, Celia had never seen her do anything particularly special to her appearance.

"I meet with my attorney today. He has an attractive assistant," Natasha answered the unspoken question.

Laughing, Celia sat down and turned on her recorder. She slid two new packs of cigarettes to Natasha and wrote the date at the top of her notebook page. "I do like the hair."

"Thank you. You wouldn't believe how I had to charm a guard to allow me to have a few bobby pins."

"I think I don't want to know."

Natasha laughed and leaned in for a light. Once she had begun smoking, she sat back again. "So is your admirer still determined as ever?"

"Oh God, yes. I'd never have gone out with him if I had known he would be impossible to get rid of. And there's nothing that can be done. He plays just barely inside the lines."

Natasha pointed her cigarette finger and scolded. "You shouldn't dismiss him. Men like him are bad for all women."

Celia waved a hand and fiddled with her notebook. She didn't want to discuss Bart with anyone, even Natasha. Besides, she wasn't going to let him ruin her day and good news. He was much more than an annoyance, but she'd handle it in her way, once she figured out what that way was. Today Celia didn't want Bart in her headspace. "I've got it under control."

"You know, I believe you do." Natasha tucked a bit of hair behind her ear. "So who are we killing today?"

Celia laughed and then caught herself. Murder wasn't supposed to be funny. "You do have a way of putting things, don't you?"

"I try to be direct," Natasha teased.

"We haven't talked about Julian Hedges."

"Oh, that we didn't have to talk about him," Natasha said dryly.

"There was speculation in some of what I read that your motive for murdering him was connected somehow to organized crime. Of course, the official record states there was a long-standing grudge over misconduct."

"Julian Hedges should have been disbarred years before he died. He was a seedy little man, a transplant from Michigan. He was crooked, and he used his skills and position to threaten and betray others. The organized crime bit was just a means to ensure his death."

Natasha was referring to the anonymous note that she had sent to a known criminal who Julian represented. He was rumored to be under investigation by the FBI. According to court records, Natasha had doctored a couple of photos so it looked like Julian and an agent were having a conversation. This man didn't bother checking the validity of the photos or the note. Julian was found dead in his townhouse a week later.

"So what did Julian do to you? What happened, and when?"

"Julian came to my father and me early in my career, offering his services. He had quite a few clients who were models, and he handled some of the legal aspects of their finances and taxes. The three of us met frequently, as my career took off rather quickly."

Natasha nodded for Celia to continue.

"So you were present at the attorney meetings? Weren't you underage?"

"I was, but I insisted on being present. My father has always been most concerned with himself. I didn't want the two of them benefitting at my expense. This did not please my father, so Julian was privy to more than a few heated discussions. He probably observed the two of us more than anyone."

"That makes sense. And he was bound by the attorney-client privilege."

Natasha chuckled as she flicked ash on the floor. "Regarding our specific business, yes. He seemed to think that the relationship between my father and me was more of a gray area."

"So he spoke to the press? Someone else?"

"Poor Julian had a gambling problem. He also had two ex-wives. When a magazine came asking for information about me, he was only too happy to accept their generous offer and betray me."

"Which article was that?"

"One of those rags for celebrity-worshipers. They played up a passionate feud and dysfunctional father-daughter relationship, with hints of more. They never revealed their source, but I knew who it was. It could have only been Julian."

"Did you confront him at the time?"

"I did. He dismissed me as dramatic and told me he was sure he wasn't the only one who could describe my relationship with Father. He also let me know his take on attorney-client privilege and how unfortunate a messy lawsuit could be."

"What a douche," Celia said before she caught herself.

"Exactly. I wanted to pursue it, but my father insisted I let it go. He was always worried about anything curtailing my fame and the money."

Celia thought about a couple of incidents in her past. "I don't think I'd be able to let that go easily. It was an ethical breach at the very least. Not to mention bullying tactics."

"Yes. As a model, I watched all of the editing and retouching that goes into photographs. Photography began to fascinate me."

"Yes, I had forgotten. You are somewhat of an amateur photographer. I've seen some of your photos; they're very good."

"Thank you, yes. I learned to use editing tools as well. It took some work, but I thought the photos of Julian talking with an agent were very convincing, as was the note."

Linguists and writing experts had examined the note closely. However, there had been no fingerprints on the paper or envelope. If detectives had not found the photos, they would never have known who wrote it.

"Were you at all concerned that the organization might target the agent as well?" Celia asked.

"I did consider that. But it's much easier to just quietly take care of a civilian. Killing law enforcement brings attention most criminals don't want."

"Of course, Julian left behind a wife and two children. Did that bother you?"

Natasha straightened. "I met his wife, a tanned, bleach-blond woman with no will of her own. Do you know why Julian moved? He moved to isolate his wife, to better control her. He wouldn't even allow her to answer questions for herself in conversation. I am sure that after the grief faded, his family felt freer than they had in years."

Natasha's matter-of-factness concerning her crimes still took Celia aback sometimes. However, there was an objective logic to her thinking too. Rather than seeming calculating, sometimes it almost seemed laudable. "So Julian got his due, and no one would think to connect you at all."

"Not until I was arrested for my father's murder and they began digging through everything, including my external hard drive."

"So that is where they found the photos?"

"Yes. I had told my father to get rid of it, but he kept it. He probably thought it would make good blackmail, should he need it."

This was new information, and Celia leaned forward with interest. "Blackmail?"

"My father is a selfish man, but he is also observant. And he knows me better than anyone. After I killed Roland, he became suspicious and tried to catch me in a slip of the tongue. When Julian was killed, he became even more suspicious. He went through my things while I was away for a premier. Tore the place apart. He found the drive and the photos."

"That must have been… Were you worried about what he might do? I mean, I know he was your father, but the way you've described him…"

"I was not afraid of him, afraid that he would disclose what I had done. After all, he was just as culpable as I was, and just as Machiavellian. Perhaps it was his hypocrisy that killed him. I do know this." Natasha pushed the ashtray aside and sat very straight in her chair, her gaze boring into Celia. "The writer, James Baldwin was wrong. The only thing more dangerous than a man with nothing to lose is a woman who refuses to lose and who is not afraid to take someone with her if she does."

Celia sat back in her chair, trying to give Natasha some space. "So is that why you killed your father? Because he knew? Were you afraid he wouldn't stay quiet? Because you must know that no one would have ever caught you had you not decided to kill him."

Natasha slowly twirled the butt of her cigarette into the ashtray and looked at the table. Silence had never been unusual during their interviews, but this silence seemed strangely thick and tense. Celia realized she was seeing one of the only glimpses of feeling anyone had likely ever observed in Natasha, and she wanted to lean forward, to watch closely. However, Natasha was so visibly uncomfortable that Celia had to look away out of some strange sense of sympathy.

"I have thought about many things over the years I have been here. You are correct. I would have been undetected had it not been for my father's murder. Of course, psychologists said that I killed him because I needed the world to know what I had done. That is not true. I had no need for anyone to know."

"So why kill him?"

"Because he lied."

Chapter 18

When Celia returned from lunch, Gladys was sitting at her desk, and she looked up and grinned. "You're late!"

"What? Late for what? My meeting with the CEO isn't until 3:00."

"Well, your 1:00 was been waiting for almost fifteen minutes," Gladys countered.

Celia stopped at her door. "I don't have a 1:00." She looked through the oblong glass window on the door. "Oh, god, no."

"He said he had an appointment. He showed me a text…" Gladys said meekly.

"It's okay," Celia replied. "Just don't go anywhere. If he isn't gone in five minutes, call me for a meeting somewhere."

Gladys nodded, and Celia walked into her office, keeping her door open. "Bart, why are you here, and why did you lie to my assistant?"

"I had to see you. You won't talk to me or answer my messages, so I had no choice. You shut me out."

"I didn't shut you out. I told you how it is. I also told you not to contact me."

"You don't control me, Celia. You don't make decisions for me."

"No, I make decisions for me," Celia responded. "And I have decided I do not want you in my life. At all."

Bart stood and walked toward her. Celia refused to move. "Celia, we have to talk. We can make this work if you'd stop being so stubborn."

Celia stepped forward, thankful she wore heels. They put her eye to eye with Bart. "There is no 'this.' There never will be. But you need to understand something. I have every communication, every message. Including your little note."

"You don't know what you're talking about," Bart sneered.

"You can walk out of my office right now, or I can call security. And my next call will be to your boss."

"This isn't done," Bart said. "And by the way, I know about your little meeting at the coffee shop."

"Good for you. Worried I might have learned something?"

"I'm not worried. But Stewart should be."

"I said this is over. Get out."

"And I said this isn't done. Not by a long shot."

"It's done, or the police will be visiting you. I have plenty to give them."

Bart smiled and stepped back. "Fine, Celia, I'll leave." He walked to the door and stopped. "Have a great afternoon," he said before taking something out of his pocket and tossing it into the trash.

Once he left, Celia closed her door and leaned against it. What an ass. She looked down and noticed a crumpled envelope in her wastebasket. She fished it out and smoothed it on her desk. It was the note Bart had sent her, the one she had ripped and thrown away at her house. It was taped together. Celia held her breath as she reread it. Bart had been in her house.

Celia sat at her desk and scrolled through her contact list until she came to the number she needed. As it began to ring, she sighed heavily.

"Good afternoon, City police department front desk. How may I help you?"

"Yes, my name is Celia Brockwell. I'd like to speak to Detective Wilson please." Frank Wilson was one of her contacts at the station, and they had developed a rapport. If he couldn't help her directly, he would know who could.

"Wilson speaking," Frank answered.

"Frank, it's Celia from the Post."

"How are you? What can I do for you? Got a new story brewing?"

"Actually, I have a personal favor to ask. What do I need to do to file a report of stalking? Maybe get a restraining order?"

"Is someone bothering you?"

"Yes, there is. I thought I could diffuse it myself, but it's getting out of hand."

"Tell you what, come on down to the station. I'll call one of our best guys. He can take your statement, and I'll fill you in on the rest of the process."

"Thanks, Frank. I'll be there soon."

Celia arrived at the station fifteen minutes later and knocked on Frank's door. He was talking to a colleague, and when he stood, Celia secretly hoped he was the "best guy" Frank had mentioned. The man was probably in his late thirties, and he was at least 6'3" tall. It was obvious he spent a lot of time at the gym too. His presence was intimidating, to say the least.

"I'm Walter. Walter Robinson." The man extended his hand and Celia shook it. "Have a seat."

Celia took the remaining chair, and Walter sat down as well. "I appreciate both of you seeing me."

"No problem, Celia," Frank replied. "You've given the department a hand on more than one occasion. Tell us what's going on."

Celia told them about her brief pseudo-relationship with Bart, the calls and messages, the repeated attempts to see her. She showed Frank and Bart the screenshots and messages. She also showed them the handwritten note.

"You sure he wrote this?" Walter asked, scrutinizing the note.

"I am. I have something to compare. Here." Celia handed him one of the cards he'd written, attached to one of the many flower arrangements he sent. "He signed this, and the writing looks the same."

Walter looked at both notes and nodded. "This is good. The anonymous note ups the threat level, and this card is a good handwriting match. Have you filed for a restraining order?"

"I haven't yet. I was hoping it wouldn't get that far. But when he lied his way into my office today, I got rattled. I think it's time."

"You think your assistant will corroborate his lie?" Frank asked.

"Oh, I'm sure she will. She was upset that he fooled her."

"So here's what you need to do," Walter said. "You need to go to the courthouse and fill out the paperwork. Get your secretary to file an affidavit too. Hang on to all this documentation and anything else that might happen. You'll need it for the hearing."

Celia sighed. "Ugh, a hearing."

"Yeah," Frank replied. "You're essentially asking the court to restrict his freedom. They'll need evidence."

"In the meantime," Walter said, "I'll go down to his firm, try to catch him as he goes outside, and have a polite but firm talk with him. I can be imposing when I need to be."

"I'm sure you can." Celia smiled. "You're quite a presence."

Walter smiled. "Yeah, I'm part of the goon squad when I need to be."

Celia nodded. They chatted for a few more minutes, and then Walter left.

"You need anything else?" Frank asked.

"No, I'm good. I appreciate this."

"Stalking is no joke," Frank said. "You're doing the right thing."

Once Celia left the office, she decided to see about getting her cell number changed. It would be a pain in the ass, but Bart would have more trouble contacting her. She was about to unlock her car when she felt an uncomfortable presence, so she looked up and around her.

Bart was across the street. He didn't try to approach her; he just leaned against the crosswalk sign and watched her. When their eyes met, he smiled. Celia looked away quickly and got into her car. She didn't want him to know he'd rattled her. However, at least now he probably knew she had contacted the police. Maybe the idea of legal trouble would make him back off. Somehow Celia doubted it. She made sure she pulled away slowly so that he wouldn't have the satisfaction of thinking he made her run.

At 3:00, Celia met with William, her new boss, and they discussed some of her duties as Editor-in-Chief. He wanted to know all about the projects she was working on, and Celia talked him through all of them. All of them except one. John had never put her interviews with Natasha on the books, and neither had she. For some reason, she wanted to keep it quiet. Once she knew a little more about how William did things, she'd let him in on the story. No matter how Multicorp Media usually did things, Celia knew her contract with Natasha regarding secrecy wasn't going to change. Now that she and Natasha were in the middle of the process, Celia didn't want to jeopardize anything.

"I think this new partnership is going to benefit us both, Ms. Brockwell," William said, standing. "I look forward to seeing some great things."

"Thank you, Mr. Keller," Celia replied, reaching forward to shake his hand. "I appreciate the opportunity."

"You've been bigger than your previous role for some time. And please, call me William."

"I will if you'll call me Celia."

"Deal." William smiled. "Well, I have about four other meetings before my day is done. I'll let you get back to work."

Celia sat down and consulted her laptop. She could probably get the first draft of her latest story done before she left if she stayed late. It drove her crazy to leave work without a good stopping place. She pulled up her notes and began typing. She was in her flow when Gladys interrupted her.

"You have a call," Gladys said tentatively. "It's um… It's John."

"I'll take it." Celia sighed. "Might as well get it over with."

Gladys closed the door and forwarded the call. "Hi, John."

"Well, I guess you got what you wanted," John said curtly.

"What are you talking about? I had no idea this was coming."

"Sure," John laughed. "I guess that fancy prison story worked its magic."

"I told you before, John, there is no agenda behind that story. William doesn't even know about it."

John laughed again. "Yes, he does. I told him."

"You did? Why?" And why hadn't William mentioned it in their meeting?

"He didn't seem surprised either. Even he knew you pushed me out."

Celia fought the urge to curse. "John, I didn't push you anywhere. How could I? I do my job every day, and you did yours. There is nothing else to say. I had no control over this."

"Yeah, I know you and your little friend Marlene are close. I'm sure she told you all about the real reason she left. And even with the gag order, I bet you know about the money."

Celia sat back, her head spinning with questions. "John, I have no clue what you are talking about. Yes, I'm friends with Marlene. No, she hasn't told me any big secrets. She always wanted a restaurant. She got one. End of story."

"We'll see. You'll see," John said. "Running things isn't as easy as you think it is. Don't expect any sympathy from me when you fail."

"I won't fail. I don't fail," Celia snapped. "I'm a hell of a lot more qualified than you ever were. Go to hell, John." And with that, Celia slammed the phone onto the receiver. The sound was a hell of a lot more satisfying than a simple swipe, she thought. "Gladys, hold all my calls," she told her assistant before silencing her cell and getting back to the article. She'd had enough crap for one day.

She got home at 6:30, and the security company van pulled up at 6:45. The officer she talked to had suggested Celia get cameras installed, and so she called Keith to find out who could do it well and do it fast. One of the other guards did security on the side, and Keith assured her he was one of the best.

Chad, the guard, asked her what she needed, and they discussed packages. In the end, she chose a camera for both doors, attached to the doorbell, a motion light for the front, and a plan that allowed her to access the footage from anywhere. By 9:00, Chad and his crew were done, and Celia had installed the app on her phone and tablet.

After her shower, Celia made a sandwich and watched a bit of television. By 10:00 she could barely keep her eyes open; she hadn't slept well the night before. She checked the cameras before turning out the light, glad she could rest a little easier.

Chapter 19

Celia was so buried in new responsibilities and deadlines, she wasn't able to interview Natasha for the next two weeks. William had met with her several times, and she had met with every staff reporter. Between meetings, there were stories to finish and assignments to make. A part of her understood why John was sometimes such an ass. However, she also managed to unravel some of his lack of organization, and Celia was certain that given time she would have things exactly the way they needed to be. It didn't hurt that most of the staff seemed relieved to have him gone, and they admired her.

The busyness had also kept her from thinking too much about Bart. He'd been threatening when she initially got the restraining order, but after a stern talk from a police officer, conveniently timed while he was at work, he settled down and had left her alone. Oh, Celia had seen his car nearby when she went for coffee, and she was sure he was likely still driving down her street. But there were no calls, messages, or visits. Keith had come by to install a new lock and a couple of cameras. Celia knew he was attracted to her, but she kept him at an appreciative arm's length. She needed an ally, not a lover.

Celia used her time in the evenings to create a special baked dessert for her friend Marlene's housewarming and gender reveal party. Despite her inability to recreate Marlene's grandmother's

Italian cheesecake, Celia was determined to visit the spirit of the dessert with her own flair. Marlene was a fan of fresh fruits, so Celia tried several combinations until she created something she hoped Marlene would find irresistible. It would please the host and garner some recognition as well.

Celia arrived at the gathering at 8:00 sharp, and when Marlene saw her with a cake box, she squealed. "You baked! I can't wait to try it!" Celia allowed herself to be hugged before breaking away and walking toward the kitchen. There was an abundance of food, which was no surprise, but there was also an array of liquor. Celia was a bit surprised. Marlene couldn't drink, of course, and David wasn't much of a drinker. "My step-father brought the bar," Marlene said wryly.

"In that case, I'll try not to let it go unappreciated." Celia took a high-priced craft beer out of an ice-filled bucket and popped the top. "I've been wanting to try this."

"I hear congratulations are in order," Marlene said, opening a tonic water and clinking it against Celia's beer. "To the new editor-in-chief."

"Thank you. It was a surprise, but I think I'm getting used to it."

"You'll do things with that publication that John would have never been able to do."

"I sure hope so," Celia replied. "There's a lot of potential there. And with Multicorp's backing, I think real growth will happen."

"I'm just glad they finally did it."

"Finally? What do you mean?"

"I mean there have been other media organizations that have wanted to take us on through the years, but John wouldn't hear of it. He liked his little kingdom."

"What an idiot. He could have made so much more money!"

"John had plenty of money already, though I'm not sure where it all came from," Marlene said, her expression darkening.

Celia was interested in hearing more. "Oh really? And how do you know this?"

Marlene waved the topic away. "Oh, that's a boring story for another time. Come on, I want you to see the nursery."

The nursery was bright and welcoming, with green and yellow everywhere. No doubt Marlene had picked the color to avoid any gender stereotypes. There were ducks painted along the base of one wall, and the picture window on the opposite wall had gingham-covered blinds, probably specially made. There was a phrase scripted in Italian over the bed: *Chi si volta, e chi si gira, sempre a casa va finire.*

"What does that mean?" Celia asked, pointing to the script.

"No matter where you go or turn, you'll always end up at home," Marlene replied.

"That is lovely," Celia smiled. "And you look lovely as well."

Marlene laughed. "I can't wear my favorite jeans anymore. But at least I'm done throwing up every day."

"I'll drink to that!" Celia laughed. "I'll drink for both of us."

The house filled with friends and family, and after a bit of eating and socializing, Marlene's mother produced a large ceramic egg. It was painted with flowers and butterflies, and she explained that the couple would break the egg to find out whether they were having a girl or a boy. Celia was glad they were going with something classy and unique rather than the typical powder or confetti explosion. The couple took a small mallet, held it together, and struck the egg a few times before it finally cracked open. Inside was a small pink doll. They were having a girl. Everyone applauded, Marlene cried, and Celia went into the kitchen to retrieve another beer. She was looking for the opener when her phone began to vibrate.

It was the alert for her camera system. Someone had approached her front door. She clicked on the icon, and the camera opened. Someone was standing at the door, trying to use a small device to get inside. She didn't have to see the face to know who it was. The build was exactly like Bart's, and the hair was short and dark. Cursing, she clicked on the option that caused a light to flash and a small alarm to sound. The figure turned to reveal sunglasses, and he spotted the camera. He lifted a gloved hand and flipped a bird for whoever was watching, and then he quickly ran out of camera view. The video was automatically saved.

Keith and Walter had been right. The cameras were a necessity. Celia saw the notification pop up asking if she wanted to forward the video to the security company. She opted to save it instead. However, her evening was ruined, and she was ready to get away from all the emotions. She found Marlene and David, told them she wasn't feeling well, and she slipped away quickly.

It didn't take long for Celia to drive home, and once she got there, she saw something sticking out of her mailbox. It was a hastily scrawled note:

Really, bitch? A camera!

There was no doubt it was Bart, though the handwriting was overly large and careful. Celia took it into the house and placed it in the folder Keith had set up for her. She was tempted to watch the footage again, but instead, she made sure every door and window was secure before getting ready for bed. Once she was settled, she decided to work on Natasha's story. Bart was not going to intimidate her, and she was not going to succumb to fear. Staying pissed off was much better. She considered calling Keith, but he would probably want her to file another report, or he might want to come over and check on her. She wasn't in the mood for that. What she wanted to do was find Bart and acquaint him with the gun she kept locked in a box in her closet, but she knew that wasn't rational. Anything she did out of emotion would be foolish. Celia had learned that lesson the hard way once. She didn't want to risk it again.

"Celia, did you hear about Candace?" The receptionist asked.

"What happened?" Celia asked.

"Candace had an accident last night. She was on her way to the courthouse to cover that shooting."

"Oh wow, is she okay?"

"She is, just a few bumps and bruises. Apparently, her brakes locked or something. She's kicking herself for not getting the first look."

"I wondered how I managed to beat her," Celia replied.

"You know, I kind of wondered if someone did something to her car. It was a pretty big story."

"That would be a dumb thing to do," Celia remarked quickly. "Let me know if she needs anything."

The receptionist nodded, and Celia walked down the hall to her office. Once inside, she sat and collected herself. Candace was okay, the wreck wasn't serious, and Celia had gotten there first. She'd be the first to break the story. She just hoped that no one else was as suspicious as the receptionist had been.

Chapter 20

As usual, Natasha was waiting when Keith and Celia arrived in Room 4. Keith had quizzed Celia about the camera incident. He had Chad set it up to send alerts to his phone as well. She assured him that she was fine, but he wanted her to file it. Bart had broken the restraining order whether she had been there or not, and everything needed to be documented. Celia promised him she would take care of it.

"At last you arrive," Natasha teased. "I need a smoke."

"I came prepared, as always," Celia said, and she took out the cigarettes and a small lighter. Keith raised an eyebrow but didn't comment.

"You've got him wrapped around your finger I see," Natasha remarked.

"As if you didn't already have him wrapped around the other," Celia responded.

"Well, he is a good ally to have."

"Yes, he is that. He's helped me with a few things around the house. I mean home security," Celia clarified when Natasha grinned.

"Good. I asked him to insist on it. You are not taking your spurned suitor seriously enough."

Celia shook her head and turned on the recorder. "So I have to admit, two weeks ago, you left me with a cliffhanger. You said your father lied, and then our interview ended."

"Once an actress, always an actress." Natasha shrugged.

"Yes, I know. It's not the first time. But we only have a few interviews left. I want to spend some time talking with you about your time in here for the story, but, to put it into your terms, we have to kill everyone first."

Natasha laughed. "Very nice. I have trained you well."

"That's a rather scary thought, I think," Celia joked. "So what did your father do? How did he betray you in a way that merited his death?"

"He lied about my mother."

"Your mother? She left when you were young. Did something happen to her?"

Natasha smoked in silence, and Celia could tell she was crafting the opening of the story inside her head. Celia could understand that. Talking about the hard things always took mental preparation.

"My mother was always a gentle person. From what I understand, it was her family who helped my father defect from Russia and into the United Kingdom. They married, and one year later I was born.

"My father was not a gentleman. He kept my mother under tight control. At home without him, she was a creative and interesting woman. Once he came home, however, she retreated into herself, capitulating to whatever he demanded. As I got older, I began to see her weakness. Around the time I was ten, their relationship became more tumultuous. My mother became unpredictable and sometimes disappeared for days. Of course, she was punished when she returned. Sometimes, however, she fought back. Her anger at my father occasionally turned on me. Still, she was too afraid to stand up for him when she calmed, so she stayed.

Our home became a place I hated. And so when my father told me she had returned to England to be with her family, I was not even upset. I had lost respect for her."

"I'm sure that was difficult. Did you ever hear from her?"

"I never did, which just solidified how I felt about her. Even when I began to gain some notoriety, and I thought she might return to get something from me, she was silent. She walked out when I was ten and never looked back."

"I'm sorry."

Natasha shook her head. "That isn't necessary."

"So she was in England all this time? Is she still there?"

"I began to wonder years ago. As I became famous and the pressure for interviews grew, my father wanted the money they would bring. We argued, and he would tell me, 'You are stubborn and crazy like your mother! You will go crazy and we will lose everything!'

"I decided to research. At first, it was difficult, but money talks and money silences. I managed to determine that she never left the country. I thought perhaps my father lied about where she went to spare me from looking for her as a girl. If she was an entire country away, it would be impossible. I realized once I discovered this that I would have to confront him to find out the truth. I knew he had lied, but I couldn't find more answers on my own.

"Did you think your father would give you the answers?"

"I wasn't sure, but I also had leverage. By this time he was dependent on me, and he was aging. If he lied or refused to give me answers, I could cut him off completely. He would be homeless with no resources."

"And were you prepared to do that?"

Natasha crushed the cigarette she was smoking and pulled out another. "Of course," she said, leaning forward for a light. "Even though my mother had problems, she was still my mother. Telling me she had fled to England benefited him. If that was a lie, she might have remained in my life. He removed my choice. And so I confronted him with what I knew and demanded the truth."

Celia leaned forward slightly. However, Natasha crushed her cigarette without taking a drag and sat back in her chair. Celia was used to dramatic pauses or thoughtful silence, but this was different. For the first time since the interviews had begun, the actress looked troubled. It was strange considering sharing the details of four murders didn't seem to trouble her at all. Celia sat back as well, trying not to speculate. She was determined not to push.

Finally, Natasha took another cigarette and leaned forward again for a light. She pointed it at Celia. "You told me last week that I had somehow gotten you to talk too much during our interviews. You have done the same to me. This is not something I prefer to discuss. It is no one's business. I want no one's pity."

Celia took a calculated risk. "Natasha, I will not pressure you to continue; however, you should know that I do not pity you."

It was quiet, and Natasha studied the reporter carefully. After a few minutes, she smiled and placed the burning cigarette in her mouth. "I know," she said, blowing a slow stream of smoke. "I knew you wouldn't. That is why I approached you. I saw our similarities." She held up her hand before Celia could interrupt. "So I will continue. But I ask that you not record this. We can record my account of my father's murder. But not the information about my mother."

In any other situation, Celia would have tried to negotiate. She would have pushed her subject to allow her to record. She might have even pretended to put away the recorder, leaving it on secretly, or just made a special note to remember so that she could put it in the story anyway. In this case, she turned off the recorder and put away her notebook. Celia wouldn't be taking notes, and this would not be part of her story.

"I wondered at times if my father had been unfaithful. I have learned that certain men need admiration and need a challenge. My mother provided neither. We had a variety of housekeepers and other staff in our home, and they were usually attractive.

"My father was unfaithful, it turns out, but not just with these women. He visited prostitutes as well. High-class ones at first I think, then the dirtier ones you see on the streets.

"When my mother became erratic and her behavior became volatile, he took her to a doctor." Natasha looked out the small window. "She had syphilis. The doctor prescribed medication for both of them, but my mother's brain was already damaged. Instead of taking responsibility for her health and sanity, my father put her in an institution across the country. Or rather, he had one of his shady friends do so."

"Oh my God." Celia could barely speak. "Did he tell you where? Did you—"

"She died when I was twenty. She spent nine years alone in an institution and then slit her wrists."

Celia sat back in her chair and watched Natasha. She was angry at her father's deceit. Anyone would have been angry. To discover her mother had been in the country, in an institution, and had committed suicide… It would devastatingly shake a person. Celia's eyes were narrow, but she was calm.

"How did you find out all of this? I know you researched, but… Did you have help?"

"I did. I got help from someone I learned I could trust. I realize now that I allowed my anger at my father to make me foolish."

"What do you mean?" Celia could tell Natasha didn't want to betray her source.

"There were several ways I could have responded to his lies. I could have cut him out of my life. I could have made him suffer financially. Killing him was irrational and stupid, and I am rarely stupid."

The familiar knock and the guard's presence signaled that the interview was over. Celia inwardly cursed, but Natasha just stood calmly and tossed her cigarette onto the floor before stepping on it. As always, a guard removed her from the room, and Keith escorted Celia back down the hallway.

Celia was distracted as she walked to her car. She didn't see the note on her windshield until she had already fastened her seatbelt. Annoyed, she got out of the car and retrieved it, cursing when she saw the handwriting. Bart had left her a note at the prison. It was infuriating. He had written the time at the top: 1:32. He'd left it right in the middle of her interview, and because she was deep inside the prison, he had technically been 500 feet away from her, as the RO advised. The police would do nothing. Again.

They had advised her to keep all correspondence, so Celia placed the note in her purse, though she didn't see how it would help. It was just one more impassioned plea from Bart asking her to call him or meet him. Looking around, she wondered if he was watching. How did he even get into the lot, and how did he know she would be there? She hadn't even told him about the interviews. There was no way he could know she was interviewing Natasha, could he? The only person who knew outside the prison was John, and he had no idea she had been dating Bart. He didn't even know Bart as far as Celia knew.

A notification went off on Celia's phone, and she checked it. It was reminding her of a 3:00 appointment. It hit her as she swiped to dismiss. The calendar app. She had it on her laptop, and it synced to her phone. Bart had been in her home. Had he hacked her laptop somehow? Celia was careful to have security in place and anti-virus and anti-malware protection. She'd even been known to use a VPN. But not always. She immediately locked the doors of her car and called Keith. She knew it would go to voicemail, but she needed his help. He knew how to check to see if her technology had been compromised.

Keith called her back less than ten minutes later. "Celia, what's up?"

"I hate to be a pest, but I may have a problem."

"What's going on?"

"When I left the prison, there was a note on my windshield. It was from Bart."

"What the hell? How did he even know you were here?"

"I wasn't sure until I got a notification from my calendar app. He was in my house at least once. I think he might have tried to hack me. I have no idea if he did or how far he got."

"I'll be over right after work. I get off at 7:00. Or I can try to have someone cover –"

"No, no don't do that. I'm not going to panic. But if you could come by and check, that would be great. I'm sorry you keep getting sucked in."

"Don't even worry about that. I'm glad to help." Keith laughed. "Besides, Natasha might murder me if I don't make sure you're safe."

"I highly doubt that," Celia chuckled.

"I mean it. She's been fascinated with you for years. I wasn't a bit surprised when she wanted you to be the one who interviewed her."

Celia wasn't sure how to respond to that, so she ignored it. "Well, I really appreciate this. I'll be home before 7:00, so I'll be there before you arrive."

"See you then. Watch your back in the meantime. I mean it."

"I will, thanks." Celia ended the call and looked in her rearview mirror. No one was following her, and she felt a little sheepish. Bart hadn't actually confronted her. He'd left a note on her empty car when she wasn't around. He wasn't violating the order, just skirting its limits. Still, Celia would feel better once Keith had given her computer and phone a once-over.

At 7:15, Keith knocked at her door. She let him in and showed him where to find her laptop. Before he took a look, he checked her router, the wall behind her desk for anything that didn't belong, like Ethernet or a fiber optic cable. He explained that worst-case scenario, he might even be streaming from her webcam. Celia had to sit down when she heard that. The idea of Bart watching her made her instinctively cover herself.

"You're okay," Keith finally said. "He hasn't wired into your place. That's a good thing. Let me check your laptop and phone. I promise not to look at anything weird."

Celia laughed. "Weird? What do you think I do online?"

"I don't know, maybe nothing," He grinned. "Maybe your write steamy crap novels under a pen name. I don't judge."

Celia punched him and then went to the kitchen to make them both a drink. She played on her phone while he went over her laptop and tablet, and then she handed him her phone. He was engrossed in his search, so she decided to watch a little TV.

"So, you should be okay now."

"Now?" Celia asked. "You mean I wasn't?"

"It could have been worse. He didn't get full access. But He did manage to get to your appointments and a few other things. No email or other access though. I plugged the holes and upgraded your security."

The idea that Bart had been able to invade any of Celia's privacy made her angry. Keith seemed relieved it wasn't worse, but all Celia could imagine was Bart's head on a stake. "That bastard."

"That's an understatement. I printed out the documentation, and I'll be glad to make a report personally. This is absolutely a violation of the order. Not to mention a few other things. If it were me, I'd push this. They need to pick him up and put the fear in him."

"Oh, I'll be reporting it for sure. I'm tired of this. What's his problem anyway? It's not like I'm the only woman in the city."

"Well, you are a cut above most," Keith smiled. "But guys like him, they get fixated. They're narcissistic and unstable, and they convince themselves it's a relationship and that you are just playing coy." He put a hand on her shoulder. "But it won't be pretty when he finally realizes your rejection is real. You need to be careful."

"How do you know so much about this?"

Keith turned and sat on the sofa. He put his elbows on his knees and sighed. "I was the one who found my sister after her ex broke her jaw."

"Oh my god!" Celia sat beside him. "That's awful!"

"Yeah, it was about 7 years ago. He was always a jerk, but when she broke up with him, he wouldn't accept it. He pulled some of the crap Bart has. Suzie wouldn't report it. She thought she could reason with him. After he beat her up, she finally had him charged and got an order."

"Thank goodness."

"Yeah, he violated it a couple of times, so big brother had to have a talk with him."

"A talk," Celia said, raising an eyebrow.

"Well, he didn't talk for a while after that. Hard to talk with your lip busted and a couple of teeth gone."

"Dang, I'm glad you have my back."

"He got really angry when he couldn't get to Suzie, so he went after another girl. Raped her."

"Good God, what happened?"

"She pressed charges, and my sister testified as well thanks to his crappy attorney opening the door. He's in prison. Won't get out anytime soon with his temper."

Celia sat in silence, thinking about Keith's sister and imagining Bart with a few fewer teeth. "You're a good man, Keith. You know that?" She placed her hand on his.

"Why thank you, ma'am," Keith replied in an exaggerated drawl. He placed his other hand on hers, and they sat that way for a while. Finally, Keith stood. "Well, I better go. You're good now, and I need to head home."

Celia was a little disappointed. "Okay then. Hey, wanna grab dinner Saturday? I'll buy."

"You don't have to do that," Keith replied.

"Hey, what are friends for?"

He cocked his head a bit and then smiled. "Sure, sounds good, Just call me."

Once Keith had left, Celia went to her laptop to type up the notes from her interview with Natasha. Even though Keith assured her it was fine now, she felt a bit naked booting it up. Bart had seen inside her life in a way that she never intended. She felt stupid and violated. And angrier than she had been in a long time. One way or another, Bart was going to need to go away. And sitting there as she checked her email, Celia didn't much care what it took.

Chapter 21

Celia was working, but in the back of her mind, something was bothering her. She'd had several meetings with her new boss, and he had never mentioned her interviews with Natasha. According to John, he knew she was talking with the actress; however, William had never asked a single question. It was going to be a big story. Celia thought he would at least be a little curious. Maybe he was waiting for her to mention it. Did John imply she was keeping it a secret? Was William testing her to see if she would bring it up during their meetings? Whatever was going on, it made Celia uncomfortable. She decided that when they met later in the day, she was going to talk with him about the story. She'd just have to hope he didn't want to leak it the way John had.

Meanwhile, Natasha's revelation about her mother still had Celia stunned. No matter how controlling Mr. Bronlov had been, Celia couldn't believe he would hide Natasha's mother away and lie about it. Was his obsession over image really that insidious? The more she learned about Tasha's father, the easier it was to see why Tasha was so calculating. With a Machiavellian father and no access to her mother, all Tasha saw was manipulation and self-interest. It wasn't the theme of Celia's article; however, she couldn't help wondering how the actress's killer mind had been created. If someone had known both Tasha and Celia growing up, they would have deemed them very much alike. But Celia didn't plot murders.

Maybe she pushed a little too hard to get ahead, but she never killed anyone.

Celia's cell phone rang, and when she looked at the screen, she was relieved to see that it was Marlene. Shaking her head, she wondered how long she would have the moment of stiffening her spine just in case it was Bart.

"Marlene, good to hear from you. I haven't had a chance to call you since the party. It was great, by the way, and I am so happy for your two."

"Thanks, Celia," Marlene responded. "We're pretty excited. Dave keeps wanting to buy pink, and I keep telling him not to. But the truth is, I kind of want to go pink-crazy."

"Celia laughed. "I say go for it. No shame in your baby girl being pretty in pink."

"Thanks," Marlene chuckled. "I actually wanted to talk to you if you have a few minutes."

Marlene's change in tone told Celia it was more serious than baby colors. "Sure. What's up?"

"Have you…" Marlene hesitated. "Have you heard anything from John since he left?"

"Oh, he called me once. Tried to get into my head. I haven't heard from him since."

"I wonder if he's in town or if he's moved on."

"I'm not sure. I'm sure he still has his cell phone if you need to talk to him."

"Oh, I don't want to talk to him."

After sitting in silence, Celia asked, "Is something wrong?"

"I'm not sure. I don't think so."

"Marlene, something is going on, I can tell. You said something at the party that made me wonder too. Did John do something?"

"Has your new boss said anything to you about why John left?"

"At the first staff meeting, he made some vague statements about new opportunities. But he wasn't specific. And I get the idea he isn't John's biggest fan."

Marlene laughed. "No, he's really not. John kept him from buying things up a few years ago. I'm not sure how he succeeded this time."

Celia shook her head. "I never understood John's control issues. Being a part of Multicorp can only be good for everyone."

"Yeah, but being part of a big company like that also brings more scrutiny."

"What do you mean?"

Marlene cleared her throat. "Let's just say that it was easier for John to get away with some things with no one was looking over his shoulder."

"Okay Marlene," Celia said. "Now you have to tell me what is going on."

"I can't say much. But I would like to talk. I just want to make sure none of this will blow back on Dave and me."

Celia stood and closed her door. "What do you mean? What could blow back on you?"

"Look, I can't talk right now. I have to get to the restaurant. But are you interested in a late dinner?"

"Yeah, I can swing that. Are you okay in the meantime?"

"Oh, I'm fine. I just want to make sure all my bases are covered."

"Well, I'll come to the restaurant at closing then. 10:00?"

"Great. I'll save some of your favorite."

"Sounds good. Let me know if anything changes."

After they exchanged goodbyes, Celia sat back in her chair and thought about John. Where was he, she wondered. And what in the world was Marlene worried about? She and John had seemed to get along fine. Looking back, she had resigned a little unexpectedly, but then again, Celia knew she and Dave had been planning a restaurant. Now, however, Celia wondered if there was more to the story. If John had a grudge, it certainly wouldn't be too surprising if he looked for a scapegoat. Shaking her head, Celia redirected her thinking. There was no use speculating between now and 10:00. Besides, she needed to get some work done.

One of the things Celia did after taking over as editor-in-chief was to create a content calendar that could be accessed by the entire staff. It was set up so that each writer could add to or update the status of their own projects, but only she could change the master calendar. John had tried the old-fashioned paper calendar method, and it had been very inefficient, not to mention confusing. It was as if he didn't trust some of the writers to manage their projects. As far as Celia was concerned, a writer who couldn't be trusted didn't need to be a writer. So she gave them more ownership of their work, and it cleared her plate for other things. She was hoping William would feel the same way.

At 2:00 that afternoon, William walked into her office and cracked the door. She noticed he rarely fully shut the door when meeting with her or others. Maybe it was a precaution. At any rate, they exchanged the normal small talk, and then William pulled out his tablet and became businesslike.

"It looks like your system is working well," William said. "And I appreciate being kept in the loop. It builds trust, and it helps Multicorp promote the publication."

"I'm glad to hear that," Celia replied. "I always thought setting up a calendar that could be partially modified was a good idea, but I could never convince John."

William laughed. "I'm not surprised. John has never been a fan of any idea that wasn't his own. It's part of the reason I knew I'd have to replace him if we acquired The Journal."

Celia studied William for a minute. "Can I ask you something?"

"Of course."

"Well, John called me right after he left."

"He did?" William interrupted. "He didn't harass or threaten you, did he?"

"No, nothing like that," Celia answered. "I mean, he tried to get into my head a bit, but that's just John. That's actually what I wanted to ask you about."

"Okay, go on."

"Well, there's one story I've been working on that we haven't discussed. I've been interviewing Natasha Bronlov. I didn't say anything because she made it clear there could be no advanced promotion or leaks of any kind. Anything like that and her permission and access to her is gone."

"That makes sense. You were protecting your source."

"Yes, well, when John called, he said you knew about the interviews. He said he told you. And yet you've never mentioned it."

William sat back and looked out the window. He seemed to be annoyed, but Celia didn't sense he was annoyed with her.

"Well, being professional certainly never has been John's way. Celia, I didn't ask about your interviews because I know how pushy John had been. I knew if Natasha said no leak, she meant no leak. She'd do exactly what she said she'd do. I figured you would tell me about it once you had the whole story."

His response surprised Celia. She was also flattered that he trusted her judgment. It was refreshing.

"I appreciate that, William. I want us to communicate. But this story with Natasha –"

"Is big. Maybe your biggest so far, considering the mystery around her and her upcoming execution."

"Exactly. And I know it's twisted, seeing that she's a serial killer, but I want to respect her boundaries."

"Nothing twisted about that," William said. "Choosing to respect someone isn't about the other person deserving it. It's about who we choose to be. I'm sure Natasha appreciates it." William smiled. "And that's another reason I knew you were the right choice for Editor-in-Chief."

"Thank you."

"You're welcome." William pushed himself out of the chair and buttoned his coat. "Well, I have to charm a rich bastard. It won't be as much fun as this meeting, but it has to be done."

"Ugh, better you than me," Celia said. "Enjoy!"

William laughed and left the office, closing the door behind him. She heard him speak to Gladys, who laughed in response, and then he walked away. Celia smiled. It was no wonder Multicorp's stock kept rising. The man knew how to work a room. Celia was also relieved to know he was fine with the story. She'd have continued either way, but it helped to know her boss wouldn't try to sabotage her. In fact, he seemed to understand exactly how Tasha felt. Almost like he knew her personally. On a hunch, Celia pulled up a document listing links to articles and photos she'd collected. After a few minutes of searching, she found what she was searching for.

There they were. There were several photos of Tasha and William chatting at various events. There was a picture of them dancing, and at one of the events, he appeared to be her escort. She was a newly minted actress then and several years his junior. William and Natasha had known each other quite a few years. It made Celia more than a little curious.

Was that why he was fine with Celia's secret, because he knew Tasha well enough to value her privacy? Were they friends, or had they been more? It was long rumored that William was gay, but since he was almost as private as Tasha, no one was sure. Then again, Celia had never shied away from seducing men to her benefit. If that was the case, however, Celia doubted William would care much about respecting her boundaries. It didn't matter, Celia supposed. However, Celia never liked the feeling that she didn't know all she needed to know.

Talking to William more about it was a bad idea, Celia decided. But she was certainly going to probe Natasha at the next interview. If something was going on, she wanted to know about it.

Just before 10:00, Celia slipped into the restaurant and sat at the bar. It was almost empty, and servers were already beginning to clean and sweep, removing condiments and centerpieces from the tables. The bartender smiled and brought Celia a glass of wine, and then she began to cash out her register. Marlene was probably still in the kitchen, Celia thought. She sipped the wine and waited.

"Good to see you, Celia," Dave sat beside her.

"You too," Celia replied. "I didn't expect to see you tonight."

"Yeah, I'm not always here, but I knew Marlene wanted to talk to you. I guess I'm here for moral support."

"Wow, there really is something going on, isn't there?"

Dave smiled and glanced at the bartender. "I'll let Marlene tell you once it clears out here."

The two of them chatted for about fifteen minutes, and then Marlene appeared from the kitchen, sweaty and disheveled from an evening of supervising. She grabbed a bottle of water from behind the bar. "Let's go sit at a booth"

The three of them settled into a booth in one of the closed sections that had already been cleaned. Marlene gave Dave a quick kiss and then took a swig of her water. "Thanks for coming," she told Celia.

"No problem. Looks like you had a busy night."

"It was very busy. Which is a good thing for the bank account." Marlene sniffed her shirt. "And a bad thing for personal hygiene."

Celia laughed. "Nothing a shower can't fix. So tell me what's going on. I have to admit, I'm a little concerned."

Marlene smiled. "I don't want you to worry. It's just that now that John has been fired, I think someone needs to know a few things."

"So John was fired, then," Celia said. "That was the idea I got too."

"I can guarantee that John never would have left The Journal. He had too much to lose."

"What do you mean?"

Marlene hesitated and looked at Dave.

"It's okay, Marlene. Celia needs to know. It's past time somebody knew." Dave looked at Celia. "Marlene is worried about the NDA she signed."

"Wait, what? When did you sign an NDA? Was it when you left? Was he worried about a story or something?"

"No," Marlene said flatly. "He didn't want me to sue him."

Celia slid her wine glass away and leaned forward. "Why would you sue him? What happened?"

"It started about two years after I went to work there. John went through a crappy divorce. He cheated one too many times, I suppose. I tried to just not listen when he griped, and I did my job. I'd heard things before about his flirty behavior with others on staff. I would bet a couple of other people who left while I was there did so because he made passes. But he'd never been inappropriate with me. At least not until his divorce."

"He flirted?"

"At first it just seemed like he wanted a shoulder. Or maybe dating advice. Sometimes I was a little uncomfortable, but it wasn't until he started drinking even more that it got weird."

"Define weird," Celia asked.

"He started asking me what I would look for in a man if I was dating. He'd ask inappropriate questions about Dave. I asked him to back off more than once. He'd pretend I misunderstood and lay low for a day or two."

"What an ass," Celia said.

"You're not wrong," Dave quipped.

"Anyway," Marlene continued. "One night he was obviously drunk. It was at the end of the workday, and as I was about to leave, he told me I needed to stay over to make sure a story was ready for the next day. I protested, but he acted like he had told me and I forgot. He was belligerent, and I figured it would just be easier to do what he asked."

Celia felt herself getting angry. She knew where the story was going.

"Once it was just us, he started getting in my personal space, trying to rub my shoulders as I typed. I excused myself to go to the restroom, took my purse with me so I could just slip out. I'd already talked to Dave about what was going on."

"And I had told her more than once she had my blessing to quit. She didn't want to put us in a financial bind, but I told her I didn't care about money. I cared about her."

"He did, that's right. I was just stubborn."

"Surprise, surprise," Celia smiled.

"Who me?" Marlene tried to smile. "Well, I walked out of the restroom, and there he was. He pushed me back in, started trying to kiss me. His hands were everywhere. He called me a tease, along with some other choice names. I went full-on fight mode, slapped him across the face. That made him mad, and he punched me. It really rang my bell. Things got blurry, but I knew I couldn't lose it. I flung my purse in his direction, it made contact and he fell backward."

"I guess it was a good thing she has a monster purse," Dave said, taking Marlene's hand.

"True," Marlene agreed. "I ran. I drove home and told Dave what happened. He wanted to call the police. I begged him not to do that."

"But why?" Celia said. "He assaulted you!"

"He didn't punch me hard enough to leave any marks. I stayed late voluntarily. By that time I knew he'd hit on others, and nothing had ever been done about it. I agreed to talk to our attorney, though, just to get an idea of what I would be in for if I reported it."

"And how did that go?"

"He was no help at all," Dave said.

"He was just blunt," Marlene said. "He was honest about what would happen, how I would be questioned, what John's side would do, and how it would all likely play out. I promised Dave I'd think about it, but it all turned out to be moot anyway."

"Moot?"

"I missed the next day, took a sick day, which must have made John nervous. When I went back to work, he asked to see me in his office. I knew something was up."

"Because John never wants to meet in his office," Celia said.

"Yep. Well, his attorney was there, and they had this paperwork all laid out. I could resign quietly, sign an NDA, and he'd give me a nice chunk of money for my trouble."

"No way!"

"Yes, way. Like I said, I have no doubt this had happened before me. It was almost like he knew the drill. I told him I needed 24 hours. Boy, he did not like that. But I'm not making any choice like that without talking to Dave."

"I still wanted to pursue charges, but I also knew Marlene didn't want to go through all that. And I knew how badly she had always wanted a restaurant. So we decided to look at the offer as an opportunity that came out of something crappy."

"So you signed, and you used the money to open this place," Celia said.

"We did." Marlene cringed. "Do you think I'm terrible? A coward?"

"God no!" Celia said. "Look, I wish John would get locked up for his behavior. But I read the papers. Hell, we write stories like this. He said she said after hours. No marks. No complaints filed officially. I think you did exactly what was best for you. That is all that matters. I just wish I had known what you were facing."

"I couldn't say anything. I signed the NDA. It still makes me nervous, but him being out there and angry makes me more nervous. He gets angry when things don't go his way."

Celia looked at Dave and Marlene. They still seemed to be holding back, and Celia was hoping it wasn't what she feared. "You've seen him, haven't you?"

"The week after he left the paper, we were in the middle of the lunch crowd, and he walked in. I was helping out at the bar that day. Someone was out sick. He asked the hostess to seat him in the bar section. Since she had no idea who he was, she did."

"Had he ever been here before?"

"Never. In fact, I don't know that I have even run into him since I left the paper. But that day he sat there and ate the slowest lunch anyone has ever eaten here. And he just stared up at the bar. I knew he was watching, so I just avoided looking in his direction. I was supposed to go home between lunch and dinner, but it made me so nervous, I just stayed. I didn't know if he was waiting outside or what."

"Has he been back?"

"No, he hasn't. But I have no idea if he is still in the city or if he has left. I watch everything around me when I go out, and I hate thinking about having to serve him again. But I can't throw him out. People would wonder why."

"And he made sure you couldn't tell them, or you'd be in breach of that agreement."

"Exactly."

"What an ass," Celia said. "Look, I'll see what I can find out. In the meantime, document every single thing that even feels off. And never be here alone."

"No worries there," Marlene smiled. "Dave has been hovering since I found out I was pregnant."

"Not hovering!" Dave protested. "Just…protecting."

"Good," Celia said. "I have to go. But I'll be snooping, and I'll let you know, okay?"

"You don't want anything to eat?" Marlene asked.

"I'm not hungry. Besides, if I eat garlic and then go to bed, I'll regret it in the morning." Celia hugged Marlene, nodded at Dave, and left the restaurant.

Chapter 22

Keith and Celia decided to meet at a local Tex-Mex place. At 7:00, Celia arrived to see Keith already seated, sipping a Michelob Ultra. She tapped him on the shoulder, and he turned his head quickly. "I didn't peg you as a light beer guy."

"Celia, glad you're here." He flexed a bit. "Yeah, gotta watch the figure."

"Oh brother," she rolled her eyes. "A macho cop."

"Gotta stay ahead of the bad guys. Want something to drink?"

"I'll take a margarita."

Keith flagged down a waiter, and Celia ordered her drink. She grabbed a chip and looked at Keith. "So this is you relaxing. I'm glad to see you actually do it."

"I try to as much as I can."

"Yeah, I'm sure things at the prison aren't always calm."

"Believe it or not, now that I work in Natasha's section, it's much better than I worked with the general population. Who knew women could be so violent."

"That's a little sexist, don't you think?"

"I didn't mean it that way. It's just, my first job was at a men's jail. Those guys were rowdy and always up for a fight. You could never let your guard down. I mean, they'd crack a guy's head open if he got more eggs than they did. It's been my experience that most women aren't that ridiculous. That smarter sex."

"Nice save," Celia teased. "No, sadly, women can be just as petty and ridiculous. We just do it over different things sometimes. Though if someone got between me and a really good western omelet, I might punch them."

"I'll remember that. Figure or not, I'm thinking you might take me."

"I could."

Their food arrived, and they ate in silence for a few minutes. Keith put down his fork and waved at their waiter to request another beer. "So what made you want to be a journalist?"

"I've always had a gift with words. I guess it's corny to say, but I've loved words since I was little. But I didn't write stories or poems like most kids. I liked finding things out, writing down what I saw. I was an avid reader too."

"Wow, you were the smart kid."

"I did well in school. I wasn't much of a social butterfly, especially once we all hit puberty and most of the girls in my class became obsessed with makeup and boyfriends. I guess I was a bit of a nerd."

"Nothing wrong with nerds. They change the world and make the money," Keith laughed. "So you were the scholar and not the cheerleader."

"I started a newspaper in high school. We'd had one before I got there, but when the English teacher who headed it up retired, no one wanted to take her place. I hounded the principal until he relented and said it could be completely student-run."

"I can see that. You're pretty determined."

"It used to drive my parents crazy. My mom said I could charm or argue anyone into or out of anything."

"Ha!" Keith laughed. "I'm surprised you didn't become a lawyer."

"My parents were hoping for that. But no. Too much drama and ass-kissing."

Keith blinked. "Tell me how you really feel."

Celia laughed. "The law is fluid. That's one thing I've figured out. Not that it upsets me. I just don't want to be part of all the constant scrutiny and politics."

"That's interesting," Keith said. "I'd think your job involves a lot of scrutiny."

"True, but I'm the one doing the scrutinizing." Celia sipped her margarita. "So what about you? Why corrections?"

Keith shrugged. "I started out thinking I'd be a cop. But then I did some work in a juvenile facility. Sad to say, a lot of the people I worked with were frustrated guys who hadn't made cops."

"Yeah, I could see that."

"The kids were just…too much for me. But the prison system itself? I thought I could do some good. I wasn't thrilled that my first job was at a women's prison. But as it turns out, it was the perfect job."

"How so?"

"After what my sister went through, I guess I saw women a bit differently. Not as weak or in a bad way. But women don't get the respect they deserve all the time in the system. I wanted to be different."

"I'm sure the women appreciate that," Celia smiled.

"Not all of them. Criminals can be rough regardless of gender. But I can at least treat them like humans, not hit on them, and keep the peace with some dignity."

"No wonder Natasha likes you."

Keith chuckled and shook his head. "Here I was hoping it was my great physique."

"Well, that probably doesn't hurt," Celia replied playfully.

"Yeah, right." Keith rolled his eyes. "I think I'll order some dessert."

Chapter 23

"How's it going?" Keith asked as he and Celia walked down the hall toward Room 4.

"Pretty good," Celia answered. "It's been busy. I didn't realize how being Editor in Chief would change things."

"I'm sure you're up to the task. Any news with your little problem?"

"Not lately, thank goodness," Celia said. "But that reminds me. I hate to ask, but I need a different favor."

"Sure. What is it?"

"John, my old boss. Can you find out if he's still at his place? He's been giving one of my friends a hard time. Not dealing with his career change well."

"No problem. Is your friend okay?"

"I think so. I just want to make sure."

Keith nodded and opened the door, where Natasha was already waiting. Celia thanked him, sat down, and began setting up the recorder.

"You and Keith seem quite friendly," Tasha remarked.

"That is because we are friends," Celia said. "And nothing more."

"Such a shame," Tasha sighed. "Maybe after our interviews are over you'll give him your number."

"He already has it. But somehow I think you already knew he did."

Tasha laughed. "I'm afraid I've been a little too forthcoming in our interviews. You may actually know me well now." She raised an eyebrow. "Of course, I know you as well."

"Perish the thought," Celia smiled. "So last time we talked about your father. We were interrupted before you told me about his murder."

"Yes, sometimes I wonder if Keith listens in and opens the door on a cliffhanger."

"True," Celia laughed. "If he weren't so law-abiding, I wouldn't put it past him."

Tasha chuckled but didn't comment. "So I knew I'd have to be careful with my father. He knew I was angry, he suspected things, and he knew murderers. Who knows, he may have been one."

"You think your father killed people?"

"My father did whatever he had to in order to ensure things went his way. I do the same, as do you."

"I haven't killed anyone," Celia argued, a bit uncomfortable.

"Not yet," Tasha said. Then she laughed. "Relax, I'm kidding. Like I said, I knew I should be cautious, but I was also angry. I was angry when I killed the attorney and the reporter too, but this was different. This was about betrayal."

"That's understandable."

"First, I tried to access one of my father's guns. I knew the combination to his safe; it's how I got the gun for the first murder. But when I went to the safe this time, the combination had been changed. I realized then my father was afraid of me."

"Well, he should have been. It was a pretty significant lie."

"Yes, it was. However, that should have given me pause. If he was taking precautions, then the chances of me killing him without getting caught were pretty slim. But I was blinded. So I had to find another way to get a weapon."

"Sadly, that isn't as difficult as we would like it to be, is it?" Celia said. "It's harder to walk into a store and buy one legally than it is to get one in an alley."

"Exactly," Tasha nodded. "But of course I could not do that. I was able to get a revolver, however. For several days, I attempted to talk to my father about my mother. I told him I was angry, but I knew he was trying to protect me. It was stupid, but it came from a good place. I told him I wasn't sure I could have him in my life anymore, but I wanted to try."

Celia nodded. Somehow she knew where Tasha was leading him, so she waited for the actress to continue.

"The idea that he might be cut out of my life upset him. His fear of being cut off superseded his suspicion of me. I knew it would. He began to beg for a second chance. So I told him I wanted to go together to see my mother, to at least see where she was buried and say goodbye. He readily agreed."

"So you went to the cemetery where she was buried."

"We did. The trip took a couple of days. He didn't want to fly, and I didn't question it. We used the GPS on my phone."

"I see," Celia said. That explained how the police knew where to find her.

"My father got a phone call while we were at the cemetery. It seemed innocuous as if it was from one of his friends. He told them he was on vacation and would take care of whatever they were talking about when he returned."

"But it wasn't innocuous."

"No, it wasn't. I had brought flowers for each of us to place on her grave. When he knelt to lay his bouquet on the ground, I shot him in the back of the head. Then I took everything from his pockets, his glasses, and the keys, and I drove to a hotel. Fifteen minutes after I checked in, the concierge knocked on the door. When I opened it, he stepped aside, and the police were there."

"Were you surprised?"

"It's funny. I was a bit surprised when the concierge stepped aside. But as soon as I saw the officers, my first thought was to chastise myself for being so idiotic. While I was manipulating my father, he was manipulating me."

"And did you still have the gun?"

"Stupidly, I did. I had planned to take a different route home and discard it the next day. But there wasn't time. My father had one of his friends tracking my phone, and when he did not call the friend back within half an hour, the friend called the local police and told them a murderer was at the hotel. He gave them my description and the location of the cemetery."

"Damn," Celia said softly. She had read an anonymous tip led to the arrest, but the reporter had no idea the plan was so elaborate. Like father, like daughter, she supposed.

"Yes, my father was smarter than I had believed. Underestimating him was a grave mistake. I should have known better."

Celia made a few notes, and Natasha smoked in silence. Her father had betrayed her twice. First, he lied about her mother. Then he trapped her into being arrested. Celia felt a bit sorry for the actress. She looked up to see Tasha staring at the wall. She almost looked vulnerable. For a moment, Celia wondered whether she should bring up the topic of William after such a revelation, but the clock was ticking, and she had promised herself she would ask about him if only to see Natasha's reaction.

"I hate to turn the subject on a dime, but I'd like to ask you something."

"A change of subject would be appreciated," Tasha said.

"William and I talked about my projects earlier this week. I had not told him about our interviews because I wanted to respect your privacy; however, he already knew because John told him."

"Of course he did."

"Yes, well, William didn't seem at all upset that I kept it secret. In fact, he was pretty accommodating. He seemed to be glad that I cared about your privacy."

"Almost as if we knew each other?" Tasha smiled.

"Exactly. I've seen some photos of the two of you. It seems like you were friends. Or maybe more?"

Natasha crushed her cigarette and laughed. "Surely you know that I am not William's type."

"I had heard that, but I wasn't sure. Look, it doesn't matter, I guess. But it felt like there was something there I didn't know about, and I am not fond of that feeling."

"I understand that. And now that we have talked and I know that I was right about you, I'll be glad to fill in the missing pieces."

"I'd appreciate that."

"I have known William for years. He approached me at a premier event, and we became friends. My father seemed to take an instant dislike to him, so of course, I spent lots of time with him after that. He took me to my first awards show."

"Yes, I saw that photo."

"People speculated, but I knew William was gay. He was always very respectful and kind, and he shielded me from a lot of probing eyes and ears. He couldn't stand my father, which I enjoyed immensely."

"Really?"

"Yes, he was very upfront with me about it, He thought my father was using me. He was the one who suspected my father might compromise my privacy if it meant notoriety. "

"Wow," Celia said. "Then again, he does seem pretty perceptive."

"He is. We remained friends, but I didn't advertise it. Neither did he. I didn't want the press hounding him the way they did anyone they thought would give them a quote. I tried to distance myself after my arrest. But we remained in touch. He was the one who gave me information about my mother."

Celia was shocked at the revelation. It made sense that William would know a lot of people. But Tasha must have really trusted him if she reached out to him in that way. After all, it could have clued him in to her plans, and she could have been exposed.

"I never doubted I could trust William," Tasha seemed to read Celia's mind. "When I was arrested, he got a message to me right away. Let me know he was there for whatever I needed. I wouldn't let him visit during the trial, though. I didn't want anyone harassing him."

"So did you ask him about who should do these interviews? He does run a media company. I'm a little surprised you chose me, even now."

"William has tried to acquire your paper before. It's on the cusp of rivaling publications like US News and Global Times. Your old boss was an idiot, however, and blocked it."

"I'd heard that," Celia said.

"This time though, he did lots of homework. He knew where John's weaknesses were, and he knew his secrets. He was going to acquire the paper, and he wanted to be the one to tell my story, should I ever decide to share. I was glad to give him that."

"It makes sense. He was a good friend. But that still doesn't explain choosing me."

"I noticed your writing in the wake of 9/11. Of course, I was busy with my own life, but your writing struck me. There was a familiarity about your voice."

"Familiarity?"

"Yes. You were pragmatic. You didn't spin things with emotion. In fact, you didn't seem to be swayed by emotion at all. It stood out at the time because everything was a drama."

"And that was familiar?"

"Yes. It reminded me of me. When I was sentenced, I began researching you in earnest. I had some help. And I began seeing connections."

Celia thought of Paul. "What kind of connections."

"Well, there were little things. But when I realized that we had both known Paul, it seemed like a sign, if I believed in signs. It wasn't hard to realize you had likely found a way to win that internship."

Celia looked away. She was both impressed with Tasha's intuition and bothered by the fact that Tasha seemed to be drawing parallels between them. It wasn't as if Celia hadn't done the same throughout their interviews, but she still wasn't crazy about the comparison.

"There's no need to be offended. We are led to think that everyone is supposed to cry over sad movies and moon over puppies and feel guilty when we take those grapes from the produce section of the grocery store. But not all of us feel that way. Once you realize it doesn't make you a monster to not be ruled by emotion, it's actually freeing."

"But," Celia hesitated. "Isn't what you are describing exactly what it means to be a sociopath?"

Tasha laughed. "You've watched too much television. People like us don't go around murdering everyone we don't like. We just see more clearly."

"You did," Celia half-joked.

"Oh honey," Tasha said. "If I killed everyone I didn't like, there would have been a lot more than five. What I did was self-preservation. Tell me you wouldn't do anything to protect yourself."

Celia didn't want to head any further down the road Tasha was traveling. "So you researched me, and for whatever reason, you thought I could tell your story best because…you think I am like you."

"A little over-simplified, but that is the gist. I also knew William was going to become your boss. And I wanted him to be a part of this. He deserves that. I wasn't sure when he would make his move, but I knew it would be before you wrote my story."

Though she pretended to be making notes, Celia just doodled in her notebook. Knowing what she knew, it made more sense that Natasha reached out to her instead of a reporter who might want to inject emotion or outrage into the story. However, the idea that a sociopathic killer had chosen her was less than comforting. And while she had no doubt William was a good person, it bothered her that he had been planning part of her life for her, at least in a sense. Celia had lived most of her adult life doing everything she could to make sure she was in control of her choices and life. This made her feel a bit like a puppet.

Then there was the assurance Natasha seemed to have that they were alike. Yes, Celia had been a bit…aggressive in her pursuit of success at times. However, she had never hurt anyone. Paul's life wasn't over because of one internship, or it shouldn't have been. He would have done well if he had been surer of himself. And her colleague's accident? There was no way Celia could have known that would happen. She certainly didn't intend harm. And then there was Bart. True, she wouldn't mind if a bus hit him, but if she was truly like Tasha, Bart would already be dead.

"You're upset," Natasha said. "Understand, I had to be careful. I'm a good judge of people, but I'm not psychic. And I knew you would benefit as well. No one has told this story. No one knows what you know. In fact, you have carte blanche to write everything. Even the pieces that weren't recorded."

"Thank you for that," Celia said. "I do understand why you were so careful. I'm just not used to parts of my life being orchestrated."

"You could have said no to my letter," Tasha smiled.

"Only an idiot would have done that," Celia smiled back. "So now I know that backstory."

"Yes, you do. It was something I had not planned to tell you, but here we are. And now it's your turn. What about this stalker? Is he keeping his distance?"

"He hasn't directly violated the order if that's what you mean. I'm being cautious."

"That means he is indirectly violating it. You know he will not stop. If he didn't stop when you told him to, when you threw him out of your office, and when you filed an order, he is not going to stop."

"I hope that isn't true. I have security measures in place."

"And you have Keith."

"Yes, I have Keith. He's been a big help. Did you know his story?"

"I assume you mean his sister. Yes, I know. Despite the television portrayals of riots and girlfriends and such, there are many very slow, dull hours in a women's prison. And I have no one to spill any secrets to. Except maybe you, but you already know."

"I'm actually honored if that makes sense. But I do have one more question."

"I'll do my best to answer."

"You said William helped you find your mother. I understand he has a lot of connections, but your father went through a lot of trouble to hide her. How did William find her?"

Natasha bit her lip, one of the only signs she gave that she was hesitating.

"I don't mean to pry too much about it."

"No. it's a fair question. I should have expected it.

"We can wait until next time…"

"William is my brother."

Keith knocked on the door then, and Celia began to gather her things as he walked into the room. She reached for the recorder, and Natasha grabbed her hand. It was the first contact they'd had, and Keith nervously touched the gun on his hip.

"I trust you," Tasha said. "I'm trusting you."

Celia nodded, took the recorder, and followed Keith without answering. They walked down the hall, and neither of them commented on Natasha's violation of no-contact or her parting words. Keith kept walking with Celia until they were outside.

"You okay?" He asked.

"I'm fine. I promise."

He nodded and walked back inside, and Celia walked to her car, a bit overwhelmed with all she learned during the day's interview.

Chapter 24

Celia led her first staff meeting on Friday morning. It wasn't the first time she'd organized a group or spoken in front of one, not by a long shot. However, it was her first meeting speaking as Editor-in-Chief, and she wanted it to go well. The feedback was good, and everyone was on board with the new calendar. Even the staff who had been skeptical or envious the day William had announced her promotion seemed amenable. When she returned to her desk, Gladys was smiling.

"Well, that's the first time I haven't heard some sort of yelling from the conference room." She joked.

"I'll try to do better next time," Celia laughed.

"You know, now that I'm assistant to the Editor-in-Chief, I think I deserve a raise."

You know," Celia said, pausing at the assistant's desk. "You really do."

"Oh, I was teasing," Gladys blushed a little.

"No you weren't," Celia replied. "Schedule a meeting between the two of us on Monday, and we can talk about it."

"I'll be glad to!" Gladys smiled and pulled the calendar up on her computer.

Celia chuckled as she walked into her office. Gladys had been there for a while, and as a result of Celia's additional duties, Gladys had additional duties now too. Celia wasn't sure what the protocol was for giving her a raise and how much she could decide on her own, but Gladys deserved it. She probably needed to look at some of the staff as well. John certainly never thought about their actual value.

Once the morning's busyness was over, Celia decided to work on her article about Natasha. The draft she had begun was already becoming unwieldy. She'd either have to end up cutting a lot of it or making it a series. Thankfully, now that she knew William and Tasha were friends, she was fairly certain he'd give her a good bit of latitude. There was so much more to Tasha's story than the drama or the facts of the five murders. Much of Tasha's early life was tumultuous, and the models she watched made it clear: weakness was dangerous, and power and control were the only way to security. When you are weak, you have no say, and then you disappear. When you have power, you are seen, and you decide your own fate.

Celia could relate, even though her upbringing had been less trauma and more typical dysfunction. Still, even Celia understood the principle behind her thinking. Emotion, trust, vulnerability…they all came with strings. And people who were led by them were easy targets. Celia had seen it in the lives of her friends and family. Even Marlene's situation. The first time John tried to use his sad-sack routine with Celia, she would have seen right through it. Marlene was a smart woman, but she wore her heart on her sleeve too much. It was how John was able to manipulate her. Not that he wasn't an ass who needed to pay for it.

Even Bart had that weakness. He caught feelings, and he wouldn't let go. Of course, he was in a whole different category. He thought he was entitled to Celia, that he owned her. No thanks. Celia had to wonder if the reason he was so stubborn was that she was the first woman who didn't fall for his obsessive love-bombing. Whatever the reason, it had taught Celia a lesson. Relationships were liabilities. They were messy. She was better suited for hot men in pool halls.

Celia's office phone rang, startling her a bit. "Celia Brockwell."

"It's Keith," his voice was short. "Don't you have your phone?"

"I do, it's right here," Celia replied. "Oh, I had it on silent for our staff meeting and didn't turn it back up. What's going on?"

"I've been calling and texting for almost an hour. Your alarm went off, and I'm at your house right now."

"What? What happened? Is everything okay?"

"I think you better get over here."

Celia hung up the office phone and gathered her purse and phone. "Gladys, something is going on at my house. I'll be back as soon as I can."

"Oh no, I hope everything's okay!" Gladys cried. "Let me know."

"Thank you, I will."

Celia punched the code into her phone and looked at her notifications. The alarm system had notified her several times, and she could see missed calls and texts from Keith. It looked like a back door had been opened. Could it have been a delivery? A break-in? Was it Bart? Celia drove faster, hoping her last thought wasn't the case.

Keith was waiting for her, and his expression wasn't good. He motioned for her to follow him, and she could see that someone had pried the back door open. The camera above the door was smashed. Celia cursed and followed Keith inside. Then she stopped and gasped.

There were flower petals all over her floor, leading from the back door toward her bedroom. She followed their path and saw a package on her bed. Police were inspecting it, and she asked them to step aside so she could see. There were some discarded roses on the bedding, but it was the item in the box that chilled Celia.

It was her neighbor's cat. It looked like the neck had been broken. There was no note or name, but Celia knew exactly who had left it there. She felt nauseous for a minute, and then anger took over, and she whirled around to face Keith.

"I want to see the footage."

"Celia, there really isn't a good view," Keith said.

"I don't care! I want to see it." She followed him into the living room, and they pulled it up on his tablet. A man wearing a ski mask walked to the back entrance. He held up the cat in front of his face, and then he threw something, probably a rock, at the camera. After that, there was only snow. Keith pulled up the view from inside the living room, but all they could see was someone's back carrying the box and dropping flower petals. It was Bart; Celia knew it was Bart.

"It's Bart."

"I'm sure it is, but his face isn't anywhere. It'll be hard to prove it's him."

"I know that's who it is. No one else would do that."

"Could it possibly be your old boss? He's pretty ticked, isn't he?"

"It's too tall to be John. Not fat enough either. And this isn't his style. He'd come closer to trying to steal a story than this. This is Bart."

An officer approached them then. "What makes you think it's Bart?"

"It's his build and height. And no one else has been stalking me, following me, and trying to hack into my computer. He's obsessed. And this clearly violates the order."

"What about your neighbors? Could any of them have seen something? Do any of them also know Bart?"

"Not really," Celia started to pace. "Wait, I'm pretty sure Lucille met him. Oh God, poor Lucille. She loved that cat. Has anyone talked to her yet?"

"We tried, but no one is home right now. We'll follow up. Maybe she noticed something."

"I can't believe he was this bold."

"It's not that unusual. He's been escalating all along, Celia." Keith said.

"I've done everything I should. Changed my number, installed alarms, locked up my computer like Fort Knox. And he still got in!" Celia stopped pacing. "How the hell am I supposed to stop him?"

"Okay, let's just take it a step at a time. You'll need to follow through with a report. Let the police do their job here thoroughly. And I can fix the door." Keith looked around. "But Celia, you really don't need to stay here."

"Where am I supposed to go? I'm not letting some psycho jackass run me out of my home!"

Keith led her to the couch and sat her down before continuing. "I get it. You don't want to give him the satisfaction. But this isn't a note or a bit of hacking. He broke into your house and left the neighbor's cat. This guy is seriously unhinged."

"Then we fix the camera, I get a dog. I buy a gun. But I'm not leaving my house."

"Celia, all of those things are good ideas. But for tonight, at least for a few days, you don't need to be here. Please."

"I wish I'd been here. I'd have killed him myself."

"Or he would have killed you. He's desperate."

Celia pressed her fingers against the sides of her head. She knew Keith was right, and it made her angrier to admit it. She needed to stay away for a couple of days, at least until the door was fixed and the camera was replaced. But where would she stay? She wasn't going to ask Marlene. Putting a pregnant woman in danger wasn't happening. Celia wasn't the kind of woman who had lots of female friends. She supposed she could rent a hotel room, but that seemed even less secure than her home.

"You can stay with me. I have an extra room." Keith offered.

"I don't know if that's a good idea."

"Oh come on, Celia, we're adults. I'm not going to try anything, and neither will you," He grinned. "It's just for a few days."

"Are you sure?" Celia stood up. "I really hate this guy."

"I know. Pack a bag, and then we can go to my place."

"No, I have to go back to the office. I'll pack a bag and then come to your place after work. I'm sure you have to get to the prison."

Keith frowned. "I'd rather not leave you."

"There are police here. I'm fine. I have to get things done today. I'll see you tonight."

"Okay then," Keith said. "Call when you get to your office."

Celia nodded and went to her bedroom to pack a few things. As she tossed her toiletries into a bag, she tried to stop fuming. Losing control wouldn't help anything. And what if he was watching somewhere? She wasn't going to leave the house in a panic. No one was going to make her panic, least of all some idiot with a bruised ego. Once she'd finished packing, Celia left her house, still being scoured by police, and drove back to work.

"Everything okay?" Gladys asked when Celia walked by her desk.

"Yeah, just a broken light," Celia lied. "No biggie." She closed her office door and sat at her desk, trying to refocus. She'd stay with Keith, she'd keep working, and she'd keep her eyes open. She'd been serious when she mentioned a gun to Keith. However, if she decided to get one, it wouldn't be from a store. Celia would have to figure another way to get one. Because if Bart pulled something like that again, Celia would shoot to kill. And she'd do it when no one was around.

By the end of the day, Celia had calmed some, and she was ready to head to Keith's house and relax. It still irked her that she couldn't go back home, but she knew she'd be on high alert all night if she was alone at her house. And there was too much to do to walk around sleep-deprived. She knew Keith would be true to his word and give her privacy, and she had to admit she had mixed feelings about that. She needed to blow off some steam and get some stress relief. However, she knew that would be stupid. Bart wasn't going to make her stupid.

Keith was cooking dinner when Celia arrived. He showed her to the bedroom, and when she had put her bags down, she walked back into the kitchen.

"There's beer in the fridge," Keith said as he stirred vegetables.

"Great," Celia said. "You didn't have to cook."

"It's relaxing," Keith replied. "You can clean up."

"Yippee," Celia laughed. "What are we having?"

"Sweet and sour pork with vegetable stir fry. Haven't had Chinese in a while."

"You want me to do some fried rice?"

"That would be great. I have some rice cooked already, in the fridge. Everything else should be in there too. The pans are to the left of the sink."

While Keith finished the vegetables and pork, Celia got the pan hot and then began making the rice. Keith's kitchen was surprisingly well-stocked, and she added to the rice until it rivaled any takeout place. Within 20 minutes they were seated at his small table.

"This is good," Keith said, taking another bite of the rice.

"Thanks, you're a pretty good cook too. I don't even mind cleaning up."

They chatted about nothing, and Celia could tell Keith was trying to keep her distracted. She helped herself to another beer, and when they were done, she shooed him out of the kitchen so that she could wash the dishes. He walked into his den, and Celia heard a ballgame on the television. Probably basketball, she thought. Keith loved the NBA.

After she finished cleaning, they both watched the ballgame for a while, until Celia couldn't sit still anymore. "I think I'm going to go to bed and try to get some sleep. Thanks for dinner and the extra room."

"Sure," Keith didn't look away from the television. "Let me know if you need anything."

Once Celia was settled in the bedroom, she opened her laptop and began looking through her email. Most of them were about articles or stories in various stages of completion. She had one email from Marlene asking her to come over for dinner. Keith had sent her a few emails about the fiasco at her home. Lucille had returned and was distraught over the death of her cat. Celia shook her head picturing the old woman in tears. Hopefully, she had seen something. Whether Keith liked it or not, Celia was going to try to go back and talk to the neighbor herself tomorrow.

Chapter 25

Celia was surprised to see Room 4 empty when Keith opened the door. Tasha was almost always waiting for her to begin their interviews. She looked at Keith, but he just shrugged and closed the door. Celia set up the recorded and read over some of her notes as the minutes ticked by. When it was ten past the hour, Celia began to wonder if Tasha would arrive at all.

"I'm sorry to be late," Tasha said as a guard walked her into the room. "I had some business to take care of before we met today."

"I hope everything is okay," Celia said.

"Oh yes, as fine as one can be on death row," Tasha answered dryly. "I should ask about you."

How did Tasha always seem to know? "I'm doing fine, regardless of what you may have heard."

Tasha shook her head. "No, you are not, but I know that expression. I've had it myself more than once."

"The police are taking care of it. I appreciate your concern though."

"Let's hope they can do their jobs."

"Yes, let's." Celia nodded. "I'm not turning the recorder on yet. I wanted to talk about what you said at the end of our last visit."

"About trusting you? I do."

"Thank you. But I meant the part about William. How did you find out he was your brother?"

"He told me."

Celia sat back. "The recorder can stay off for this. As far as I'm concerned it's not part of the article. When did he tell you?"

"He'd known for a long time. I started to have doubts about my father. As you know, William didn't like him. At all. And that made me curious too. It wasn't all that strange for my father to dislike someone. But William seemed to like just about everyone. I wondered why they had such animosity between them."

Celia understood that. She'd never heard William express dislike for anyone, even John, except for his criticism of the former editor's professionalism.

"So how did he find out?" Celia asked.

"William was adopted. When he was 18 years old, he started searching for his birth parents. It was hard. There was no internet, of course. But he knew his adoptive parents had been overseas when he was adopted. He finally found the catholic organization in Belfast where he was adopted."

"He was adopted in Belfast? But I thought Natasha's mother was in England."

"She was, but her family had family and connections. So they sent her to Ireland to have the baby. William's parents adopted him there, and when he was three years old, they moved to the United States. The same year I was born."

"So…was your father William's father?"

"We don't know. I don't think so." Natasha sighed. "There was no father named on the birth certificate."

Celia shook her head. No wonder William felt so protective of Natasha.

"But what about your mother? Does that mean he knew she was in an asylum? Why didn't he tell you?

"I was only a teenager when I met William. He worried about what my father would do if he told me. Not just to him, but to me or our mother. When I asked him to help me find her because of his connections, he told me the truth."

"I'm sure that was shocking.".

"It was. He was so afraid I would be angry. But I wasn't. It explained why he and my father hated each other. And it confirmed my suspicions that my father was a liar."

Celia could tell by Natasha's slouched posture and tight fists that the memories bothered her. It was time for a change of subject.

"I wanted to talk some about the trial today if you don't mind," Celia picked up the recorder. "I know it isn't the thrust of the story. But you were silent through most of it. You gave no comments. I'd like to know a little about what you were thinking and feeling during the process."

"Thank you," Tasha smiled. "I can understand that. After all, I wouldn't be here without the trial."

"Yes," Celia said. "So let's go back to the arrest. Were you initially just arrested for the murder of your father? That was what I understood."

"That is what I was Mirandized for, but it became clear that they were also looking into others. They had already searched the house and apartment. My father was the first domino, but the others were about to fall."

"And did that frighten you?"

"I wouldn't say frighten," Tasha sat back in her chair. "But once I realized they had found a few strands of connection, mostly compiled by my father, I guess I was…resigned? They wanted to upset me. They wanted a confession spilled out of fear and emotion. That was something I would not give them."

"So they presented what they had, you made them work for it."

"I asked for an attorney once it became clear where they were going. Once my attorney was in play, I stayed as tight-lipped as possible. In the beginning, my primary concern was privacy. That privacy was very expensive."

Celia had wondered about that when the story was breaking. Tasha confirmed her suspicions. Money bought the silence. She wanted to ask how much, but she doubted Tasha would tell her. "So you circled the wagons, so to speak, and let the detectives figure it out without any help from you."

"That would be a good way to describe it. While they were scrambling and diving for evidence, I was talking with my attorney. He came highly recommended, and he was trustworthy. I told him what I believed would help him. He kept probing until I told him what he needed to know. He was very patient. I do not trust easily. He wanted to use trauma as a defense."

"Trauma?"

"Yes, the trauma of being assaulted, the trauma of my childhood, not having a mother, the trauma of being used by my father. I didn't think it would work. However, I was willing to talk to the experts he suggested."

Celia took a few notes and considered how to carefully word her next question. "Have you ever thought that your privacy and aloofness may have hurt you in the courtroom? That maybe you weren't as sympathetic as a defendant because you had always been so guarded?"

Tasha sat silently, and Celia wondered if she was offended. She didn't seem angry, but it was hard to know what the actress was feeling. Celia knew from experience that an absence of emotion sometimes put people off and made a person seem cold. She'd gotten that reaction from others before when she didn't react in the way they expected to a tragedy or injustice. Being pragmatic had its price.

"I wonder sometimes if being more human, for lack of a better word, might have made a difference. People certainly do seem to rely on emotion, even when they are directed to only consider facts. Would the jury have acted differently if they had known me better? Who knows? It may have had the opposite effect. Neither you nor I are very warm and fuzzy, are we?"

"True," Celia replied. She didn't like it when Natasha compared them, but she'd grown used to it over the weeks. "I suppose we could spend time speculating, but it doesn't seem to make a difference now."

"Exactly. The attorneys did their jobs, and the jury decided I was guilty. I let my closeness to my father make me stupid. In the end, I can only blame myself for their verdict."

"And, of course, you did it."

Natasha laughed. "Well, yes, there is that." She shifted and leaned forward. "Now I want to ask you, what are you going to do about Bart?"

"I'd rather not talk about that."

"I've been trying to figure out why you are so hesitant to take action. It's clear that restraining orders and alarm systems aren't going to stop him. If you can divorce yourself from what is acceptable, surely you can see what is logical."

"I know you think we are alike, and maybe we are in some ways," Celia said. "But we are also different. I won't deny I've wanted him dead. I admit that in the past I've been ruthless from time to time. But everyone has their line in the sand."

"And murder is yours," Tasha said.

"Yes, I guess it is."

"Even if it costs your own life?"

"I hope it doesn't come to that."

Tasha sighed and leaned back. "I'm going to miss our interviews."

"We still have a couple left. Need a cigarette? You usually ask."

Tasha nodded, and Celia handed her one after she lit it. "I don't have friends. Well, there's William, I suppose. But I consider you a friend. Someone I wish I had met before all this."

"I appreciate that. I know it's a gift you don't give many."

"No, it isn't," Tasha agreed. "But it's a pretty useless gift at this point. It won't keep me alive, and it won't solve your problem."

"True, but still, friendship is valuable. My circle is small too. That is part of what makes them valuable."

"I won't ask if I am part of that circle. But I like to think I am, even if it is in a strange way." Tasha smiled. "I suppose friendship with a serial killer isn't all that attractive."

"There's more to you than that label." Celia held up a hand when Tasha shook her head. "No, it's true. I admit when I started this process, I thought of it as an opportunity to get the story no one had. But I think the media did you a disservice, reducing you to a killer ice queen. You matter to people. You mattered to your mother, you matter to William, I'm sure you mattered to the couple you saw at the diner every week. And even though he was a controlling ass at times, I have no doubt you mattered to your father."

For the second time, Natasha reached across the table to grasp Celia's hand. "Thank you." Celia thought she saw tears, but Natasha blinked, and they were gone. "I do have one request."

"What is it?"

"Make me another cake before we finish our interviews?"

Celia laughed. "Of course."

The two women typically talked until Keith knocked, but today it seemed as if there was nothing more to talk about, at least for now. Tasha seemed quiet. Celia gathered her things, stood, and knocked on the door. Keith opened it, a little surprised.

"I think we're done for today," Celia said.

"Sure thing," Keith nodded.

"I'll see you next week, Natasha."

"I look forward to it, Celia."

"Everything okay?" Keith asked as they walked down the hall.

"I think so. Something is on Natasha's mind."

"There's less than a month until her execution, and her attorney isn't having any luck with last-minute measures, I don't think."

"It's strange. She's so controlled and so determined to win. But she seems resigned to the execution. I would have thought she'd fight it until the end."

"Never let them see fear," Keith said.

"What?"

"I think Tasha would rather not let them rattle her. That's her way of winning."

"She did say something like that a few weeks ago. I guess it makes sense. But I don't think I could just give up."

Keith shrugged. "She's been here at least a decade. Most of that time she's had almost no contact with anyone but guards, her attorney, and you. Maybe she's tired of it."

Keith walked her to her car, and then he watched her drive away. Celia felt unsettled. Was it Tasha's demeanor, the business with Bart, or something else? Maybe she was going to miss Natasha. The actress was right; being friends with a serial killer was odd. However, it was the most up-close Celia had been with someone who seemed as dispassionate as herself. As uncomfortable as comparing the two of them made her, it was also educational. Besides, being unemotional didn't make someone a murderer. Natasha dealt with her threats by killing them off. Celia had never done that.

After work, Celia decided to go by her house to check on things. There was still tape on her front door. She pulled into the drive, and as she stepped out of her car, Lucille came around from the back of her house.

"Oh, Celia, dear, I'm so glad you're okay." Lucille took Celia's hand. "It's terrible, just terrible."

"I'm so sorry about your cat," Celia replied.

Lucille wiped away a few tears. "Poor Jerry. He was old, but he was still kicking. Who would do such a thing?"

"I don't know," Celia lied. "I'm glad you weren't here when it happened."

"I wish I had been. I noticed you hadn't been back. Are you staying with your friend?"

"You mean Keith, the man who put in my alarm system?"

"No, that other fellow, the handsome one I met when you came home a while back. Brent? Brett?"

"Bart," Celia replied. "No, we stopped seeing each other."

"I'm sorry to hear that. I noticed he'd been by a time or two."

Celia felt a chill. "When was that?"

Lucille put a finger to her chin and thought. "Well, I saw him in a car once or twice. He didn't stop. And then last week he came by while I was out with Jerry. I waved, but I guess he didn't see me."

"Did you tell the police about that?"

"Well no," Lucille said, looking puzzled. "Should I have? Surely he didn't do this!"

"Lucille, we need to call them. Bart wasn't very happy when we broke up. I think they need to know."

"Oh my goodness!" Lucille cried. "Oh my goodness! I didn't even think of it when I saw him. I didn't know."

"That's okay, you didn't know. How could you? Can we go inside your house and call them?"

"Yes, of course," Lucille nodded. "Come in and I'll make tea as well."

The police came by about 10 minutes after Lucille called. Lucille held Celia's hand while she recounted seeing Bart in his car and outside the house over the past couple of weeks. They showed her pictures, and she confirmed that he was the man she saw. They thanked her, and then one of the officers walked Celia to her car.

"It's good you talked to her," he said. "This points to him. And since it violates the restraining order, we can pick him up. He isn't supposed to be on your property at all."

"Thank God," Celia said. "Maybe getting arrested will send him the message."

"Hopefully," the officer said. "Sometimes it does, sometimes it doesn't. After tomorrow you should be able to go back home."

Celia thanked him and drove toward Keith's house. Thank goodness she'd decided to befriend her neighbor. Lucille's account gave the police what they needed. It was one thing for the police to talk with him but being arrested would surely deter Bart from going further. He was an attorney; he didn't need legal trouble. For the first time since the stalking had begun, Celia felt certain it might actually be over.

Chapter 26

Celia had baked Tasha her promised cake, and she was cleaning the kitchen counter when her phone rang.

"Collect call from Baylor Women's Correctional Facility for Celia Bronlov from an inmate. Do you accept the charges?"

"Yes," Celia answered, dropping the dishtowel she'd been using and sitting at the table.

"Is this Celia?"

"Natasha? I didn't think you could make calls."

"I can't. Thanks to our friend who bent the rules, I have just a few minutes. There is information you need."

"What kind of information?"

"Your Bart is a financial attorney, yes?"

"Yes," Celia sat a bit straighter.

"I have limited contact with others, but I need you to know that he attempted to visit a prisoner today. Another woman on death row."

"What? Who? When was this?"

"It was yesterday. It was caught because she told the officer he was not her attorney. I don't know how he thought he could fool someone. I don't know how he knew who to try to visit. But I do know that he was trying to visit her."

Celia sighed and took the phone off speaker. "Oh my god."

"I don't have long. But you needed to know. I was not sure Keith would tell you."

"He probably would have."

"Yes, but he would not tell you this. If you want help, I will help you. Men like this Bart must be dealt with."

"I appreciate that. I need to call Keith. I probably need to make sure the police know as well."

"I can't talk more. But I knew you would want to know." Tasha hung up the phone.

Celia sat quietly for a moment, trying to decide what to process first. A death row inmate had just called her on the phone. Bart tried to access the prison. A murderer just offered to help her. She had to chuckle. This is why I don't do drama and emotional stories. Whatever Celia decided to do, it wouldn't be done tonight, she thought. So she walked back into the kitchen and finished the frosting. She'd let the cake cool overnight and frost it in the morning before she went to work.

At 1:00 pm, Celia was walking down the prison hallway to Room 4 for the last time, carrying a homemade cake. The clerk had allowed her to bring paper plates this time, along with two plastic spoons, providing she returned the spoons. Keith made it clear he expected a large piece of the cake after her interview, and Celia promised he could have whatever was left over after the clerk had a slice. This time when he opened the door, Natasha was waiting, and she clapped when she saw the cake.

"I was hoping you remembered. I didn't want to miss my last dessert."

"Well that's certainly morbid," Celia replied. She set up her recorder and then cut a piece of cake for the actress.

"This time you must have a piece too. I will not eat alone today."

"Okay, you twisted my arm," Celia laughed. "I confess red velvet is my favorite."

"And appropriately macabre, don't you think?"

Celia shook her head as she took a bite of the cake. She knew Tasha was stoic, but Celia wasn't sure she was truly as flippant as she tried to appear. This was their last interview. She had less than two weeks to live, barring a last-minute reprieve, which was not likely to come. However, she'd let the actress play her part. They both enjoyed the cake in silence.

"So what is today's topic?" Natasha asked as she finished her last bite.

"Honestly, I didn't make a plan. Though I would like to know what you are thinking. I'd like to know if, knowing what you know now, you would have done anything differently."

"Ah, yes, deathbed regrets."

"Not quite that trite. Just some last assessments of your situation, I guess. What do you want readers to know?"

Tasha slowly licked the last of the icing off the spoon and slid the empty plate to Celia. "The readers will conclude what they will conclude. However, your question about what I would do differently is interesting. It's something I have considered many times over the last decade.

"I don't regret killing any of them, not really. But I do wish I had given more thought to my father. I could have avoided that mistake had I not allowed anger to drive me. I could have made him pay in other ways. Taking action without thinking things through is foolish. That is the main reason I am here."

"So you believe they deserved to die?"

"That is a moral judgment, which I didn't expect of you," Tasha said. "What do any of us deserve or not deserve? Did I deserve to be at risk? Did I deserve to have my privacy invaded, to be assaulted? Actions have consequences. Tom's actions in high school ended with the consequences in the parking garage. When Julian betrayed me and his ethics, he had to know there would be consequences. And even me. When I killed my father out of anger, I chose these consequences. I knew it when I was arrested, and I chose to control the way I responded."

"Surely it isn't that simple," Celia countered.

"Why not? Isn't that how you approach your stories? A CEO is deceptive and unethical. It is logical that he should suffer the consequences."

"I'm not talking about cause and effect. I'm talking about the pragmatic way you appear to be reacting. If these men truly deserved to die, then doesn't being put to death over it make you angry? Doesn't it seem unjust? I guess I expect more…fight? Rebellion? Something."

Natasha smiled. "For most of my life, others wanted something from me. I wanted something from them. This is how we live. I wanted the things I wanted, so I did what I needed to do. I gave others, including my own father, what they wanted when it benefitted me. And when I didn't want to give, I withheld. The public wanted to know things about me that were none of their business, so I was silent. The police wanted to know why, they wanted me to incriminate myself, so I was silent. When there was no recourse left, they wanted to watch me crumble and protest and panic. So I was silent. I may die, and my story will be told. But it will be told on my terms, on my timeline, and it will be told by the person I chose."

Celia took notes as Tasha watched. "So you made the choices you could make. You took your power by not giving them any."

"Exactly. My choices were my power."

Celia nodded, making more notes.

"And now I must ask you something." Tasha waited until Celia looked up to continue. "I would like for you to be here next week."

The request didn't surprise Celia. For whatever reason, Natasha considered her a friend. Celia had never attended an execution, and it wasn't something she had ever wanted to do. However, she had been thinking about it since her first interview with Tasha. Lethal injection was said to be virtually painless, though Celia doubted that. She would have no interest in watching an electrocution.

"I thought you might ask," Celia said. "And yes, if it is important to you, I will be there."

"Thank you. I am not typically sentimental. But I have trusted you with many things. I would like to have you there."

"I understand."

"Now for my other question. I need to know you will take some sort of action to stay safe, even if it is extreme."

"I am taking every precaution," Celia began.

"I think we both know that isn't enough. I have told you I would help you if you would like my help."

"How can you help me? There is nothing you can do from in here."

"I have some friends. Not many, but a few. They would help you if I asked them. I know you don't think you can take drastic action. I assure you that you can. You are at least as strong as I am."

Celia knew what Natasha meant. And it wasn't as if Celia wasn't considering it. It was simple for Natasha. She had grown up in a cutthroat world with a father who used violence. Celia understood competition, and she'd bent the rules to get where she was. But she wasn't like Natasha. It wasn't about morality or compassion or emotion. Celia wasn't a killer.

"I understand what you're trying to do. What you think I should do. And I confess, it would be a solution. It's one I've thought about before. But I can't. That is one line I can't cross. Even to save myself."

Natasha sighed. "I think I knew that. We are the same, but we are different. You aren't ready. Your own preservation isn't enough." She smiled again. "In that case, I would like more cake."

Celia laughed and cut another slice. They sat in comfortable silence until Keith knocked at the door. Celia gathered her things and stood. She wasn't sure what to say. What does someone say to a convicted killer who has become a strange type of friend? Especially with a corrections officer listening. "I'll see you next week, Natasha."

"Thank you," Natasha said. "Thank you for the company and conversation. I am glad to know you will handle my story with care. I want to find some way to repay you for that."

"You can repay me by asking your attorney to find some way to intervene before next Friday."

Natasha chuckled. "Oh, he's already trying."

"Good," Celia said.

"You know, unless the governor steps in, nothing her lawyer does will help," Keith said as they walked side by side.

"I know, but it's just too strange. She's so calm about the whole thing."

Keith shrugged. "It's her way of coping."

"I guess so."

The clerk was ready with a plate when they got to the reception area. Celia laughed as she cut a piece and Keith protested it was too big. The receptionist scolded him, called him greedy, and then began eating. There was still 2/3 of a cake on the platter, and Celia called him greedy as well.

William had called during the interview, so once Celia started driving back toward the office, she returned his call.

"How does she seem?" William asked.

"She's calm, poised, and pragmatic as always."

"I don't usually ask about the interviews, I know. But before she was an interview subject, she was my friend. She doesn't want me to visit. She definitely doesn't want me there next week."

"I told her I would be there. She asked." Celia hesitated. "I'm not sure I'll feel comfortable writing about that."

"I understand. If it was Charles Manson, maybe. But, profession aside, I don't know that I want my friend's death detailed for the voyeurs."

"I understand, William. You care about her." Celia wondered if Natasha had told him that Celia knew their secret. She wasn't going to ask. "Some things should be kept private."

"Thank you," William said hoarsely.

An alert indicated that Celia had another call. She recognized the number of the police department. "I'm getting another call I need to take. I'll talk to you later this afternoon." She swiped to answer the call. "This is Celia Brockwell."

"Yes, Ms. Brockwell. It's Officer Stanfield. I wanted to let you know that Bart Vandiver is out."

"Yeah, I figured. I'll be careful. Is anyone on him?"

"We're going to be watching. Are you back in your house?"

"I'll be going back tonight."

"I don't suppose I could talk you out of that."

"No, you, can't. I'm not letting him disrupt my life."

"Well, just be vigilant. Make sure that system is on. Do you have any time to come by the station? There are a few things we've uncovered, and I'd like to talk to you again."

"Um, I don't have anything for a couple of hours. Is now okay? It'll be about 20 minutes."

"That'll work."

Celia ended the call. What had they found? Bart was out, so she'd have to watch her back. She knew they wouldn't hold him long. He'd make bail, which wasn't very high, and he would either back off or not back off. Celia hoped it was the latter. She thought about Tasha and her advice. Even though Celia had accepted that she and Tasha shared a common...dispassionate rationality, murder was an entirely different thing from breaking a few rules or stepping on a few toes to get ahead. Bart wasn't worth the risk.

"Thanks for coming in," Walt Stanfield shook her hand, and they both sat. "How are you doing?"

"I'm fine. Hoping an arrest has knocked some sanity into him."

"Me too. What do you know about his first wife?"

The question surprised Celia. "Not much. I know they were married for five years. She had a car accident. He apparently is still close to her family."

"Actually, he's not. They don't think too much of him, but he tends to show up at public events. Likes to keep an eye on them."

"That's weird."

"Indeed. And I got an accident report. It's a little strange."

"What do you mean?"

"She was driving a curvy road at night. But there weren't really a lot of skid marks. No real evidence, but you can't rule out car tampering just reading the report."

"No one investigated?"

"At the time, it seemed clear, I guess. Bart seemed devastated. That road was known for accidents. Nobody really pushed. Honestly, I probably wouldn't have either. But looking at it in light of his stalking…"

"It makes you wonder. Yeah, I get it. How was their marriage?"

"No idea. But I'm going to try to find out. If my gut is right, you need to be very careful."

"Yeah, I know. Thanks for filling me in."

He nodded. "I know Keith has been helping you out. I really wish you'd stay with him a little while longer."

"I can't do that. I'm not going to hide in someone else's house."

"Okay then. Just be aware of your surroundings at all times. Call if you even think something is off."

"I will."

Celia drove back to her office, her mind spinning a bit. What the hell had she gotten into when she agreed to go out with Bart? Were there red flags she had missed? She really couldn't think of any. He seemed normal, charming if a little overly affectionate. His connection with his former wife's family had seemed endearing. Now it just seemed creepy. Hoping he murdered her was a bit morbid, but Celia was hoping that was the case and that Stanfield found evidence to support it. The reality was that Bart would never stay behind bars for stalking. But he would for murder.

It occurred to her that her father might know more details about the accident, so Celia called him, not knowing whether he was still in the city or not.

"Hello. Can I help you?"

"It's Celia."

"Oh! I didn't recognize this number. It's good to hear from you."

"I changed it. Sorry I didn't let you know."

"Did you change it -"

"Because of Bart, yes. Look, we may have a way of getting him. Apparently, Judith's family isn't alone in wondering about her accident."

"Really?"

"Yes, but I need to talk to you again. Are you still in town?"

"I'll be here three more days. How about dinner?"

"Sounds good."

"I have to meet a couple of clients tonight, but we could meet tomorrow night if that works for you."

"Perfect. There's a place my friend owns. I'll text you the address. 7:00?"

"I'll see you then."

Celia ended the call and smiled. Between the police, Stewart, and her special folder, there was finally a light at the end of the crazy tunnel. She headed to Keith's house feeling very hopeful.

Chapter 27

Celia had hoped to get away from Keith's house before dark, but he had grilled salmon, so she couldn't resist staying for dinner. By the time they had eaten and cleaned things up, it was after 8:00. She thanked him again for his hospitality and headed to her house, glad that she'd be sleeping in her own bed again.

When she was about halfway home, Celia noticed a car following her a little too closely. Ugh, she hated tailgaters. After a mile or two, she got tired of being blinded by the driver's halogen lights, and she lightly tapped her brakes, hoping they would back off a bit. It worked, and she was glad to be rid of the blinding light. However, then Celia noticed the car, a nondescript sedan, made every turn she made.

Was it Bart? It couldn't be, could it? He drove a Mercedes, and he enjoyed the status of nice things. He wouldn't own a car like the one behind her. But she knew she wasn't imagining being followed. She'd made too many turns for it to be a coincidence. Celia decided that if someone was going to follow her, they'd be following her to the police station. She adjusted her route accordingly.

When she was a few blocks away from the station, the sedan moved to the right lane; apparently, he had realized where Celia was going. The light turned yellow and then red, and they both stopped.

Celia wanted to stare straight ahead, but she couldn't resist a glance to her right.

It was Bart. He was staring straight ahead, but he seemed to sense it when Celia looked at him, and he turned his head. He smiled and waved. Celia quickly dug through her purse to grab her camera so that she could take a photo. But as she held it up to take Bart's picture, he turned right onto another street.

"Psycho," Celia said, gunning her engine when the light turned green. She drove to the station, walked inside, and asked for Walt. Within a couple of minutes, he was out front to greet her.

"Ms. Brockwell, is everything okay?"

"Bart tried to follow me home. Once I realized I was being followed, I just drove here."

"Why don't you come on back, and I'll take your statement."

They walked back to Walt's desk, and Celia sat in a folding chair.

"So tell me exactly what happened. Start at the beginning."

"Well," Celia began. "I left Keith's place a little after 8:00. I was planning to go back home to stay."

"When did you notice someone behind you?"

"I guess a couple of miles from Keith's. A car started tailgating me, and he had those awful headlights."

"Halogen, yeah. People complain about those all the time."

"At first, I just thought it was some jerk driver. I tapped my brakes a little, and he put some space between us."

"You know," Walt smiled. "You're really not supposed to do that. It's a good way to get read-ended."

"Yeah, I know. I was annoyed."

"What did the car look like?"

"It was a sedan. That champagne color. I think it was a Camry? Or it might have been an Altima."

He took some notes. "So when did you realize it was Bart?"

"Well, he figured out where I was headed, and he moved into the right lane. We both got stopped at the same red light. I looked over, and he looked at me and smiled. The bastard waved at me."

"Did he try to say anything?"

"No. I tried to get my phone out to take a picture, but he turned right before I could get one."

Officer Stanfield kept writing. "We've got some traffic cameras at intersections. We should be able to find the two of you. I'll have a tech take a look." He looked up and frowned.

"But?" Celia said.

"We might be able to get him behind you and beside you. But, I mean, it's the city, and you both live here. He could claim you just ended up at the same red light."

"I *know* he followed me, probably all the way from Keith's." Celia protested. But she knew Walt was right. Unless other people saw the car, there would be no way to prove anything. He could claim it was a coincidence.

"I'll definitely get as much traffic footage as I can. Maybe we can at least track him following you in the city."

"I appreciate it," Celia replied.

"Is this a car he normally drives?"

"I've only seen his Mercedes. I don't even know if it was his car."

"If it was a rental, there will be a record. That would help. I mean why would a guy with a car rent something else to drive around town?"

Celia had thought of that as well, and while she hoped it was the case, she had a feeling Bart was smarter than that. She doubted there would be a rental record.

"Just be careful. I'll promise we'll do everything we can to track this. And I'll keep you informed. Do you have somewhere to stay?"

"You know, I'm just gonna go home. The alarm system is fixed, and I'll lock my bedroom door too."

"I'd be glad to follow you home and check things out."

"No, I don't want you to do that. I'll be fine. He probably thinks I'll go back to Keith's now or something."

"That's actually what I'd recommend. At least call him when you arrive home. Or call me. I'll have someone drive by your house a couple of times."

"Thanks. I mean it." Celia stood and shook his hand. He picked up his phone to call about the cameras, and Celia walked herself out of the station and back to her car.

When Celia got home, she went inside and immediately rearmed the system. She left the lights on outside both doors, though she knew the light would make it harder to sleep. Taking a knife from a top drawer in the kitchen, she went through every room and closet just in case. There was no doubt in her mind she'd use the knife if she needed to do so. Once she was satisfied no one else was in the house, she got ready for bed. Even though she needed to do a bit of work, she wasn't in the mood. Instead, she took a sleeping pill and watched trash television until she felt drowsy. She was almost asleep when she realized she hadn't called Keith. After sending him a short text, Celia fell asleep.

At 9:00 the next morning, Celia was checking email in her office when the phone rang. It was Keith.

"Hey," She answered the phone. "Sorry I didn't call last night. I was beat. Did you get my text?"

"I did. I got it last night." Keith replied. "I talked to Walt this morning."

Shoot, Celia thought. "Yeah, sorry I didn't tell you about that last night. I didn't want you to worry."

"He didn't call me. I called him. When I went outside this morning, someone had keyed my truck and slashed the rear tires."

"Oh my god, Keith! Do you know who it was? Was it Bart?"

"I'm not sure, but I wouldn't be surprised. If he followed you from here, he probably figured you'd come back here instead of going home."

"It's a good thing I didn't, then." Celia was a little smug.

"Yeah, right, not my point. He probably came back here to wait for you. Since you didn't come back, he thought he'd send a little message."

"Oh, Keith, I'm sorry about your truck. What a bastard."

"I'm gonna report it. They know you've been staying with me. Maybe they can connect the dots."

"I hope so," Celia replied. "And Keith, can I ask a favor? I know Natasha grills you for information. Don't mention this."

"Yeah, she's a bulldog. She has a way of fishing…"

"So that you say more than you meant to. I know. But don't tell her this."

"I'll keep it quiet."

"Thanks, Keith. I've got a meeting, but I'll call later."

After she ended the call, Celia cursed to herself and broke a pencil. It didn't solve anything, but she felt better. It was almost 9:30, and she was meeting with Julia at 10:00. Julia had been an underused talent when John was in charge, and Celia had been meaning to talk to her about a byline. She'd been one of Celia's biggest supporters, and she deserved a reward for her loyalty.

At 10:30, as Celia was wrapping up her meeting, Gladys interrupted. "I'm sorry to disturb you. But you have a call. I think it's an emergency."

"Your life is never boring, is it?" Julia chuckled.

"You have no idea," Celia rolled her eyes. "Let me know what you decide. I'd like to start this at the beginning of February."

"It's the police," Gladys said softly as she transferred the call to Celia's office.

"This is Celia."

"Celia, it's Walter. We…we had a call this morning from the Garden Inn. The one on Kennedy.

That was where Celia's father was staying. "What happened?"

"Well, the housekeeper went into your father's room this morning to change the linens, and she found him unresponsive in the restroom."

"Unresponsive?"

"Yes, it seems he slipped. They took him to General."

"I'll head there now," Celia said. She still hadn't forgiven her father. But something in her gut told her there was more to the story.

"Do you need a ride?"

"No, I'm good. Are you sure he slipped? Is he okay?"

"Just tell them who you are at the nurse's desk. They'll give you all the details."

Celia told Gladys she had to meet someone and left before her assistant could ask any questions. She made it to the hospital in record time, and when she asked about Stewart Marshall, the nurse showed her to a waiting area and promised to call the doctor.

"Ms. Brockwell?" a middle-aged woman called her name a few minutes later.

"That's me. I'm Stewart Marshall's daughter." The words sounded strange.

"Follow me, and we'll talk. Your father is in ICU."

"ICU? From a slip in the bathroom?"

"Did you know your father was diabetic?"

"Yes, he told me. He said he was using some sort of insulin pump."

"He was. I'm just not sure if he made an error, or there was some sort of malfunction."

"What do you mean?"

Well, his type of pump also monitors blood sugar. When his sugar is too low or too high, he receives a notification, even an alarm if it's severe. It looks like he gave himself a large bolus."

"Bolus?"

"A dose of insulin. Perhaps it was at dinnertime? At any rate, he had too much. His pump should have notified him that his sugar was dangerously low, but apparently, it didn't."

"What does that mean?"

"It means your father went into a coma. His body began shutting down after his sugar bottomed out. And he wasn't found until this morning, which means there is significant damage."

"How significant?"

"I'm afraid his organs are failing."

Celia didn't respond as the doctor led her through a set of doors and down a hallway. They stopped in front of a small room.

"He's in here. You may go in for five to ten minutes, then we'll talk more. We've notified his children and ex-wife. They should be here this afternoon."

Celia entered the small room and sat in the chair next to her father's bed. His face was slack and pale, and it was obvious he was in serious condition. Monitors displayed his blood pressure, heart rate, and oxygen level. He had an IV, and he was being given oxygen. She could also see a catheter bag at the foot of his bed.

"What happened, Dad? Did you take too much insulin? Was it you who overdosed? How did you fall?"

There was no way to know, but Celia couldn't help thinking it was pretty convenient that her father was in a coma. Bart knew he was in town; did he know they were going to meet? Was he stalking her father the way he'd been stalking her? And even if he was, where was the proof?

"I don't know what to do, Dad. We're basically strangers. Your real family isn't here yet. Why did it take you so long to figure out how bad you screwed up?" Celia took his hand and tried to feel something. She couldn't. Maybe if they'd had longer. Still, she didn't want to watch her father die. After a few more minutes of silence, she squeezed his hand and left the room.

"Ms. Brockwell," a nurse called as she walked down the hall. "Would you like for me to contact you when the rest of your family arrives?"

It's not my family.

"No thank you. Just call me if his condition changes. Or I'll check."

She pressed the button to open the double doors and left the ICU.

Chapter 28

There was less than a week until Natasha's execution. Celia hadn't heard anything from her, and she had to admit she was a little surprised. Of course, she didn't really have phone call privileges, and she'd never sent a letter to Celia before. However, the two women had developed an odd sort of friendship, and the actress had seemed sad at the prospect of not speaking again. Celia was planning to attend the execution, but it wasn't as if they would chat *there*. Celia had researched the protocol for that last day or so, and she knew a bit about what Natasha's day would be like. It was strange to think of it. Maybe it didn't make sense, but Celia was a bit sad as well. There was a kindredness about Tasha that both disturbed and comforted Celia.

It comforted Celia because she wondered over the years if she really was an ice queen, as a few people had told her. The term didn't bother her; she was who she was, and her nature was part of what made her successful. However, it hadn't escaped her notice that most people, especially other women, tended to be more emotional than she was. That emotion had always seemed to be a handicap in Celia's estimation. Tasha understood that. Of course, Tasha was a serial killer. She'd been described as a sociopath, even a psychopath. Celia didn't think the actress was the latter. However, Celia had wondered more than once if she herself might be the former. Looking back over her own choices, there was certainly manipulation there, along with a lack of regard for others. But certainly, everyone looked out for number one most of the time. They had to; how else could one achieve real success?

The phone startled Celia out of her ponderings. She saw Andrew's name. "Hello, this is Celia Brockwell."

Ms. Brockwell, it's Andrew, Ms. Bronlov's attorney."

"Yes, hello. How can I help you?"

"Well, Ms. Bronlov has given me her list of requested visitors for next week. You are on the list."

"Oh, really? Well, how does that work, exactly?

"Well, you'll arrive at the prison several hours before the execution. You'll have 15-30 minutes to visit. There will definitely be a partition this time, I believe. I'll send you the details if you like."

"That would be helpful, yes."

"I am still hoping for a last-minute reprieve, of course. But it doesn't look very hopeful."

"Well, I for one hope you can pull a rabbit out of the hat."

"As do I. I oppose the death penalty on principle. I'll send you those details. Feel free to call me with any questions you may have."

Celia ended the call and sat back in her chair. Tasha wanted to see her on the day of the execution. She wondered who else was on the list. There was no family to visit, and Natasha didn't have many friends. She couldn't help but wonder if William was on that list. But then, he had said he didn't think he could bear to watch the execution. He might visit her, however, to be supportive. It would be tasteless to ask him, Celia thought. Still, she was absolutely curious.

The email notification pinged on Celia's laptop, and she opened the message. It was from Tasha's attorney. He reiterated the actress's invitation and attached what Celia assumed were the standard guidelines for visitors. Celia opened the document and began to read.

Celia would need to arrive around 1:00. She would be allowed to visit with Natasha briefly, under supervision, and with a partition. She couldn't bring any items with her or receive any items from the actress. The visiting window was narrow. Natasha would have her last meal at 4:00 pm. There was information regarding what the prisoner would wear, the preparation and visit from the Warden and a chaplain. The chaplain could be refused, and Celia suspected Natasha would do that. Natasha would be allowed a shower and a different garment, and then she would be prepped for the injection.

One of Celia's early pieces for The Journal was about the death penalty, so she knew what a lethal injection would entail. Still, reading about it this time was different. This time Celia would be observing, and the recipient would be someone she knew, someone she had come to respect in her own way. The journalist wouldn't have admitted it to anyone else, but she had come to regard Natasha as a friend.

Pushing the execution out of her mind, Celia spent the rest of the day reviewing pitches for stories, editing some of her own work, and looking through a stack of resumes. She needed to hire a couple more staff members. By the time she finished, it was after 6:00, and she was starving. Keith wanted her to call every time she left work, which Celia thought was a bit much, but she swiped his number as she walked toward the elevator.

"Celia, hold up a minute," William called out to her as she pressed the down button. He caught up with her and pressed the button again. "Heading home for the day?"

"I am," Celia replied. "It's been a long one."

"Have you had a chance to look through any resumes?"

"I have. I've narrowed the huge stack to a smaller stack. There are about a dozen who look pretty promising."

"Good. Let me know if you need anything. I want us to be ready for what's next."
"Good thinking."
"How are the interviews going?"
"I've finished the interviews, and I've been crafting the article. It's strange, and a bit sad."
"Yes, it is," William sighed. "She committed terrible crimes, but she is not a terrible person. I confess I'm feeling some grief. I've had friends die, but not this way."
"Yes, it's not the same as cancer or an accident. She will die at a prescribed time and place at the hands of the state."
"You sound troubled by that concept."
"You know, I never really had much problem with the death penalty. You take lives, you forfeit your own. But knowing the story behind the crimes, and knowing that sometimes murder seems like a real answer, it isn't as cut and dried."
"I'm not sure I agree that murder is the answer, but I do understand why Natasha felt so betrayed, especially by her father."
"You knew about that?"
"I helped her find out the truth about her mother. She was controlled, of course, but when she was arrested for her father's murder, I knew immediately what had pushed her over that edge."
Celia didn't respond, but she did wonder exactly how much William knew about the actress's life. She was impressed that he never exploited that relationship as a member of the press and CEO of a media organization. She respected his loyalty to a friend. The elevator opened then, and she and William said goodbye.
Celia had been home for less than five minutes when someone knocked on her door. She looked through the peephole and saw Lucille holding a kitten in one hand and a box in the other. *Oh great, another cat,* Celia thought, but she put on a friendly smile and opened the door.

"Hello, dear," Lucille said. "I was waiting for you to get home. You have a package, and they put it on my doorstep by mistake. I thought it might be important."
"Thank you," Celia replied, taking the package. "Who is your new friend?"
"Oh, this is Tom. My friends at bingo gave him to me." She nuzzled the kitten and sighed. "He'll never replace Jerry, of course, but he can keep me company."
"That's nice. I'm glad you have a new companion."
Lucille stood outside the doorway, waiting. Celia could tell she wanted to know what was in the package, but Celia wasn't going to open it in front of her. There was a fine line between neighborly and nosy.
"Well, I'll let you get back to your evening," Lucille said, sounding a little disappointed. "You have a nice night."
Celia closed the door and took the package into the kitchen. She hadn't ordered anything; however, she did occasionally get promotional items. Her address was there, but the return wasn't familiar, and the postmark looked odd. The box was small and light. Taking a knife, she cut the tape and opened the flaps.
Two Ziploc bags were nestled in some tissue paper. One of the bags held her toothbrush, and the other held a pair of her underwear, neatly folded. She dropped the bags quickly and closed the box. How had Bart gotten into her house? He couldn't have! There were no alerts on her phone, and Keith hadn't called her in a panic. She knew she'd armed it before she left. Celia pulled up the camera app, but Lucille's front door wasn't in view. There was no way anyone had been in her house today, she thought. Did Bart take them when he broke in before? She pulled her phone from her purse and called the police station.
"Yes, I need to speak with Walt Stanfield, please."
"May I ask who's calling?"

"It's Celia Brockwell, and it's urgent." She didn't want to panic, but Celia was shaking with rage.

"Celia, It's Walt. What happened?"

"Someone put a package for me on my neighbor's front doorstep today. She thought they delivered it to her by mistake. I opened it, and it has things from inside my house. I know no one has been here. My alarm was on, and there's no one on either camera. I think Bart must have taken things when he broke in before."

"What was in the package? Did you touch them?"

"My toothbrush and a pair of underwear. They were in Ziploc bags. I know what you're thinking, but I'd bet you won't find any prints. The underwear was folded like it had been washed. I only touched the bags and the outside of the box."

"Stay there, and I'll be over with someone. Do you think anyone is around your house now? He might be watching, wanting to see your reaction."

"I didn't notice anyone," Celia walked toward the door. "I'm going to stay on the line and check."

"No, Celia don't go outside-"

"It'll only take a minute." She walked out of her front door and looked up and down the street. There were no unusual cars. Then she walked back inside and checked the back porch and yard. There was nothing out of place. "No one is here."

"Stay inside and lock your door until I get there."

"I will." Celia hung up and looked inside the box again. She couldn't remember if the underwear had been in her drawer or the hamper. The idea of Bart taking clothing out of her hamper was disgusting. And why hadn't she noticed the toothbrush? Was it because she had more than one sitting in the holder? She couldn't remember. Sometimes she would keep the old one to clean her jewelry. Regardless, Bart had not just left Jerry on her bed and roses on her floor. He'd gone through her things.

Walt and another policeman arrived quickly, and Keith wasn't far behind them. Walt must have called him. The police began examining the box, and Keith took her into the living room to sit.
"So do you think he took your things when he was here before? You haven't forgotten to arm the alarm, have you?"
"No way, I arm it every morning and every night," Celia replied. "It must have been when he broke in before. Ugh, he went through my drawers…or my hamper. And why my toothbrush?"
"They're both personal. He probably thought you'd notice the toothbrush."
"I can't believe I didn't. Why keep them and send them to me? And how did he send them? Why did they end up on Lucille's step instead of mine?"
"My guess is he knew he'd only get one shot in your house, but he wanted to prolong it. So he took a few souvenirs that he could scare you with later. You should probably go through the house and see if anything else is missing."
"Hey, guys, you two should see this," Walt called from the kitchen. They walked into the kitchen, and Walt's partner was taking photos of the box.
"See this?" Walt pointed to the postmark. "It's not a real postmark. This box never went through the mail."
"What? You mean he brought it here himself?" Celia asked
"Probably so."
"Wouldn't that be risky?"
"Well, he probably knows how far the view of your camera goes. My guess is he knew no one would see him going to your neighbor's door. That would explain why he put it there instead of at your door. Delivery men make mistakes all the time, so no one would think anything of it."
"I assume you'll run prints and DNA on everything," Keith said.
"Yeah, but I'm not hopeful. He probably wore gloves and made sure there weren't any. My guess is that the only prints we'll find are

Celia's and the neighbor's. We'll take it with us and check everything, though. And Celia, you need to go through this house with a fine-toothed comb. We need to be prepared for any more special deliveries."

After the police left, Celia let out a string of curses. "That was very eloquent," Keith laughed.

"Why thank you. I have more if you'd like to hear them."

"Nah, I'm good. If I wanted more I'd have joined the navy."

"The navy," Celia chuckled. "Yeah, I'd like to see Bart buried at sea."

"After walking the plank?"

"That's not the navy, that's pirates," Celia teased. "But they'd work too."

Keith folded his arms and looked at her. "So are you going to pack a bag?"

"Why would I pack a bag? I'm not going anywhere." Celie pretended not to know what he meant.

"God, you're stubborn!"

"I'm not running away every time he pushes a button. He doesn't get that power."

"It's not about power. It's about safety," Keith countered.

"I *am* safe. He put the box at Lucille's door because of my alarm system. He knew there were cameras. He can't get in here without tripping the alarm and being caught on camera. This is probably one of the safest places I could be right now."

"I thought you might say that. I'll be right back." Keith walked out of the house and walked back in after a minute or two. He was carrying an overnight bag. "So I'll stay here."

"I don't need a babysitter," Celia argued.

"I'm not a babysitter. I'm the muscle." Keith flexed. "Think of me as the bodyguard."

"Oh god," Celia laughed. "Well, if you think I'm gonna sing to you like Whitney Houston, you're wrong."

"You're too young to know that movie."
"I have cable, and I don't sleep much," Celia laughed. "It's not gonna be comfortable. My office couch is a pullout, and it's lumpy."
"I'll survive." Keith tossed his bag through the door of her office and then rubbed his hands together. "So what's for dinner?"
"I'm not about to cook. So I guess we get to choose from the stack of delivery menus in my top drawer over there."
Keith opened the drawer and looked through the stack. "Pizza, pizza, Mexican, Italian, Chinese, oh look, more pizza. Hey, this sounds interesting. Barbecue?"
"Oh, that one I've never tried. It was in my mailbox one day." She walked into the kitchen and looked over his shoulder.
"My dad had this big smoker when I was growing up. A couple of times a year he'd stay up all night sitting next to it, making the whole neighborhood hungry. I wonder if this place is any good."
"Go ahead and call if you want. Do they have chicken? I'm not a big pork fan."
"Yeah, they do. This actually looks good." Keith punched the number into his phone and waved away Celia when she tried to hand him her credit card. He ordered pork for himself, chicken for her, and several sides. He topped it off with dessert.
"You a little hungry?" Celia teased.
"Hey, I gotta keep my strength up. I have to protect a damsel."
"Oh good grief," Celia rolled her eyes. "Should I faint now?"
"It would help set the whole mood, yeah."
Celia punched him and grabbed each of them a beer from the fridge. They sat on the sofa to wait for their dinner, and Celia grabbed the remote. Keith took it from her. "How are you really?" He asked.
"I'm angry. I'm frustrated that this whole thing is still going on. It's absolutely ridiculous."
"Are you afraid?"

"I guess I am in a way. I just don't know what he'll do next, ya know? I have no say, and that drives me crazy."
"Yeah, I've noticed you like to be in control of a situation."
"Doesn't everyone? I mean, I hate the idea of life happening *to* me. That's not the way it's supposed to work."
"And yet sometimes it does," Keith adjusted so he was facing her. "I get it. We all like to know what's coming next. But a lot of times we just don't. Sometimes you just have to wait and see."
"It just feels like I'm waiting for Bart's next stunt. And what if he gets tired of leaving things on the doorstep or slashing tires? You can't be around every minute, and it's not your job to take care of me."
"Maybe it's not my job, but it's what a friend does, isn't it? You'd do the same for me."
Celia laughed. "I don't think you'd need my help against a stalker."
"Maybe not, but there have been times in my life it sure would have been nice to have a scheming mind like yours."
"Scheming mind? Is that supposed to be a compliment?"
Keith laughed. "You know what I mean. You read people. You plan and figure things out. Look at how you immediately jumped into your new role at work. You've got a quick mind."
"I wasn't very good at reading Bart," Celia muttered.
"Yeah, that's because your libido got in the way."
"Don't remind me," Celia groaned. "I may never have sex again."
"Now, that *would* be a tragedy," Keith laughed.
"Shut up, perv," Celia chuckled. "Give me the remote. I need some trash TV."
After their supper arrived, they decided to move to the kitchen to eat. Celia was amazed at how much food Keith could put away. Obviously, he worked out enough to compensate for the calories. He offered her some dessert, but she declined. Once the dishes were done and the leftovers wrapped up, Celia decided to do some writing while Keith watched a game. He complained that he should

have brought his 72-inch television with him. What was it about guys and televisions, Celia thought. Then again, she had enjoyed watching a couple of movies on his giant screen. She shook her head as Keith shouted at a referee and then turned her attention to Natasha's article.

It was a little surreal to be writing an article about someone who was going to be executed in a matter of days. It was even more surreal that Celia was actually feeling down about the whole thing. After all, the actress had killed five people. And Celia had never felt strongly about the death penalty either way. It didn't affect her. Besides, if someone was dumb enough to get caught, there were consequences, right? Now, though, Celia felt a little strange about how flip she'd always been.

And then there was Natasha as a person. Celia knew that Natasha considered her a friend, and Celia could admit to herself that she felt the same way. Sure, Celia had other friends, like Marlene or Julia. But honestly, those friendships had always felt lopsided. Marlene almost saw Celia as a sister, which was sweet, but Celia had never felt the same closeness. Not just with Marlene, either. She never shared much of herself with others. Luckily most people didn't notice. Celia noticed that most people spent more time talking about themselves than probing others. That was fine with her.

But Natasha was different. Nothing about Celia shocked Tasha, and the actress seemed to know more about Celia than she said. Even though they had grown up in different families, their childhoods had been remarkably similar. And their young adult years were the same as well. They were driven, single-minded, focused on doing what needed to be done to take control of their lives. Celia never would have told Marlene about the way she got inside Paul's head, for example. And she certainly wouldn't tell anyone about the accident her colleague had.

Natasha wouldn't judge. Natasha had done the same types of things for her career. The press had referred to Natasha as a sociopath, even a psychopath. As if that was the worst thing a person could be. The two women were pragmatic, Celia thought. In life, it paid to be pragmatic. She thought about people like John, Lucille, and even Bart. John was so paranoid and worried about everything. He was constantly on edge. Lucille missed her daughter terribly and felt rejected by her. Celia had heard her cry about it. She pined for a child who didn't even bother to visit.

And then there was Bart. He had to know there was no long-term potential between them. His emotions had wrecked things, and then his emotions made her life hell. He still visited his dead wife's family, for God's sake! And based on what the police had told Celia, his emotions might have gotten the better of him in that situation as well. Pragmatism was absolutely preferable.

Refocusing on the article, Celia wondered what Natasha was feeling. Was she as calm and stoic as she liked to appear? Or was she secretly hoping her attorney could stop things? It was unlikely the governor was going to step in, given the publicity the case had received and the fact that five people were killed in cold blood. Natasha had certainly never expressed any remorse. Maybe Celia could ask Keith to probe a bit. The actress seemed to like and trust him.

After a couple of hours, Celia closed her laptop and joined Keith on the couch. They finished the game. Watched a bit of news, and then watched the late-night host's monologue before Celia finally stretched and said she was tired. Keith thoughtfully turned off the television and said he'd retire as well. After he grabbed the rest of the dessert. That man could eat!

When Celia checked her phone before turning off the lamp, there were three missed calls and two voicemails. She punched in her password to listen to the first message.

"Ms. Brockwell, this is Amelia Thompson calling from Jefferson General Hospital. Please return my call at this number, extension 4208."
"Ms. Brockwell, this is Ms. Thompson from Jefferson general Hospital again. It is imperative that you call as soon as possible. Extension 4208."
Oh no…
Celia dialed the number and waited, holding her breath.
"Jefferson General Hospital, 4th-floor nurse's station, Candace speaking."
"Yes, this is Celia Brockwell. I had a message to call Amelia Thompson."
"Oh yes, Ms. Brockwell. We've been trying to reach you. I'm afraid Ms. Thompson is with a patient."
"I assume the message was regarding my father?"
"Yes, well…I'm sorry to inform you, Ms. Brockwell, but Stewart Marshall passed away earlier this evening. His liver and kidneys failed, and he was unable to rally. I'm so very sorry."
Celia leaned against her pillow. "Oh, okay. Thank you for letting me know. Do you know…is his family still there?"
"No, I'm afraid they have left. Is there anything I can assist you with?"
"No thank you."
Celia ended the call and closed her eyes. She had questions, but she knew the nurse would not be able to answer them. What had the doctor's name been? Could she tell Celia more? Knowing her father had died was unsettling, partly because she couldn't help but wondering what really happened? Did he truly misuse his insulin pump? Wouldn't he have realized his sugar was dropping? In the movies and on television, they always got agitated or started sweating or *something*, didn't they? Did he pass out and fall, or was he already unconscious when his pump delivered the insulin?
And did Bart have something to do with it?

Chapter 29

William caught Celia as she was coming out of the elevator the next morning. "Have you talked to Natasha by chance?"
"I haven't. I am not scheduled to see her until the day of her execution. Is something going on?"
"I sent a letter to the governor. Again. I've talked to her attorney to see what else I can do. We're running out of time."
"I know. I hope your letter does some good. Have you seen her?"
"I'm supposed to see her the day after tomorrow. The stubborn woman hasn't let me visit in years, and now she wants to see me. I'm just glad she relented. I'm hoping I can talk her into pushing her attorney harder. I can't believe she is actually resigned to this."
"She's been calm about it throughout the interview process. I admit it surprised me too."
"Well, let's cross our fingers. Life in prison is a hell of a lot better than death." He headed down the hallway.
Celia thought about what he said. She wasn't sure Natasha would agree that spending the rest of her life in a cell was the better of the two options. Of course, almost everyone had a sense of self-preservation when push came to shove.
Gladys already had several messages for Celia when she reached her office. "They're starting early this morning."

"Thanks, Gladys," Celia said as she took them. "I'm going to get these taken care of first thing, and then I'd like to be undisturbed for a couple of hours."

"Sure thing. Need coffee or anything?"

"No thanks."

Celia closed her door and looked through the messages while her laptop started up. William wanted her to call, and Celia wondered if they'd already had the conversation in the hallway. She'd put him off a bit. Two of the staff had questions about articles that were due at the end of the day; questions usually meant delays. That would need to be a priority. One of her sources for a story wanted to reschedule their meeting. He was probably getting cold feet. Celia would need to work her charm to keep him on board.

The last message was from Marlene, asking Celia to call her. It was unusual for Marlene to call her work number, so Celia was curious. She decided to call Marlene first.

"Hey, Marlene, what's up?" Celia asked.

"Pull up the link I sent you. It's in your personal email."

Celia opened her inbox and looked for Marlene's message. It was just a link.

Former Journal Editor Arrested for Fraud and Embezzlement."

"Oh my," Celia said. "This is interesting."

"Keep reading," Marlene replied.

According to the story, John Talbot had been arrested on charges of fraudulent business practices and the embezzlement of almost 100,000 dollars. In addition, he was being investigated for harassment.

"Well, I guess you don't have to worry about him anymore. Unless you're one of the complainants?"

"I'm not. I was ready to be if he came back to the restaurant; money be damned. But now I don't have to."

"William didn't say a word about any of this, even when I probed him about things."

"He probably couldn't."
That was true, Celia thought. She did wonder who had filed the harassment charges, but William would probably keep that quiet too. He'd want to protect whoever it was for as long as possible. No wonder Natasha trusted him, she thought, her respect for the man growing.
"Well, I'm glad for your sake that he's got more on his plate than stalking your restaurant."
"Me too," Marlene replied. "I'm getting too fat to outrun him!"
"I doubt that," Celia laughed.
"I'm serious. I'm having more and more trouble seeing my feet every day. But I love it."
"Better you than me. But I'm glad you're happy."
"Thanks," Marlene said. "I know you're in work mode, so I'll let you get back to it. I just wanted to share."
Celia hung up the phone and reread the story. It was brief, but she had no doubt the speculations would fly around the office. Maybe she could charm some more details out of William later in the day.

By lunchtime, Celia had gotten her writers back on schedule, reassured her source, and unsuccessfully tried to pry information out of William. He wasn't sharing, and while it frustrated her, it did give her insight into his character. Again, she thought about how valuable his friendship must have been to Natasha.
At 2:00, Natasha's attorney called. Celia sighed when she saw the number. "Hello, this is Celia Brockwell."
"Andrew McMillian here. I wanted to talk with you about Celia's impending execution. I think we may have to work together to stop this."
"What is it you'd like to do?"
"I can arrange for you to visit Natasha. This afternoon if necessary. We need to convince her to allow you to publish at least part of her

story. If you can paint her in a sympathetic light, maybe it will make a difference to the governor."

"Have you talked with Natasha about this? What does she want to do?"

Andrew sighed. "I've tried more than once. She won't listen to me. But I think she'd listen to you. For whatever reason, she seems to trust you even more than she trusts her legal team."

Celia ignored his tone. "So you're saying she's made her wishes clear."

"She has, but she isn't thinking clearly. She's so stubborn and...arrogant. I can't believe she's willing to die to prove a point."

It isn't to prove a point, Celia thought, but she knew her attorney wouldn't understand. Celia was never going to beg for her life. She was going to be in control of it in whatever way she could be. Keeping her silence had been part of her control.

"I'm sorry, Andrew. If Natasha asks to see me or get my help on this, of course I'll go. But if she's clear about this story, I am not going to interfere. To be blunt, I work for her, not you."

She heard him curse under his breath. "Fine. You two are peas in a pod, you know."

"Thank you. Now I have work to do."

Celia cursed too after she hung up. The attorney meant well, but he was also stubborn and arrogant. From the beginning, Tasha had been very clear about the timing and parameters of her story. Even if Celia thought she was crazy, she wasn't going to do anything except what the actress asked. It wasn't just because of Natasha's wishes. Celia knew if she pushed her, Natasha would take the article off the table completely. Not that Celia couldn't decide to publish it after her death anyway, but it wouldn't change anything now.

At 6:00, it was time to shut things down and head home. Since Keith had insisted on staying the night again, Celia decided to pick up her favorite pizza on the way home. It was fine for him to stay and be the protector, she thought, but she wasn't going to let him buy all the dinner.

Julio's Pizza was Celia's favorite splurge. It was a great place for deep-dish Chicago-style pizza, and Julio knew her by name. He greeted her warmly when she walked into the restaurant.

"Celia, my love! Vegetarian for you, yes?" He always greeted his patrons with an exaggerated and completely fake accent.

"Not today, Julio. I have a dinner guest, so I'll have your special."

"It must be a man guest if you are ordering Italian sausage, pancetta, and pepperoni."

"Just a friend," Celia laughed.

They chatted while the pizza was baking, and Julio showed her the latest photos of his daughter and grandchildren. Celia noticed a new photograph of his wife above the wall menu. She had died two years before, and Julio periodically changed the photo, wanting to share all of her beauty, he said. He handed her the large pie and then returned to the kitchen to yell at the staff, most of whom were family members.

It was almost 6:30, and since Julio's was in the opposite direction of home from the office, it would take Celia over half an hour to reach her house. She zipped around cars and tried to make up a little time by pushing the speed limit. When she crested a hill and saw a backup of traffic, probably due to a rush-hour fender bender, she sighed. The pizza was going to get cold. She took her foot off the accelerator and prepared to stop.

Nothing happened. The car didn't slow at all. Trying again, Celia pressed the brake pedal harder, and it just sunk to the floor. The wall of cars was approaching fast, and Celia tried to think of a way to avoid them. No matter how hard or how many times she pressed the pedal, the brakes were not going to respond.

Finally, she swerved over to the narrow shoulder, hoping her car would fit. It almost did, but the roughness caused her to swerve a bit too far, and she began driving down the deep embankment, bumping up and down. One particularly large jolt snapped her neck forward, and her car lurched over, finally coming to rest on its side in the deep ditch. Her ears were ringing, and dots began to cloud her view before everything went dark.

Chapter 30

The first thing Celia noticed was the smell – that strange, slightly burnt chemical smell from the airbag. The car was on its side, but she was still fastened into her seat belt. Thank goodness it rested in the passenger side, she thought. It took a bit of doing, but Celia was able to unfasten her belt, get the door open, and climb out of her car, taking her purse with her. Traffic was still moving inch-by-inch on the road, and a few people were rubbernecking to see her emerge. Celia pulled out her cell phone and dialed 911 to report the accident. Then she called Keith.

"Hey, Celia, when is that pizza gonna be here? I'm starving!"

"Well, I think it's all over the car interior. I had a little problem."

"What's wrong?" She could hear the change in his voice. "Are you okay?"

"I am, but my car isn't. I ran off the road and went into a pretty deep ditch. The car's on its side. Can you come to get me? I should be close to mile marker 14."

"God, Celia! Yes, I'll be right there! Did you call the police? Is anyone hurt? Are you okay?"

"It was just my car. I couldn't stop so I had to get on the shoulder."

"I'll be there in a few minutes. Stay put."

Keith arrived just ahead of the police car. Celia waved him over, and he jogged down the embankment, concern on his face. He

helped Celia up and checked her over. "How's your head? Can you track my fingers?"
"I'm fine, just a little jangled."
"What happened? You said you couldn't stop."
"Yeah, I crested the hill and noticed the stalled traffic, but my brakes wouldn't work. I pumped them and such. No luck. So I tried to ride the shoulder, but apparently, it's too narrow, or I was going too fast."
"Your brakes didn't work? Have you been having trouble with them?"
"No, not at all."
Keith went to her car and began inspecting its underside. He managed to get the hood partially open and looked around a bit. Celia's fog cleared, and she realized he was looking for evidence of tampering. He and the officer were chatting, and then he pointed to something. Celia felt a sinking in her stomach, and she knew what he was going to say before they came back over to her.
"Someone messed with your brake line," Keith said flatly.
"By someone you mean Bart."
"Well, we can't prove it at the moment, but that would be my guess."
"Dammit! Would somebody please just kill him for me?"
The officer with Keith chuckled a bit. "I'll chalk that up to a head injury."
"You need to get checked out. Do you need an ambulance?" Keith asked.
"No way. No ambulance."
"Well, either way, you need to get checked out. I'll take you after we finish here."
While the officer took down Celia's account, Keith went back to the car, took out his phone, and took a few photos. By the time they were ready to go, a wrecker had arrived, and Keith told them

where to take her car. The two of them climbed into his jeep and headed to the ER.

"Thanks for coming," Celia said.

"No problem. So no problems until just now with the brakes?"

"No, everything was fine. I didn't notice anything until I crested that hill and tried to stop."

"Well, the hole is small. You could have been leaking all day, or even more than a day. You'll have to make a list of every place you've been. I'll see how quickly Walt can get video. If there *is* video everywhere you've been."

Celia cursed again. "I can't believe this is still happening. For an attorney, Bart is an idiot."

"He isn't thinking rationally. Whatever it was, something switched in his brain. And I don't think it'll switch back on his own. I can't believe there's no record of him doing this before."

Celia thought about his wife and her conversation with Walt. "There may be."

"What do you mean?"

"Well, I knew he had a wife. She died a few years ago. He still kept in touch with her family, which seemed kind of nice when he told me. But then Walt wondered about her accident."

"She died in an accident?"

"Yeah, apparently it was one car, at night, on a curvy road."

Keith sighed. "This isn't good."

"You think he probably killed her."

"It's not a stretch. He could have done the same thing. And depending on the extent of the crash, no one would have noticed a hole or tear in the brake line." Keith looked at Celia. "He's done this before."

"Well that's just great," Celia muttered.

"Let's just get you checked out, and then we can deal with the accident."

There was a pretty good crowd at the ER, but Keith talked to the nurse and showed her some credentials, so they took Celia back quickly. She could feel angry stares at her back, but she didn't care. She was being stalked by a psycho. That trumped pretty much everything in her opinion. A nurse took her vitals and did the usual neurological checks and asked them to wait for one of the doctors on call.

"Let's see," a middle-aged doctor walked in and picked up the clipboard with Celia's information. "It says here you had a single-car accident. Can you tell me about it?"

"I was driving home, and I tried to slow down on the way down a hill," Celia began. "My brakes locked up or something, and I couldn't stop. I swerved onto the shoulder, but I overestimated, and I went down the embankment and into the ditch. I hit a pretty big bump, and the car turned on its side."

The doctor stepped forward and took Celia's head in his hands, gently moving it from side to side. "Any pain?" Celia shook her head no. He performed the basic neurological tests as the nurse had, and then he did some writing.

"Ms. Brockwell, I'm going to send you to radiology for a couple of tests and some imaging. We'll take a look at those. No doubt you'll be pretty sore for the next few days, but if the images don't show injury, you should be fine. Are you feeling any nausea or dizziness?"

"No, none."

"Alright, then. The nurse will be back in soon to take you down to radiology. I'll also write you a prescription for pain. It isn't unusual to have a bruised sternum in these kinds of accidents, and those are painful."

After the doctor left, Keith studied Celia. "You sure you aren't nauseated, being tough for the doctor?"

Celia laughed. "I'm fine. If I did hit my head, it couldn't have been very hard. The car didn't actually roll. I figure my neck will be the sorest."

He rubbed it for a few minutes, and Celia winced. It was already getting tender.

"I'll wait up here while you get x-rays. Then we can head to your house, by way of takeout, of course." He grinned.

"Oh yeah, our supper is all over my car, isn't it?"

"Too bad. I was really in the mood for pizza."

When Celia returned from radiology, Keith was on the phone, arguing with someone. "I don't care what you have to do. Get some footage, find out what happened to that car. You and I both know it was Bart. He's crazy, and if you guys don't stop him, I will." Celia stepped backward to listen. "Yeah, thanks. Sorry, you're right. Yeah, I know she's not my sister. Just try to find something out, and soon."

Celia made some noise as she walked in, and Keith hung up the phone. "They said the doctor should be back up here in half an hour. Apparently, I'm a VIP."

"Celia Brockwell, rising star editor-in-chief," Keith smiled.

"Yeah right. More like Celia who? Friend of assertive cops."

The doctor walked in carrying a clipboard. "Well, Ms. Brockwell, it looks like you have a mild concussion. I'm not seeing any fractures or dislocations, but, as I said, you'll be sore, especially your sternum. I have a prescription here for some pain medication, and you need to be monitored for the next 48 hours."

"I can do that at home, correct?" Celia was not about to stay in the hospital overnight if she didn't have to stay. She was not a fan of hospitals.

"I wouldn't be comfortable with that if you live alone."

"I'll be staying with her for as long as necessary," Keith said. He nodded when Celia mouthed a thank-you.

"In that case, be sure to avoid sleeping for the next several hours. If you experience any severe nausea, dizziness, or vomiting, you need to come back in immediately. A concussion is not something to ignore. I would also avoid driving for several days."

Celia was about to protest, but Keith spoke up first. "She won't be going to work for a couple of days, and when she goes back, I'll be driving her."

The doctor nodded, gave some final instructions, and then he left them to prepare to go home.

"Thanks, Dad," Celia said as she gathered her things.

"Just following doctor's orders. And I'll be making sure you do too."

"So am I grounded?"

"You will be if you don't behave."

Celia rolled her eyes, and Keith laughed. They left the hospital and climbed into Keith's Jeep. Celia winced a bit as she pulled the seatbelt across her body. Okay, so maybe the doctor had a point. Her head was throbbing, and so she asked Keith if they could drop off the prescription on their way back to her house. He agreed and said he'd get back out to pick it up later. Celia wasn't used to being taken care of by someone else, but she was grateful for Keith. The whole event had rattled her, and she didn't want to be alone. It was a strange feeling, depending on someone besides herself.

"Go rest. I'll wake you with some food and your medicine in 45 minutes. Don't go to sleep."

"Yes, Dad." Celia rolled her eyes at Keith. *Ugh, note to self, eye-rolling hurts.*

"Don't make me ground you."

"Yeah, yeah," Celia closed her bedroom door. She kicked off her shoes and climbed into the bed fully clothed. *Thank goodness for blackout shades.* Surely closing her eyes would ease the pain.

"Wake up, sleepy. I thought I told you sleeping was out." Keith was nudging her gently.

"What the –"Celia rolled over. "Oh god, my head."

"I've got the stuff for that. Sit up." He pulled back the covers and lifted her into a sitting position.

"This is the worst hangover I've ever had."

"Funny," Keith chuckled. "I made you a sandwich. Grilled cheese."
"Aw, mom, my favorite."
He shrugged. "My mom made it for us when we were sick. Plus I hate to cook on short notice. Especially when there's nothing in your fridge."
"It tastes amazing," Celia pointed at him with the sandwich. "I had cheese?"
"Well, no. I got a few things when I picked up your medicine."
"What's *in* this?"
"Provolone, cheddar, swiss, and Colby. With lots of butter."
"Heaven help us," Celia took another bite. "How are you not married with three kids?"
"Just lucky, I guess. Here's some water. Once you've had a few more bites, you need to take this. It'll help with the headache. Then you probably need a shower. No offense."
"Well, *that* killed the mood," Celia snorted.
Keith left the room, and she heard him washing the skillet he'd used to cook. *Lots of butter?* Celia wondered how many groceries he bought. She finished the sandwich and took her meds.
The hot shower felt amazing. Celia stood in the steam with one hand against the wall, just in case. The steam cleared her head, and her muscles began to relax. Surveying her body, she saw a few scrapes and some marks that would probably become nasty bruises. The largest mark was between her breasts, where the seat belt had been. That's where the doctor said she'd have the most pain. Celia hadn't been in an accident since high school when her buddy had run a red light after a ballgame. No one was seriously hurt then either, but she remembered that the pain got worse before it got better.
"What are you doing?" Keith asked from the couch. He was watching a game.
"I was just going to check some things before bedtime." Celia opened her laptop.

He was out of the couch before she finished the sentence. "Yeah, no." He closed the laptop. "No work tonight."
"I'm not dying. It's a bump on the head."
"You spend time looking at that screen, you're gonna regret it tomorrow. Migraine city."
"I don't get migraines."
"You do now. At least for a day or so." Keith rubbed his head. "Trust me, I've had a few concussions."
Celia pushed the laptop away and got comfortable. "That sounds like a few good stories."
"Ah, you know, mostly football." Keith flexed.
"You played basketball."
"Reporters remember everything. It's annoying." Keith sat next to her. "Okay. I got one when I had a bike wreck in junior high school. Split the back of my head open. Blood everywhere. I was a legend."
"I bet. Boys and blood." Celia poked him.
"Then I got into a fight in high school."
"Over a girl?"
"Over my sister," Keith said. "A boyfriend forgot she had a big brother."
Celia fanned herself. "How chivalrous. I'm impressed." She sat forward with her chin in her hand. "And the other one?"
"Remember how I said female inmates can be every bit as rough as male inmates?"
"Ouch." Celia winced. "So you got beat up by a girl."
"Well, more like knocked down. Another guard and I were pulling two inmates apart. Mine lost her balance and fell backward. She was…substantial. And the floor was hard."
"You really are a concussion expert. I'm feeling lucky I just had an accident."
Keith stood and walked to the window, looking out carefully. "It wasn't an accident."

Celia joined him, and they both looked up and down the street.
"You don't think he's close by?"
"He knows my jeep. I doubt he'd risk it." Keith put a hand on Celia's shoulder. "But we've got to get the evidence he did this. He escalates with every interaction."
"That's your department, or Walt's. Or maybe Natasha knows a hitman."
Keith laughed. "I didn't hear that."
They watched the rest of the game, and Celia took another pill before going to bed. It would knock her out, but she didn't have any illusions about going to work the next day. Keith would stand in front of the door to prevent her if he had to do so. She felt strange being fussed over, but it was nice to have a friend close by, especially one with a concealed carry permit.
"*Glad you slept all night. Call if you need anything. STAY HOME.*"
Celia read Keith's note as she drank coffee. She'd slept until almost 9:00, not hearing Keith at all when he left. Other than a dull throbbing in her head and chest, Celia felt almost normal. She was tempted to go to work, but if Keith didn't drag her home, Gladys probably would. Instead, she took her coffee and laptop to the sofa and decided to do a little work from home.
"Yes, can I speak to William? It's Celia Brockwell." Celia typed a response to an email while she was on hold.
"Celia! What are you doing on the phone? You're supposed to be resting!" William scolded her. "I heard last night. Someone tampered with your brakes?"
"How do you know these things?"
"I have spies everywhere." William chuckled. "Actually, I called last night around 9:30, and Keith told me. They need to quit dicking around and catch that bastard."
"From your lips to God's ears." Celia pressed send. "I'm going to try to wrap up the piece on the commissioners today."

"Don't worry about that. We can run it next edition if we need to. You need to make sure that head of yours is okay. That head makes money."

"Ah, so that's why you're concerned!"

"Of course!" William laughed. "No really, I don't want you to push it. I'm glad it wasn't worse."

"That makes two of us. So what did you need last night?"

"I was calling to remind you that I'm going to see Natasha today. I know you're done with interviews. Anything you want me to tell her?"

"You could tell her I'm still hoping the governor will intervene, but she probably wouldn't appreciate that. I'm glad you're going. She acts stoic and formidable in there, but we both know it's an act. At least some of it has to be."

"I've never seen Natasha scared, but she'd have to be superhuman not to be afraid." William cleared his throat. "I feel so helpless."

"Seeing you will mean a lot to her. That I'm sure of, William. And we still have three days."

William coughed. "True. Well, I'll tell her you said hello. You know, she considers you a friend, and that's rare for her."

Celia smiled and ended the call. Natasha had also told Celia that she was a friend. Celia wouldn't have admitted it, but she felt honored. And she felt the same. For whatever reason, she'd found an ally and kindred spirit in the actress.

Celia was about to make herself something to eat when her phone rang again. She didn't recognize the number. Was it the hospital?

"Celia Brockwell."

"So you're still alive," a soft voice said.

Bart. "Who is this? Bart, what the hell are you doing?"

"I'm glad you're safe…for now. Too bad about Stewart."

"Bart, I swear to God, I will -"

The call ended.

Chapter 31

For the next 48-hours, Celia appeased Keith by staying home. She talked to Keith, Walter, and two other officers about Bart's latest call. Of course, the phone had been a burner, so there was no way to trace it. And Celia hadn't thought to try to record the brief conversation. They all agreed, however, proof or not, Bart was the caller. Walter promised to speak with her father's doctor at the hospital to find out more about his diabetic coma. There was nothing Celia could do but wait for news.

On the third day after her accident, she went to her office long enough to get some messages, talk to a couple of writers, and be scolded and sent home by Gladys. Gladys was a very professional assistant, but she could switch to a mother when it suited her. Celia gave up and left the office before lunchtime.

She was considering whether or not to cook that afternoon when someone knocked on her door. It was Lucille, and she was holding a basket.

"Hello, Lucille, how are you?"

"I'm just fine, but how are you?" Lucille handed Celia the basket. "That nice man staying with you told me you'd had an accident! I made some bread, and I thought I'd come to check on you. You've been so kind to me."

"Thank you. Would you like to come in?"

"Oh, no, no. You need your rest. I just wanted to see that you were alright. I need to take Tom to the vet."

She named her new cat Tom. Tom and Jerry. "Well thank you for that. And for the bread. I'm sure it's delicious."

Lucille walked back to her house, and Celia closed the door. Smelling the bread, she sighed. Her neighbor was a kind old lady. The bread would go well with some soup if Celia could find enough ingredients to make it.

"What smells so good?" Keith walked into the kitchen a while later and grabbed a beer from the fridge.

"I decided to make some soup. Lucille brought homemade bread over earlier."

"I guess that means you're feeling better." He leaned over the pot. "Looks good."

"It needs to simmer a little more. You can drink your beer and get comfortable."

Keith was already on his way into the den. *He's really made himself at home.* It didn't bother Celia, but she realized while she watched him that she was ready for him to go. Maybe cooking for him would soften the blow.

"This soup is great." Kevin got seconds from the pot. "Especially with the rain, it's perfect."

"Glad you like it. You can take some to work if you want."

"Thanks, I probably will. And this bread…I might have to marry Lucille."

"Aren't you a little young for her?"

"Who knows?" Keith winked. "Maybe she's a cougar."

"Well now I've lost my appetite," Celia joked as she took her bowl to the sink.

"That's not very nice. She'll sick her cat on you if she hears talk like that."

"Did you know she named her cat Tom? The first cat was Jerry, this one's Tom."

Keith chuckled. "That's pretty funny. Maybe tomorrow I can bring him some catnip."
"About that," Celia sat next to him. "I was thinking that since I'm okay now, you might want to get back to your place."
Keith concentrated on his soup and bread, not answering. Celia tried not to stare at him, and she could tell by the way his back stiffened that he wasn't pleased with her suggestion. He walked to the kitchen and put his bowl into the sink and then sat back down. "Are you trying to get rid of me?"
"No, not at all. I just thought…you've been here a while. My head is fine. I'm going back to work. I'm sure you would like to get back to your own space."
"Is something wrong?"
"No, why?"
"You seem off."
Celia sighed and walked toward the guest room. The bed was unmade, and clothes were hanging on the back of a chair. "You know, you're kind of messy."
"That's not it. What's going on?"
"I'm fine. I just need my space." Celia began putting the discarded clothing into Keith's overnight bag.
"This is stupid," Keith said. "I can stay one more night. You need me here, and we're going to the same place tomorrow."
Celia winced and kept packing. "You've been great, and I appreciate it. I promise I do. But I don't need a babysitter. You haven't been to your own house in days. You're too tall for this guest bed. It can't possibly be comfortable."
"Celia, stop." Keith took the bag. "What's going on? Why are you trying to get rid of me?"
She threw her hands up and stomped out of the guest room toward the kitchen. Opening the dishwasher, she began putting up the clean dishes. When she slammed a tumbler onto the shelf, it

shattered. "Dammit!" Celia ran her finger under the cold water, hissing as it stung her.
Keith took a clean dish towel from the top drawer. He turned the water off and wrapped the rag around Celia's finger, applying enough pressure to make her curse again. "Celia, talk to me."
Pulling her hand away, Celia looked at her finger. "Go sit on the couch. I'll be there in a second. She blotted the cut again and then grabbed some gauze and tape from her first aid kit before sitting beside Keith on the couch.
"Need some help?" He took the supplies. After wrapping her finger in the gauze, he taped it securely and then sat back.
"I really thought Natasha's attorney would pull a rabbit out of his hat." Celia sighed.
"He kept her on death row for a decade. He did everything he could." Taking Celia's uninjured hand, Keith continued. "I know you two formed a kind of bond, but she killed five people."
"I know that. I'm not stupid!" Celia pulled her hand back. "She also lost her mother and a life with her brother to a man who only loved her for the money!"
"What are you talking about? What brother?"
"You wouldn't get it."
"Try me. Celia didn't have a brother."
"Yes, she did!" Celia pounded the sofa. "William is her brother!"
Keith opened and closed his mouth. Celia could tell she had shocked him. *Good.*
"What? How did you find out?"
"It doesn't matter. And you can't say anything."
"And what about her mother? What did Natasha's father do to her mother?"
"I shouldn't have said any of that. You can't share it. It's from the interviews."
"But aren't the interviews for an article?"

"Not that part. Some things should stay private." Celia chuckled. "I can't believe I just said that."

"I can. You're a journalist, but you're still a good person."

"That's just it. I'm really not. I just seem that way to you because you don't get it."

Keith shook his head. "Now you've lost me again."

"I understand Natasha. I get why she did what she did, how she thinks. I get it because we're alike."

"Alike? Celia, it's one thing to see her point of view. But you're not alike. You've never killed anyone. You don't use and manipulate people."

Celia's short laugh was sharp. "Don't I? You don't know how I worked my way here. The way I played on people's insecurities, manipulated circumstances to get a story. Hell, I used Bart knowing he had feelings, and then I dumped him when he was too much trouble. And honestly, I'd like to kill him." She sighed. "He's just not worth getting caught."

"None of that means you're like Natasha. You care about people. You have feelings."

Celia stood and walked away from the couch. She spun around to look at Keith again. "I really don't. I mean, I enjoy Marlene's company, but her friendship benefitted me. The inside knowledge she had from working so closely with John helped me to get more stories and work my way up at The Journal. I don't feel anything about her life or her baby. Not really.

"And Lucille," Celia continued, beginning to pace. "If she didn't check my mail and keep an eye on things, she'd just be an annoying old lady. Her cat? Jerry? He annoyed the crap out of me. I should have been horrified when I saw him in that box. But I was just pissed at Bart and what he'd done to my house."

"Come on, Celia. The man has been terrorizing you. No wonder you didn't mourn for a cat."

"Then there's you." Celia stopped in front of him. "I'm kicking you out the night before Natasha's execution because I don't want you here. I don't want you hovering. I don't need you anymore because my head is fine. I don't want to need you around."

"Sit down," Keith ordered. He sounded like a guard instead of a friend.

Celia was caught so off guard by his change in tone, she sank into a chair and stopped rambling.

"You've got walls. You're tough. You don't express feelings, and yeah, you look out for yourself first. Hell, maybe you would kill Bart if you thought you'd get away with it. But all this stuff about being exactly like a serial killer is bull."

Celia started to protest.

"No, look at me and don't talk. I don't know what you've done or whether you feel guilty about any of it."

"I don't –"

"I said don't talk. Yeah, you do what you have to. I get that. But you're not a sociopath. Don't make that face. It's rude."

"You don't know what I am."

"I know you're my friend. I know you're pushing me away so I won't see how much this execution bothers you. I know you don't do closeness and you don't do relationships." Keith looked at Celia until she had to look away from him. "But you're not a sociopath. And even if you are, I don't much care. I'm here."

Idiot. Celia smiled. "I appreciate that. And as much as I *can* do friendship, you're the closest I've got. I mean that. But I just can't have you stay tonight."

Keith sighed and lowered his head, and neither of them spoke. Finally, he slapped his knees, stood, and grabbed his bag.

"Understood. I'll go."

"Thanks, Keith."

"What time do you visit her tomorrow?"

"1:00."

"I'll be there. I'll be there the whole day and night."
"I know. I'll see you tomorrow."
After Keith left, Celia sat on the sofa for a long time. She thought about their conversation, she thought about letting Natasha's secrets slip. She thought about all the things she knew about the actress's life and William's life. *Am I helping her die by keeping her secrets? Would betraying her confidence save her?* Probably, not, Celia thought. All her suspicions were just suspicions, and Natasha would never forgive her, even if it saved her from being executed. Celia's phone pinged and interrupted her thoughts.
"I'm home. Try to sleep." It was Keith.
Celia sighed and walked into the bathroom. She brushed her teeth, washed her face, and put on some pajamas. The pain medication was sitting on her bedside table. She'd only taken a couple of them because they knocked her out, but now she thought that was exactly what she needed. Taking two of them, she swallowed, washed them down with water, and climbed into bed.

Chapter 32

Celia woke up at 6:00 am, fighting for breath. She sat up, pulling the wet pajama top off and looking around her dim room to get her bearings. She had sweated through her sheets, and she immediately started shivering, so she threw off the bedding and stumbled to the bathroom to turn on the shower. Resting her hands on the counter, she surveyed herself in the mirror. Even with a night of heavy sleep, she had circles under her eyes, and she looked like the drugs were still working, with puffy cheeks and disheveled hair. I look like death, fitting.

The hot spray felt like heaven. Celia wasn't sure how long she stood under the steamy water, but she didn't care. It was 6:00 am, and she didn't need to be at the prison until after lunch. Even if she worked a couple of hours first, she had plenty of time. In the spirit of indulgence, Celia washed her hair twice, slathered on the fancy conditioner that cost more than a five-star meal, and shaved her legs. By the time the hot water began to run tepid, she felt as pampered as if she'd been to a spa.

She was not surprised to see a message from Keith, even though it was only 7:00 am. She pulled on her terry cloth robe and dialed his number.

"Celia, you're already awake?"

"You sent me a message."

"I hope it didn't wake you, I just wanted to make sure you woke up."
"You realize that makes no sense at all, don't you?"
"Whatever. How did you sleep?"
"Like a rock. I drugged myself and didn't move until 6:00."
"Ha! So I didn't wake you up!"
"No, you didn't, but 6:00 am is a one-off for me, just so you know."
Celia moved to the kitchen and started a pot of coffee. "Is everything quiet there?"
"I don't go in until 9:00 today. But I'll be there until almost midnight."
"Wow, why so late?"
"Paperwork. Not to be an ass, but execution days are murder."
Celia wanted to laugh, but she couldn't. Instead, she put an extra spoonful of Splenda into her coffee and stirred.
"Oh god, Celia, I'm sorry."
"No problem. I'm making coffee."
"What time will you be here?"
"My visiting time is 1:00, but I may get there early. I'd like to talk with her attorney. I was thinking 11:00."
"I figure he'll be here all day. She actually has a few people on her list, starting at 10:00."
Celia was surprised. Except for Andrew, William, and herself, she couldn't think of anyone Natasha had even mentioned in her interviews who was still alive. The morbid thought punched her in the stomach, and she poured the rest of her coffee down the sink.
"Celia, are you still there?"
"I am. I'm going to try to do a little work before I go to the prison. I figure I'll get ready here, go to the office for a couple of hours, and then head there."
"Are you sure you want to go to work today?"

"Yeah, I need to. I haven't been there since the accident. I need to get a few things done." Celia's head began to ache. "Which means I probably need to go ahead and get started."

"I'll let you go then. I'll see you when you get there."

Celia filled her coffee mug again, this time black, and grabbed a slice of homemade bread. She popped a couple of ibuprofen and started her morning routine. Once her hair and makeup were done, she stared at the contents of her closet. What do I wear to an execution? Natasha would kill her if she wore black. After sliding a few outfits back and forth along the rack, she decided on a navy blue and tan hound's-tooth jacket with dark pants. After choosing dark pumps and a blouse, she put them on while sipping the dregs of her coffee.

Gladys was watering plants when Celia arrived. "Good morning! How are you feeling? Still sore?"

"I'm much better, thanks. Just ready to get my car back. The rental isn't my style." Gladys chuckled, and Celia walked into her office and closed the door. In lieu of the fluorescent lighting, she turned on the small lamp at her desk. The hum of the lights would probably give her a headache. She saw her voicemail light blinking but decided to check email first.

Celia,

I wasn't sure you'd be in today, so I am canceling our regular meeting today at 10:00 am. I may see you this afternoon.

William

Celia wasn't surprised William canceled the meeting. She was, however, curious about what he meant by seeing her this afternoon. Has he changed his mind about going to the execution? Can he even do that this late? She assumed he was cryptic because he was using his work email.

"Celia," Julia knocked and then stuck her head inside the door. "You busy?"

"Not too busy. Come on in."

"I heard about your accident. I'm glad you are okay." Julia sat and leaned forward. "You're okay, right?

"I am. Just a little sore."

"Your brakes locked? I bet that was scary. Glad it wasn't worse. Did you get a rental?"

"I did. They gave me a Prius. It was all they had."

"Well, at least you'll get good gas mileage."

"True. You always find the silver lining."

"I try. Have you seen William? Don't you have a meeting with him?"

"He canceled it. Must have something else to do."

Julia nodded. "Well, I'll let you get back to it. We should do lunch next week."

"Sounds good."

Once Julia left, Celia locked her door and tried to focus on email. There was an email notifying her that a meeting was canceled. Two staff members sent drafts of upcoming stories. Celia opened one and tried to read it. She stared at the first paragraph, reading it three times before giving up. Reading articles would have to wait.

"Gladys," Celia buzzed her assistant. "Other than the meeting with William, my day was clear, right?"

"It is. You said you'd be leaving before lunch for an appointment, so I cleared everything."

"Thanks." Celia hung up and rubbed her temples. Why did I try to work today? Because I didn't want to be stuck at home. Sighing, she opened the folder named "NB Interviews." After putting in her earbuds, she began clicking each one in chronological order.

For the next hour, Celia listened to bits and pieces of all the interviews. The first one, when it was obvious they were sizing each other up and Natasha was deciding whether she could trust the reporter. The generalities of Celia's life that she shared with the killer to keep her talking. Then there was the comfortable banter, and the venting Celia did when Bart became a nuisance. The journey from two strangers to friends and confidantes was right there in 12 sound files on Celia's laptop.

Of course, not all the details were there. The farther along they got in the interview process, the more often Celia agreed to turn off the recorder to protect Natasha's privacy or her own. There were no recorded details about Natasha's mother or the fact that William was her brother. Their conversation about whether or not Celia could murder Bart was absent. The only people who knew those things were the two women, and one of them would die in a few hours. Celia didn't know whether to feel sad or relieved.

The alarm on Celia's phone interrupted her listening. It was 10:15, time for her to go to the prison. Depending on traffic, she'd be there close to 11:00. Hopefully, she'd have a chance to talk with Andrew and Keith and ascertain how Natasha was doing. She closed her laptop and then her office and headed to Delaware.

"Name and identification please." Because Celia was in a different part of the facilities, the receptionist was different. This woman was younger and much less friendly. Celia gave her name and slid her driver's license under the window.

"Sign the registry, please. If you have a cell phone or any other devices, you must leave them here. Then step to the side."

Celia did as the woman asked and then stepped to the side to be patted down by a guard. "Please see the receptionist." He said.

"Your appointment is at 1:00. You can wait here or go through the detector and wait in the public assigned area until you're called."

Celia opted to go through the metal detector, and then a guard escorted her to a plain room with limited seating and a couple of tables. There was a coffee machine, water fountain, and snack machine against one wall and a row of barred windows on the opposite wall. A television hung on the wall, a news station playing with closed captions and no sound.

"Glad to see you," Andrew sat down and offered her a paper cup with water.

"I was hoping I could talk with you before my visit." Celia sipped the water. "See how she's doing?"

"We talked earlier. She's not too talkative, which is understandable. I told her I'd sent another letter to the governor, and I know a friend of hers has done the same."

"Do you think it will do any good?"

Andrew sighed. "I'm not sure. I hope so, but I'm honestly not hopeful." He sat up and looked at Celia. "But you may be able to help. It's not too late."

"How can I help?"

"You have contacts. You can go to someone right now and share some of her story. I know enough about her life to know that parts of it would make her a sympathetic victim, especially regarding her father. You probably know more than I do."

Celia finished the water and crushed the cup. She walked to the wastebasket and dropped it in, trying to think of an answer for the attorney. He was watching her.

"I don't think I can do that."

"Why not? She won't know. She can't pull the story now. If it has a chance of helping with an intervention –"

"I signed a contract, and I gave Natasha my word. I may not understand why, but she doesn't want one word of that article published until after her execution. That's her choice to make. Every other choice has been taken away from her. I'm not taking that one."

Andrew cursed and stood. "Enjoy your visit." He walked away.

Why did I come here so early? Celia considered hiding until 1:00. *Maybe I can take a nap.* Chuckling, she leaned her head against the cinderblock wall and closed her eyes.

"Celia, I didn't think you'd be here yet." William startled her.

"William, you're here! Are you visiting Natasha?"

"I just saw her." He sat and gestured helplessly. "I just can't believe the state is going through with it."

"I know. How does she seem?"
He scoffed. "You know her. She's calm and sarcastic, sitting there with perfect posture."
"Hair and makeup are done, no doubt." Celia chuckled.
William laughed and leaned against the wall, closing his eyes as Celia had done earlier.
Should I leak the story? Should I do what her attorney asked even though Natasha was clear? Should I betray her wishes to try to help? Celia wanted to ask William, but she didn't. She was afraid of what he would say.
"You want some coffee?" William finally asked.
"I'm good. I don't think I need to be caffeinated."
William walked to the coffeemaker and made a cup. Then he counted the change and bought something from the machine. He sat back down beside Celia, offering her one of the stale vanilla crème cookies in the small package. She took one to be polite.
"I wonder how long these have been here," she joked as she took a bite. It wasn't too bad for a stale cookie.
"I don't want to know. He sipped from the Styrofoam cup." I do know you made the right decision about the coffee." He took another sip and grimaced.
"But you're still drinking it."
"You gotta do what you gotta do. Even bad coffee is still coffee."
Celia laughed and then noticed a door opening. Keith walked through it and caught her gaze. He smiled and nodded before picking up a phone attached to the wall. After he hung up, he went to the door where Celia had come in, met a man Celia had never seen before, and escorted him back out through the opposite door.
"Who is that?" William asked.
"I have no idea." Celia watched as the man walked with Keith. He looked to be in his thirties, and he was an inch or two taller than the guard. He wore a gray suit and purple shirt with no tie, and his dark hair was slicked back and slightly curled at the neck. He seemed to be very careful about making sure he only looked straight ahead.

"Is he going to visit Natasha? Is he one of her attorneys?"
"He doesn't exactly look like someone who would work at Andrew's firm," Celia said wryly. "Maybe he's here for someone else."
"Yeah, he looks more like an ambulance chaser."
Celia chuckled at that, and William offered her the last cookie. They sat in silence and watched the clock.

Chapter 35

Just before 1:00, a guard escorted Celia to visit Natasha. Instead of the dull, neutral scrubs-like garb she usually wore, the actress had on dark dress pants and a blouse, a bright blue that complemented her eyes. Her hair was in an updo that fit the red carpet better than an execution, and she was wearing makeup. Alicia wondered if the change in appearance was standard or if Natasha had finagled access to cosmetics. Regardless, she looked more like the star from the magazines than the convicted killer Celia had gotten to know.

"I see we both dressed for the occasion," Natasha said. "Thank you for not wearing black."

Celia chuckled. "I considered red, but I didn't want to upstage you."

Natasha laughed out loud. "You're a refreshing change from today's somber faces. Even William couldn't bring himself to be witty."

"I talked with him earlier. Is he staying?"

"He'd better not. He doesn't need to see this. He's seen enough."

"Are you sure?" Celia didn't want to overstep, but William had looked so unhappy. "I mean, do you think he'll regret it? He's…well, he's family."

Natasha's head snapped up. "That's exactly why I told him to go home. Does he know you know?"

"No," Celia replied. "I assumed you didn't want me to tell him."

"Thank you again. Maybe down the road, if you think it will help him."
"I understand."
"So tell me something good. Have you and Keith finally broken your silly rules?"
Now Celia laughed out loud. "Oh God no! He's a friend, and that is all I need. I think some self-imposed celibacy is better for me after the Bart fiasco."
"You just have to do a better job of weeding out the crazy ones. Keith seems sane. I bet he's more than capable." Natasha winked.
"Of that, I have no doubt," Celia smirked. "But I won't be finding out."
"Too bad."
Celia reached across the table and covered Natasha's hand with her own. "So what do you need? What can I do right now?"
"You're doing it. You're my friend. You're in here dressed to the nines, letting me have a laugh. And you're not begging me to fall on my sword."
"Yes, I talked to Andrew earlier."
Natasha folded her arms and scowled. "So what did he do to try to convince you to do? Seduce the governor?"
"No." Celia chuckled. "He did ask me to get part of the story out. Try to pull at the heartstrings of the public. I said no."
"As you should have."
"But," Celia leaned forward. "I could say yes. There's still time. It might help."
"No. Absolutely not."
"Are you sure?"
"I'm sure. No one reads my story until after I'm gone. You write it, they read it, and it's done. No reporters trying to get a comment or quote, trying to get another piece of me, or bleeding hearts using me as a cause."

Celia squeezed Celia's hand. For just a few seconds, she saw emotion in the actress's eyes, an emotion she hadn't seen in their interviews. It looked like Natasha might cry. Instead, she chuckled, and the emotion was gone.

"So, aren't you going to ask me about my last meal?"

Celia laughed and shook her head. "Don't tell me it's kale and avocado toast!"

"Absolutely not!" Natasha made a face. "I'm having lasagna and an Italian cheesecake."

"Oh wow! Talk about carbs!"

"Yes, I avoided pasta for most of my career. But I heard about this amazing little place called Verelli's…"

"Ha! Marlene's place! You won't be disappointed. I can't believe she didn't tell me."

"She may not know. I think a guard or Andrew makes the arrangements. I didn't ask how it would work." Natasha smiled. "And I'm not sure providing the last meal for a murderer would make the best advertising."

"You'd be surprised," Celia said.

"I want to thank you again for everything. I have no doubt it will be a great story, told the way I hoped it would be."

"I'm the one who should thank you for trusting me with it."

Once again, there was a flicker of emotion. Then she chuckled. "It's almost time for Keith to knock for the last time."

"True. I have to say, meeting him was a lifesaver I didn't know I'd need. He's practically my bodyguard."

"So you're saying he's Kevin Costner to your Whitney Houston?" Natasha teased.

"Well, I won't be singing if that's what you mean."

There was a knock at the door.

"I hate to interrupt, ladies, but time is almost up." Keith stuck his head inside the door.

Celia and Natasha looked at each other before bursting into laughter. Kevin looked at each of them, shook his head, and closed the door.

Both women stood, and Natasha began walking toward Celia. "See that camera? The person watching this is about to freak out."

"Why" Celia began. But she understood when the actress embraced her. She returned the hug.

"No physical contact! Step back!" A frantic voice sounded through the speaker.

"So predictable." Natasha chuckled.

Keith walked in and cleared his throat. Celia walked toward the door, and he opened it for her.

"I'll be there, Natasha. On the front row."

"I know," Natasha said, sitting back in her chair.

"You okay?" Keith asked as they walked away from the room.

"I actually think I am. I know what's going to happen in a few hours. But she seems okay. And I kept my promise."

"What promise?"

"One thing that was very clear in my contract," Celia said. "Not a word of the interviews or the article could be leaked or published until after Natasha's execution."

"Seems strange, but that's her call."

"Exactly. As recently as this morning, her attorney was begging me to put out part of her story to generate sympathy and maybe get an intervention at the last minute."

Keith sighed. He looked away.

"What?"

"I mean, I know you wanted to abide by her wishes. But do you think maybe the guy has a point?"

Celia closed her eyes. "Not you too."

"Look, it's none of my business. I'm just saying I can see why he thought it was a good idea. You did what you thought was right, what Natasha wanted."

"I did. It was the right thing to do."
"Okay then. I have to get back to work. Don't hang around here all afternoon. Believe it or not, there's a great café just down the road. Have a late lunch. Take a walk." Keith smiled. "Just be back before the protest crowd gets too big. Otherwise, I may have to carry you inside…like Kevin carried Whitney."
Celia's eyes went wide, and she punched him in the arm. "You eavesdropping ass!"
He walked away laughing, and Celia decided to take his advice.
At 7:30, Celia wove her way through a group of protesters outside the fence. She gave her pass to the guard at the gate, and he let her inside. After signing the register again and surrendering her personal items, Keith was waiting for her.
"I'll take you to the family waiting area. It will be away from the others."
"Others?" Celia asked. "Are there any others?"
"There are a couple of detectives, someone from the DA's office. There are also a few family members of victims."
Celia hadn't considered family members. It had been over a decade, but she'd only heard Natasha's version of the murders and the victims. Of course, they had spouses, siblings, even children who were still grieving and wanted to see justice done.
The family area had a better coffee maker, nicer furniture, and no snack machine. I guess no one has an appetite for stale cookies at this point. There were a few inspirational books, the Bible, the Book of Mormon, and the Koran. For the atheists in foxholes. Natasha would appreciate the irony.

"We can go to the observatory now." A guard Celia had never seen before opened the door and gestured for her to follow him.
They walked down a hallway, and Celia tried to step gently to soften the echo of her heels on the tile. The guard was silent, and though Celia wanted to fill the space, the small talk stuck in her throat.

Several heads turned as the guard opened the door and ushered Celia into the theater-style room. She avoided their gazes, hoping no one would recognize her. She didn't want to lock eyes with a victim's family member. Instead, she looked down at the cement steps as she walked to the front row.

Celia had spent some time researching the lethal injection process. Initially, it was for the story, but now she wished she didn't know so much. While she studied the out-of-date curtains, she thought about what was taking place behind them. There would be a gurney, and the warden, at least one guard, and medical professionals would be prepared. In a separate area, a few people would be waiting to press a series of buttons. None of them would know who had administered the poison. Celia wondered how it would feel to be one of those people, if not knowing would be enough to assuage their guilt.

Her head began to ache as the curtains opened. Natasha was there, and she found Celia's gaze immediately. There was no trace of the emotion Celia had seen earlier; she just nodded at the reporter.

Ring! Ring, dammit! Celia screamed inwardly at the white 1980s relic on the cinderblock wall. Natasha smiled, and Celia smiled back. Part of her wanted the actress to sit up and rip the IVs from her arms, break into a dramatic monologue, something. Instead, she lay there as her boy relaxed and her eyes began to close, surrendering to the barbiturate.

Once Natasha's eyes closed, it was over. Celia knew the actress's body was being paralyzed, and her heart was going into cardiac arrest even as Celia's own heart was thudding behind her sternum, which was still sore from the accident.

And then the doctor pronounced Natasha deceased. The curtain closed, people began to file out of the room, but Celia sat, fighting off nausea. She allowed Keith to help her out of the creaky chair. He led her up the steps toward the door.

"Are you okay?" Keith asked.

Celia didn't hear him. She was already on her way to the ladies' room, hoping to make it before she began to vomit. She did, but just barely.

Once her stomach was empty, Celia stood and walked to the sink.

"I'm okay. It's okay." Celia whispered to herself as she splashed water onto her face and took some deep breaths. Her legs felt like over-boiled pasta, but she felt certain she wouldn't throw up anymore.

Keith was talking with Andrew when Celia left the restroom. They both looked at her, Keith with concern and Andrew with disappointment.

"Do you need anything?" Keith asked quietly. He handed her the purse and other belongings.

She nodded.

"Ms. Brockwell, may I speak with you?"

Keith left them alone, and Celia sat on a bench.

"Is this the first execution you've witnessed?" Andrew sat next to her.

"Yes, it is."

"It's a difficult thing. I probably should have prepared you better."

Celia shook her head. "I don't think that was possible but thank you."

"I need to give you this. Natasha didn't want it inspected." He handed her a business envelope with her name written in Natasha's script.

Celia took the envelope and placed it in her purse. "Thank you."

Andrew nodded and walked away.

"Ready to go?" Keith asked. "You okay to drive?"

"I'm fine," Celia stood and smoothed her pants. "I just want to go home."

"I'll walk you back to your car."

Keith's voice sounded muffled as nausea hit Celia again. Her ears rang loudly, and she couldn't swallow the sour taste. She turned to grab Keith's arm for support, and everything went black.

Chapter 36

Keith was talking to someone, a woman. The voices faded in and out, but Celia could hear Keith asking questions and the woman's voice answering.

"It's strange that she seemed fine for days and then passed out."

"Every concussion is different. She seemed agitated last night, so we gave her something to help her sleep. She should be –"The woman saw Celia try to sit up. "Ah, you're awake! Ms. Brockwell, just lie back. Don't try to sit up."

Celia realized she was in a hospital room. She was wearing a blue gown, which meant someone had undressed and dressed her. *Ugh, great.* An IV line was taped to her arm, and several sticky pads monitored her heart rate. The machine on the right showed that her blood pressure was 97/60.

"Ms. Brockwell, I'm Dierdre. How are you feeling?"

"Okay, just a little woozy. And very thirsty."

Keith reached for the yellow pitcher and poured a cup of water for Celia.

"I'll let the doctor know you're awake. She'll be in soon." Dierdre left the room, and Celia took a sip of the cool water.

"So what happened?" She asked.

"You passed out at the prison."

"I remember feeling sick. I went to the restroom."

"After you came out, you talked to Andrew and me. I was about to walk you to your car, and you just buckled."

Celia groaned. "Please tell me you didn't call an ambulance."

"Prison protocol." Keith shrugged. "Besides, the sirens were a good way to disperse the protesters. You woke up once you got here, but you were kind of out of it. They gave you something to help you calm down."

"Well, at least I slept all night. You didn't stay here all that time, did you?"

"I went back to the prison to do paperwork, and then I came back here. I've been here about three hours."

Dierdre walked back into the room with another woman. "I'm Dr. Schuester. Glad to see you awake. Let's check a few things."

Dr. Schuester listened to Celia's heart, had her track the doctor's fingers with her eyes, and asked a few basic questions about the day of the week, her phone number, and address.

"Did I pass?" Celia chuckled.

"You did. The tests show no sign of bleeding or problematic swelling, and your blood work looks good."

"So why did I pass out, and when can I go home?"

"It looks like you may have mild post-concussion syndrome. It can happen, even with a mild concussion."

"So what does that mean?"

"You may have some lingering symptoms for a few weeks. A headache is common, along with difficulty concentrating. It typically resolves itself."

Celia nodded. "And can I go home?"

"We'd like to watch you a couple more hours. But yes, you can go home today. I'll let you get some more rest now."

Once she was gone, Keith poured her another cup of water. "Just so you know, I'll be staying with you for a few days, and I don't care how uncomfortable the bed is."

"Yes, sir," Celia teased.

Then she noticed a breaking story. Bart's photo appeared on the television screen.
"Turn that up," she told Keith. They both watched and listened.
"Local attorney Bart Vandiver was found dead in his Philadelphia townhouse last night, of an apparent overdose. Vandiver was a partner at Lewis, Tyler & Brown. He was 41 years old…"
Celia felt her heart rate accelerate. "Can I have a minute?"
"Sure."
"Bring me my purse, please."
He looked at her with a strange expression but did as she asked and then left the hospital room, cracking the door behind him.
Celia opened her purse and found the envelope Andrew had given her the night before. She muted the story about Bart, whose photo was still on the screen. Why are my hands shaking? Celia opened the envelope and pulled out a sheet of notebook paper.
A gift, because I knew you wouldn't
Celia took a deep breath and folded the paper, placing it back into the envelope. She took the remote and turned off the television.
Bart is dead. I have a note from Natasha, and Bart is dead. Celia looked around the room until she saw a small trash can sitting in a corner.
"You okay in here?" Keith knocked and then walked back into the room.
"I'm good." Celia shoved the envelope into her purse. "It was just a bit of a shock."
"I get that," Keith said. "But, and I hate to say it, at least you don't have to worry about him."
"Thank goodness," she sighed.
"I talked to the doctor while I was waiting. I told her I was going to be staying with you, and I persuaded her to go ahead and release you. If you can get dressed, we'll leave now."
Yes. Please. Celia wanted to get out of the room. "I can dress. Just bring me my clothes."

Keith retrieved a plastic hospital bag from the cabinet and helped Celia stand. "Want me to hold your purse?"
"I got it. I need a couple of things in there."
Keith led her to the restroom, and she locked the door behind her. Celia turned on the water and checked her phone. The news of Bart's death was already on the internet too. As she scanned the article, the phone buzzed.
"Willian," Celia answered. "Is everything okay?"
"You're the one I should be asking. Are you okay?"
"I'm fine. I'm about to leave the hospital."
"Have you seen the news?" William asked.
"I have. I can't believe it."
"Yes, well, now you can breathe easy."
"I got a note from -"
"Well, I just wanted to check on you. Take a few days. I'll see you back at the office." He ended the call.
That was odd. Celia's reporter's mind raced as she quickly put on her clothes. Then she took the envelope out of her purse. She read the note again before tearing it into tiny pieces. After doing the same with the envelope, she dropped them into the toilet and flushed. A quick fluff of hair and a bit of lip gloss, and she was ready to go.
"You all set?" Keith asked as she opened the door.
"I am," Celia said, looking back at the bathroom. "Thank God it's all over. Let's go home."

Made in the USA
Middletown, DE
28 April 2021